SALVATION

A REALM OF FLAME AND SHADOW NOVEL

CHRISTINA PHILLIPS

PHOENIX 18 PUBLISHING

ISBN: 978-0-6487568-9-7

Edited by Amanda Ashby
Cover Design: Covers by Christian
06/2023

PROLOGUE

NATE

Eleven Thousand Years Ago. Somewhere on Earth.

THE ARCHANGEL NATHANAEL landed on a rocky outcrop that gave him an uninterrupted view of the brawl in progress on the sandy beach below. Folding his wings, he recognized the three tormentors. They were minor gods who often hung out on Earth, and their current victim didn't stand a chance against them.

He wasn't in the mood for a fight, but three immortals against one frail human was barbaric, whatever way he looked at it. Like a lion playing with a mouse.

Sweat beaded along the human's forehead and a knife hilt protruded from his neck. Even from this distance, there was no mistake. The swirling runes on the knife handle were too distinctive. It belonged to one of the jeering gods, Maahes.

Intrigued, he scanned the creature. His aura throbbed with leashed power, the ancient, unadulterated power that only archangels possessed. *So he wasn't human.* And he certainly wasn't an archangel.

Demon.

Nate had never come across one before, although there were plenty of legends of their duplicity and how they'd corrupted and tortured humankind in the past. But since there were no witnesses of such events still alive, as far as he was concerned it was all speculation. Their goddess had banished her first children from Earth long ago, before the creation of the archangels.

That dark history, that their goddess forbade them to discuss, had always fascinated him. Why couldn't they speak of it? Most of his fellow archangels accepted Her word and had no interest in digging into a prohibited past that didn't affect them.

They were bitter enemies. As prescribed by their goddess' decree. But it was academic. Despite how their goddess maintained that if they ever met, they'd annihilate each other, no battle had been fought between their races. She was determined to keep them separated, and it seemed he was the only one who questioned Her word in this matter.

He grinned. Potential answers to all the questions he'd had over the years had just neatly dropped into his path.

It was an enthralling proposition.

A second later he materialized into the fray and narrowly dodged a curse-drenched, eight-pointed star that the goddess Inanna had hurled. She gave a theatrical groan.

"Fly away, Nate. You're in the way."

He offered her an insincere grin. "Not a chance."

Maahes spun another of his knives on the tip of his finger. "Pick a side, butterfly."

As insults went, it was one of the milder ones. "Already have."

The demon lunged for the third god, Veles, gripping his sword in both hands. "Filthy godspawn cowards."

Nate shot him a glance, as Veles parried the thrusts with his own sword. Inanna laughed, as if the whole thing was a great joke, and Maahes drew back his arm, knife in hand, focused on Nate.

Nate teleported, wrapped his arm around Maahes' throat and there was a satisfying crack before the god teleported to Inanna's side. Unfortunately it took more than that to kill an immortal, but still.

"You're *so* going to regret this, Nathanael." It sounded more like a prophecy than a threat, as Inanna held out her hand, and her star spun back to its mistress.

"Big time," growled Maahes, his fingers clutching his throat, as the crushed bones mended, before he and Inanna vanished.

Veles leaped back, landing knee deep in the ocean. He grinned at Nate, as though he found the interruption of his and his fellow immortals' fun and games amusing.

"Good hunting, archangel." There was the faintest trace of a sneer in that last word, before he, too, vanished.

Nate rounded on the stranger, who was leaning heavily on his sword and sucking harsh breaths into his lungs.

"What the hell are you doing on Earth?"

The demon gingerly touched the hilt that was still sticking out of his neck. "I pissed off the Demonic High Council. Thought I'd lay low on the last planet they'd ever think of looking for me."

"And then you pissed off Maahes."

"Bastard caught me unaware." His voice rasped and he staggered, as though the sword was no longer enough to keep him upright. "I can't even teleport."

Nate eyed the knife. If the demon couldn't teleport, there was no way he'd be able to heal himself, either. Once the knife was pulled out, he'd bleed to death.

He'd healed plenty of humans with minor injuries in the past. Even a few with life-threatening wounds. But he'd never offered to help an immortal before. Because immortals didn't need that kind of help.

"Huh." He folded his arms and glowered at the demon, because this was unchartered territory and he had the feeling if his goddess discovered his deed, she'd be severely displeased.

Then again, he did a lot of things he suspected his goddess would disapprove of. Not that he was the only one. The trick was not being found out.

Assisting a demon bordered on blasphemy. It was dangerously tempting.

"Battling your conscience?" The demon gave a feral grin. His teeth were bloodstained. "Do me a favor. Cut out my heart. This knife hurts like fuck."

The melodramatic comment decided him. Anyone who could joke at a time like this couldn't be as despicable as their reputation contended. "Here's your choice. I'll leave now, or you pull the knife and I'll fix the wound."

The demon grimaced. "And be forever in your debt."

"Yeah. Thought that went without saying."

The demon gave a pained laugh. "Deal."

It took longer than he'd anticipated to mend blood vessels, knit torn muscle and repair damaged nerves. By the time he had finished, the sun had set, and he and the demon were both dripping with sweat.

He exhaled a long breath and stepped back. He'd done all he could. "Might take you a while to regain your abilities."

The demon cautiously flexed his neck before giving him an assessing look. "My name is Dagan." He gave a mocking half-bow. "At your service."

"Nate. Not at yours."

Dagan's dark eyes gleamed in the moonlight. "It appears not all archangels are the scum of the universe that I've been led to believe."

"No. That distinction is reserved for demon kind."

Dagan gave a grunt of laughter. "In a different universe, we may have been friends."

An archangel and a demon? It was unheard of.

Forbidden.

And a perfect way for Nate to finally get answers to all the questions that had burned through his mind for centuries.

"Are you still planning to stay on Earth?"

Dagan shrugged. "Until I'm healed, I don't have a choice. But yes. I still plan to stay for a while."

In that case, Nate needed to figure out a way to keep him alive. He rubbed his brow and then grinned. "How do you feel about masquerading as a demigod?"

"The thought of possessing hybrid blood from a god and mortal coupling offends my sensibilities."

Nate snorted with laughter. Who knew demons possessed a sense of humor?

"I can't guarantee you'd be welcome in Ama-gi as a demon. But you'll pass unnoticed if you present as a demigod."

"Ama-gi still thrives on this primitive planet?"

He'd forgotten Dagan would know of the magnificent civilization from the time when demons populated the Earth over a thousand years ago.

"It does."

Dagan was silent for a few moments. "You would protect my identity, against the edicts of our mutual goddess?"

"Hey." Nate unfurled his wings. "What are friends for?"

CHAPTER 1

NATE

London, Present Day

NATE STOOD outside The Queen's Arms pub in the West End and narrowed his eyes at the unassuming club across the street. The name had first caught his interest. *Inanna.* But it was the elusive scent of demon that clung to the building that really snared him.

He was certain there was a connection that linked the club and the architect behind an immortal forged sword that had horrifically wounded one of his closest friends, the Archangel Azrael. Nate had grabbed that damn weapon and was in the process of having it analyzed but he was already sure of its origin.

Demon made. And that meant an immortal on Earth was either forging weapons capable of destroying an archangel—or someone off-world was supplying them. And somewhere in this club was his answer.

It wasn't that unusual to pick up a trace of demonic infestation on Earth. Their bloodline polluted the human race far more than any of his fellow archangels were aware. Most of the time, he ignored the signs. Because generally the hybrids had no idea what cursed DNA they possessed, and as such they posed little danger to the indigenous population.

The ones he hunted across the universe were powerful demon spawn, who not only knew exactly who and what they were but were consumed with wiping out mortals and claiming their planet for their own.

Not on his watch. He'd been burned once by their duplicity.

Never trust a demon.

He wouldn't rest until he'd crushed every seed of their rebellion, across all the galaxies except Fornax, the one they called their own.

The fact that so far his best clue was lurking inside a club called after the goddess who had warned him about Dagan, was just the kind of karmic bullshit the universe liked to pull on him.

He threw up a low-level glamour to obscure his archangelic radiance from mortals and strolled across the road. He'd visited the club half a dozen times during the last couple of weeks but apart from the traces of powerful demonic power steeped into the very brickwork, he hadn't found the answers he'd been looking for. He'd also checked out *Inanna* in Birmingham and Brighton but although the demon element was unmistakable in both clubs, it was nowhere near as potent as their London counterpart.

Once inside the club, he prowled the perimeter of the dance floor. It was like every other night he'd been here, and he raked his gaze around the oblivious humans. They were so sure of their position at the top of the food chain, they had no idea who else they shared this planet with. Which was just as well. No one needed the kind of panic that would sweep the Earth if humans ever lifted that particular veil.

Let them keep their illusion of superiority. It made no difference to him.

He was convinced the demon responsible for the attack on Az had been here, which meant Nate wasn't going anywhere.

He was certain of which demon bastard was behind it, too.

Dagan.

Bella

Isabella Beauchamp navigated her way through Heathrow Airport, collected her luggage, and went through "Northing to Declare" at Customs. Teleportation was *so* much easier, but sometimes when it came to her work, she just needed a paper trail, to avoid unwanted scrutiny.

Also, Octavia was picking her up. And while the other woman was a good friend, there were still some things she couldn't confide in her.

It was safer, that way. For Octavia.

She spied her friend in the crowd and made her way over.

"Welcome back," Octavia said, even though Bella had only been in Milan for a couple of weeks. "And congrats on clinching the deal on your new nightclub."

"The place has so much potential." Most people in the underground network she was a part of believed her string of nightclubs were a cover for her real work, but it was so much more than that. She loved renovating old buildings, bringing them back to their former glory, and then opening them to the public. It had always been her passion, even before she'd been recruited by the Watchers. But there was no denying that her businesses also served as a perfect cover if any full blood humans decided to investigate her.

Although it was the middle of March, it was bitterly cold outside, and she shivered as gusts of wind chilled her face. The demon blood in her veins gave her a lot of advantages but countering the effects of extreme weather conditions wasn't one of them.

As Octavia drove through the London traffic, Bella shared her plans for the new club. Even though they'd kept in touch by phone and texting, it wasn't the same.

She had many immortal friends from the Watchers underground network. But Octavia was different. She possessed no demon blood and while she knew of Bella's mixed heritage, she didn't have a clue that the immortal Watchers existed. More importantly, she was the only one of her friends who loved historic architecture as much as she did.

"What about you?" Bella glanced at Octavia. "Any closer to the light at the end of the tunnel?"

She didn't know exactly what Octavia had been working on for so many years, since the details were confidential. But since she was a dhampir, Bella had long ago concluded it had to involve something potentially catastrophic connected to her race.

"You could say that." Octavia frowned. "Although now a whole new level of complication has emerged. I'm leaving for Romania tomorrow."

"Good luck." Curiosity curled through her, but she'd never ask Octavia why she needed to go to Romania. If she couldn't share, there was a good reason for it.

Caution went both ways, after all.

"Hey." Octavia shot her an assessing glance. "Out of interest. Have you ever come across an archangel?"

Well, that was unexpected. She ignored the animosity that slithered through her gut at the hated word, and everything it represented. "Definitely not."

Her mentor had taught her how to read auras years ago, as a basic security measure. He'd also taught her how to obscure her own immortal heritage, an essential tool of defense against unknown enemies, and now it was second nature.

Silence echoed in the car before Octavia inhaled a long breath. "You know of the Great Massacre of nine hundred years ago?"

"Yes." It was dhampir history, but she had learned of it before meeting Octavia. Because an archangel had been involved in the slaughter of a thousand dhampirs, and anything that had occurred on Earth that involved an archangel was faithfully documented in the Watchers' archives.

"A few days ago, I met the archangel responsible."

"Oh my gods." She didn't even know what to say to that. "Are you okay?"

Octavia flapped her hand in a dismissive gesture. "Of course. Unfortunately, he wasn't the evil monster I was expecting." She sighed. "They never are, are they?"

Bella was more than sure that they were. "I hope he's being brought to justice."

Not that she was going to hold her breath. While demon kind had been defamed for countless generations by clueless humans, archangels had never been brought to justice for anything they'd done.

That doesn't mean they never will.

She hoped she was there to witness it.

"I believe he redeemed himself." There was a dry note in Octavia's voice.

"Where does he make his lair? On Earth?"

"I've no idea. Off planet, I think."

Of course he did. Archangels rarely walked the Earth anymore. They had usurped the demons from their rightful place, corrupted historical truths as victors always did, and then hadn't even stayed afterwards to nurture the planet.

She desperately wanted more information. If Octavia had met one archangel, had she met any others? She'd never mentioned having done so before, but she could've been sparing Bella's feelings. Octavia was well aware she had a low opinion of archangels.

She swallowed down the barrage of questions. It didn't matter how her soul burned for answers. She was skating perilously close to the line as it was. The function of the Watchers was to find those unaware they possessed a demonic bloodline and bring them into the fold.

The Watchers allowed no breach of their security, and if even the hint of a whisper escaped of their existence, there would be dire consequences. Bella understood the reasoning. Secrecy was vital. She could only imagine how humans would react if they ever discovered they shared Earth with the descendants of demons.

Among others.

It only took about half an hour before Octavia pulled up on the drive of Bella's semi-detached house in Richmond upon Thames. A warm glow engulfed her at the sight of the substantial Edwardian building. It had taken her years to renovate, and she still wasn't finished, but that was okay. She had plenty of time, and no intention of moving from the first real home she'd ever had.

She'd done enough midnight flits and living on the edges of society before she'd learned who—*what*—she truly was.

There was no need to live in the shadows anymore. She could hide in plain sight, and no one would ever guess her secret. It wasn't the life she'd dreamed of, but it was better than the one she'd had. And right now, that had to be enough.

It was ten that night before she teleported to a dark side road in Soho, not far from her flagship nightclub, *Inanna*. Her staff assumed she always got a taxi to work, which was fine by her since it saved a lot of questions.

A satisfyingly long queue snaked along the pavement outside the club, a converted three-story Georgian building that had been in danger of demolition before she'd bought it. Ornate iron railings prevented patrons from falling to the below ground level, where the cellar windows allowed an elusive glimpse of the state-of-the-art kitchen.

She bypassed the queue and smiled a greeting at the security guards on duty before entering the club. The Friday night guest DJ was one of the hottest celebrities around and going by the wild appreciation of the clientele had already earned his exorbitant fee.

"Welcome back." Yvette, her efficient, human, manager, who also possessed a handy psychic gift, came over to her and they made their way to the bar. "And well done."

"It needs a lot of work, but it'll be worth it."

Yvette ordered a bottle of champagne and tossed her a grin. "All your acquisitions need a lot of work. It's like you enjoy punishing yourself."

More like a reward, for all the times she'd lived in hovels and slept in the gutter. She suppressed the shudder that crawled over her flesh. Even after all this time, the terror she'd lived through still lurked in the dark corners of her mind.

Savagely, she shoved the past back where it belonged. She refused to think of it or give the memories any power. That part of her life was over, and never again would she be at the mercy of an uncaring Fate.

Except for once a year, on the anniversary of the day she'd been rejected by her own mother and flung onto the streets to survive. She needed a whole lot more than ironclad willpower, then. Because without the blissful numbing effects of alcohol, the memories always found a way to slither through her barriers.

"Any problems I need to deal with?" She knew there wasn't. Yvette was brilliant, and if anything had cropped up that needed her attention, her manager would've phoned. She topped up her glass with champagne.

"Not a problem as such." The cautious note in Yvette's voice was so unlike her that Bella forgot about her drink and frowned.

"What do you mean?"

"Some guy I've never seen before turned up here the night you left. He's been back several times. There's just something about him I can't put my finger on."

"Does he cause any trouble?"

"No. He just watches everything. He was here last night, too. The weirdest thing is, no one seems to pay any attention to him."

"That's not so weird. He's probably giving off a psychic vibe that only you can tap into. That's why you keep noticing him."

Yvette tapped the stem of her glass with her finger. "Maybe," she conceded. "But that doesn't explain why everyone is virtually ignoring him."

She laughed. "Is he that hot?"

Obviously, he wasn't. Otherwise he wouldn't be ignored. People didn't come to *Inanna* if they wanted to remain inconspicuous. They came for a good time, and her nightclubs were a magnet for the wealthy, the famous, and the beautiful.

"You tell me." There was a dry note in Yvette's voice, and she raised her eyebrows and gave a little nod across the club. Intrigued, Bella slowly pivoted to face the crowd. Would she even see who Yvette was talking about?

Her heart slammed against her ribs as her gaze riveted on a giant of a man across the crowded floor. Patrons had pulled away from him, leaving him in a shadow filled sphere, but she didn't need a spotlight to appreciate his presence.

He was magnificent. The word jangled in her head, but there was no other way to describe him. Why wasn't everyone in the club gazing at him in awestruck wonder? His thick hair was twisted into tight braids and had been pulled into a band at the back of his head, and his black eyes glinted as he swept the clubbers with a casual glance.

And caught her staring at him.

Prickles of awareness danced over her skin, her chest contracted, and liquid fire tangled low in her gut. She clutched the champagne flute as though her life depended on it and with a sense of inexplicable inevitability, watched him prowl across the floor.

Holy godsdamn fuck. He was coming her way. This was insane. She never let her emotions rule her head and she wasn't starting now. *Was* lust an emotion? Her brain was too scrambled to care. It had been way too long since that particular inconvenience had attacked her, but she sure as hell didn't remember ever experiencing anything as visceral as *this*.

She swallowed her drink in one long gulp, but the alcohol only increased the fluttering sensation that had taken up residence in the pit of her stomach. The cacophony of music and humanity faded, and all she could hear was the elevated thud of her heart, echoing around her head and pulsing through her blood.

Breathe. The harsh command from what remained of her good sense reminded her to suck in some oxygen, but it wasn't enough to clear her head. Random shafts of light glinted on black and gold jewelry in the man's earlobes and through his nose, and another streak of primitive need turned her reflexes inside out.

He came to a halt an arm's length in front of her. At five foot ten she'd never considered herself short, but he towered over her, leashed power radiating from him like a nuclear reactor in meltdown. And instead of getting the hell out of there, which was the logical course of action, she had the alarming urge to smooth her palm over his black stubble beard.

Don't. You. Dare.

From behind her, Yvette cleared her throat. Or maybe she stifled a laugh. Bella couldn't drag her fascinated gaze from the stranger to check and was only faintly aware when Yvette patted her shoulder and disappeared into the crowd.

The stranger gave a slow, infinitely sexy smile, that was so full of wicked invitation that the air evaporated from her lungs.

It was ridiculous. She didn't do speechless, or instant attraction, or any of that annoying human stuff that messed with her perfectly planned life. She didn't even do sex anymore. Not that she ever had, much, but that was beside the point.

She knew what she wanted and where she was going and being distracted by the most gorgeous specimen of mortality that had ever walked the Earth had no place in her game plan.

And then he spoke, his voice low and gravelly, like sin incarnate, and her resolve melted like snow before the sun. "Can I get you a drink?"

NATE

Nate swallowed the groan at his appalling attempt to flirt. Seriously. That was the best he could come up with? His only excuse was this woman had damn well robbed him of the power of critical thinking.

He hadn't come here tonight to interact with anyone. Definitely hadn't planned on an enjoyable hook up. But from the second he'd become aware of her from across the other side of the club, she was like a siren's call.

She was tall for a human and looked in her late twenties, and her long blonde hair, pulled back from her face into a ponytail, and big blue eyes gave her an aura of fragility. It was one of the reasons he hadn't been with a mortal in millennia because they were too easily breakable.

"Why not?" Her voice was cool, and he had no fucking idea what she was talking about. Her delectable lips curved into a smile and his cock thickened with appreciation. "On second thoughts, I've a bottle of champagne. I don't mind sharing."

He leaned his arm on the bar next to her. The humans on his other side moved further along, a side-effect of his glamour.

Which didn't appear to have affected the blonde at all. As the bartender brought him another flute, he briefly scanned her aura.

An unmistakable glimmer of psychic ability swirled, which had to be the reason why she appeared to see straight through his low-level glamour. Although that ability was common with more advanced civilizations, it didn't happen often on Earth. He'd only scanned her out of habit. Sometimes his suspicious nature was a bastard, not that it mattered. It wasn't like she was going to call him on it.

The bartender filled their flutes and Nate handed one to her. Her fingers grazed his as she accepted it, and her touch was electrifying.

"Cheers." Her voice was husky as they clinked glasses and he gazed, fascinated, as she took a long, slow, swallow of the golden liquid. He couldn't remember the last time a human had so ensnared him. Hell, he couldn't remember ever being this enthralled, period.

It was intoxicating. He grinned at her and downed half the champagne in one go. So far, he'd not discovered any sign of Dagan. One night off to pursue this delectable female wouldn't derail his plans.

"I'm Nate." He held out his hand, purely for the pleasure of feeling her touch once more and was intrigued when she didn't immediately take it.

A heartbeat passed. And then another. It was like time slowed down, became suspended within this moment, and if he wasn't so caught up in the mesmeric blue swirls of her eyes, he would've laughed at the absurdity of his thought.

And then she smiled and the vision damn near sucked the air from his lungs.

"Hello, Nate." She accepted his overture, even if she didn't give him her name. Her hand was delicate, fragile. Just as he expected. Except there was also an underlying hint of steely strength that totally belied her appearance.

Nice.

With reluctance, he released her, and didn't miss the way she flexed her fingers, as though his touch still lingered on her skin. If so, it made two of them. He smothered the incredulous laugh that threatened to escape by finishing off the rest of his champagne.

Human alcohol had no effect on him, but it gave him a few seconds to mock his unprecedented reaction to this alluring mortal. Didn't matter, though. His brain could mock him all it liked. He'd not wanted a female in his arms as much as he wanted this woman in…

Well, fuck. Forever?

"I haven't seen you here before." He picked up the bottle of champagne and topped up her glass.

"Do you come here often?"

As he filled up his own glass, he silently marveled at how she'd countered his implied question with a direct one of her own. It wasn't a usual mortal trait when confronted by an archangel. Not even from humans who possessed psychic ability.

Not that he was complaining.

"Only recently. I'm staying in the area, so just checking out the nightlife."

Yeah, well, it was better than the truth. Humans couldn't handle the truth.

"Ah." She inclined her head, as though he'd confirmed something she already knew. Curiosity spiked. Had she been in the club before and seen him, and he simply hadn't noticed her?

Seemed unlikely, considering he hadn't picked up anything of interest in the hordes of clubbers he'd scanned during the last couple of weeks. No way had he missed seeing her.

As she took a dainty sip of her drink, he ran a leisurely gaze over her. She was stunning in crimson boots that matched her sweater, and her black jeans showed off her gorgeous legs to perfection.

But her outfit was in stark contrast to everyone else, who looked right at home in one of the trendiest clubs in London, with their designer label, red-carpet worthy clothing. To complete her understated air of laid-back sophistication, her only jewelry was a silver, eight-pointed star, suspended from a silver chain.

The star of Inanna.

Maybe she worked here? Even though none of the other staff he'd encountered wore such a necklace, a lion, the emblem of the goddess, was carved into the stonework above the entrance, and embroidered on the collar of the employees' smart uniform.

He leaned in closer, and a subtle hint of her perfume wove a seductive trail through him. A smoky, woodsy, scent, with a tantalizing undertone of vanilla, that conjured up mythical groves in ancient forests.

There was something faintly familiar about her and suspicion stirred, but in his gut he knew he was right.

"You're Isabella Beauchamp." It wasn't a question. He'd researched the owner of the string of *Inanna* nightclubs, but the sparse, weirdly grainy photos he'd uncovered of the undoubted human didn't do her justice.

Fuck that, she was barely recognizable as the same person. According to what he'd discovered, she was a virtual recluse with no social media footprint—although her clubs had very active accounts. About ten years ago she'd inherited a small fortune from an obscure relative and had begun her nightclub empire.

He'd intended tracking her down, so he could eliminate her from his investigation, but he hadn't expected this wild attraction. Not that it made any difference. If anything, it could help with his investigation of who held the real power behind the clubs. Sometimes, business and pleasure could be mixed without losing sight of objectives.

"I am." If she was surprised by his comment, she didn't show it. "Why? Have you been looking for me?"

He couldn't help himself. "Only all my life."

She laughed, and the faint air of aloofness that had clung to her dissolved. "And now you've found me, what do you propose?"

"How about we get out of here?"

Bella

What the bloody hell are you doing?

Flirting, that's what. Bella squashed her flare of caution, which usually served her well, because she was in *no* danger from this guy. She wasn't on an undercover mission to assess the suitability of a potential new recruit, where there was always the possibility of an enemy lurking in the shadows.

He was merely a—

Fuck. Ice skated over her arms. She hadn't even scanned his aura. Hastily, she corrected that error and relief tumbled through her. He was just a regular human, with an indecipherable thread of immortal blood in his ancient heritage. It was amazing how many oblivious humans had traces of various immortal blood in their veins. But it was often so diluted that the only advantage was they'd inherited the capability to access psychic abilities.

He's been stalking your club for the last two weeks.

Just because Yvette had seen him in the club a few times, didn't make him a stalker.

He knows who you are. Okay, that *was* a little concerning, but only because she had a distrustful nature. It wasn't as though her ownership of *Inanna* was a secret. It was in the public records.

Honestly, why was she trying to find excuses to get away from this guy? She couldn't remember the last time she'd found someone so irresistible. Didn't she deserve a little fun, every now and then?

It wouldn't kill her.

Maybe not. But she wasn't in the habit of having fun, when it involved hooking up.

Illicit thrills chased through her blood at the imagery of *hooking up* with Nate. A one-night stand.

Incredible sex.

But it was more than that. His presence filled her mind, more potent than the finest champagne she'd ever tasted, engulfing the toxic memories. Drowning them until they were barely a shimmer on a far horizon.

She cleared her throat and refused to succumb to the overwhelming desire to wrap herself around him and to hell with the consequences. She had an ethical code to uphold. She didn't allow staff to be intimate with their clientele. Not on the premises, at any rate, and if she couldn't stick to the rules, how could she expect anyone else to?

Then again, some rules were just made to be broken.

"We could have coffee in my office." Ugh, that didn't sound in the least bit sexy now she'd said it out loud. Luckily, Nate didn't appear to find her invitation lacking, as his response was a bone-melting smile.

She *really* needed to get out more. But tonight, this was exactly what she needed.

"Sounds good." His voice sank into her like a potent cocktail of aged whiskey and smoky promises of orgasmic bliss. She resisted the urge to wipe her damp palms on her jeans. The gods alone knew why her sex drive had suddenly woken up, but she wasn't about to spoil the moment by analyzing it.

"This way." She grabbed the almost empty bottle of champagne before leading him through to the back of the bar where she unlocked the door that opened to the private section of the building. She'd never noticed how narrow the corridor was before. Nate took up way more space than was legal, and whatever cologne he was wearing should have a public health warning attached to it.

"A secret passageway." There was an undercurrent of laughter in his voice as he followed her up the stairs to the top floor, where all the offices were.

"It's not a secret." She made the mistake of glancing over her shoulder at him. Liquid heat unfurled deep inside as she caught his mesmeric dark gaze, and then the moment shattered as she tripped on the next stair. She gripped the bannister before she fell on her face but couldn't prevent herself from laughing. Because how ridiculous was it that she was so besotted with a hot stranger that she'd almost lost her balance?

"You okay?" His hand wrapped around her arm, clearly in a chivalrous attempt to steady her. All it did was catapult her newly energized libido into orbit.

"I'm fine. It's been a long day." *And it's going to be a longer night.* Thank the gods she hadn't said that out loud. There was going to be no *night*. Just a quick hook-up. Okay, maybe a *long* hook-up. She might as well make the most of it.

Once the morning came, her annual weakness would be back under lock and key and she wouldn't need the irresistible distraction Nate offered.

"I bet it has, with five clubs in your portfolio."

They reached the top landing, where she unlocked the door that led to the offices. She was nothing if not security conscious when it came to keeping out unwary humans from prying into her business.

"Six clubs, as of today." She swung around and tilted the bottle at him. "I don't usually drink while on duty."

Usually, she didn't drink much at *all*.

He took the bottle from her. "Congratulations. We should celebrate." The gleam in his eyes told her exactly how he planned on doing *that*.

Yes, please.

"Absolutely." Was that breezy voice really hers? He'd never guess she was a volcanic mess inside. "That's why we're here. For coffee, remember?"

She pushed open the door to her private office. A nineteenth century desk gleamed in the corner and the polished floorboards were covered with thick rugs while huge potted plants dotted the room. Her offices in each of her clubs were beautiful.

Most of the time, they helped keep the ugly nightmares at bay.

He kicked the door shut behind them and placed the champagne bottle on her antique desk. "I can think of a better way."

So could she. But this bantering was kind of fun.

"Sounds like someone's in a hurry."

He grinned. "Where's your coffee machine?"

Ah, okay then. She hadn't expected him to take her up on that challenge. "Over there."

He strolled across the room, and she all but salivated over the spectacular view of his rear. His black shirt fitted him like a second skin, emphasizing his broad shoulders and enhancing his breathtaking biceps. He could be a template for the ultimate specimen of masculinity, the fabled mold that had been broken and never perfected again.

"Where's this new club of yours?"

She dragged her mesmerized gaze from his large, strong hands as he deftly scooped coffee into the machine and then found cups. What was the question again?

"Milan. It's going to be fabulous."

He turned to face her. "Do you source all the properties yourself?"

She almost answered him, when her cursed caution kicked back in. "You're asking an awful lot of questions about my business."

He prowled toward her. There was no other word for it. Like he was a panther stalking his transfixed prey. The notion sent shivers of delicious awareness along her spine.

"Hey, I can't be interested in what you do?" He reached out and wound a strand of her hair around his finger. She forgot how to breathe.

"Sure." She sounded like she needed life support. *Not far wrong.* "As long as that goes both ways. What do you do?"

"I hunt violators."

What a strange way of putting it. Bloody sexy, though. "You're a bounty hunter?"

His eyes glinted, and he looked raw and powerful and utterly dangerous. "If you like."

She did like. A lot.

"That must be exciting."

"It has its moments." He crooked his finger, tugging her captured hair, sending tingles across her scalp. "Better than the alternative."

"Being bored to tears?" Why were they still talking? She could think of something far better for him to do with his mouth. She licked her lips and his intense gaze followed the tip of her tongue. It was as potent as a featherlight caress from his fingertips.

"I don't do boredom." He lowered his head and his breath fanned her face. Elusive amber flecks glittered in his black eyes. She'd never seen anything quite like it before. "You can die of that."

"Apparently," she whispered, before leaning closer and brushing her lips against his.

Danger...

The urgent warning fluttered through her mind. She squashed it flat. The only danger she was in right now was of combustion.

He wrapped his arm around her, pulling her close. His body was hard, as though his spectacular musculature was made from granite, but he wasn't cold like stone. He was warm and vital, and the beat of his heart echoed through her, filling all the empty spaces deep inside.

Stop. This was just sex. She didn't need her imagination to conjure up fanciful visions of anything more meaningful. She couldn't afford to.

An unintentional groan escaped as his lips trailed a scorching path across her jaw before gently nipping her earlobe. His hot breath was a barely-there caress and his stubble chafed her heated skin.

"Isabella." He drew out every syllable of her name, his lips teasing her ear. She'd never heard anything so erotic in her life, and she gripped his biceps. Gods, he felt even better than he looked. Leashed power vibrated through him, and when she tightened her grip, he flexed his muscles in a blatant show of masculine pride.

Feverishly, she tore open the buttons of his shirt. A magnificent expanse of chest greeted her, lightly sprinkled with dark hair, and he gave a primitive growl that was so damn hot she almost melted on the spot.

He gripped the hem of her sweater and tore it over her head. Frustration glowed in his eyes at the long-sleeved T-shirt beneath. She laughed and ripped it off. "Hey, I get cold. All right?"

"You won't be cold tonight." He appeared riveted on her crimson, push-up bra which, she had to admit, made her boobs look good. "I'm going to make you burn."

"Burning already." She went onto her toes and wound her arms around his neck. He responded by gripping her butt and crushing her against his unyielding erection. Damp heat bloomed between her thighs, and savage need clawed through her.

His hands cupped her, branding her through her jeans. And when he kissed her, stars exploded inside her mind as their tongues touched and lips melded. Her jeans were halfway down her legs before she even realized he'd unzipped her, and with a groan of frustration she broke their kiss so she could kick off her boots and jeans.

A growl rumbled in his throat as he dragged his molten gaze over her. The only reason she bought sexy, extravagant lingerie was because she loved them. Tonight, she loved them for another reason entirely.

Because Nate clearly approved of the crimson scraps of lace, too.

"You're dazzling," he rasped, as his fingers skimmed over her arms, leaving prickles of fire in his wake.

Dazzling. What a magical way to say he found her hot. She struggled to return the compliment, but it took all her effort just to remain upright. And breathing.

"So are you," she gasped, which was hardly original, but she still meant it. Her palm glided over his head, and his glorious hair sent molten waves of need from her fingertips to her toes.

Astounding.

He nibbled kisses along her throat, and one big hand cupped her breast, his thumb caressing her aching nipple through the fabric of her bra. She arched into him, needing more, her nails digging into his scalp and neck, desperate to feel every inch of him possess her.

For one night only.

His grin was satanic as he lifted her in one arm, as though she weighed no more than a feather, and set her on the edge of her desk. He stood between her spread legs, cradled her head and kissed her as though the world was ending.

She was pliant flame beneath his hands and didn't even try to rein in her overactive imagination. She could pretend whatever she liked. It was only make-believe but this incredible man could make her believe almost anything.

He wound her hair around his fist and tugged her head back, before raining scorching kisses over her throat and breasts. She clung onto his shoulders as he tore her knickers aside and teased her wet folds. Desperately, she hooked her legs around his body, but she might as well have tried to bend a mountain to her will.

That he could resist her strength was staggering but it only added to his irresistible allure.

"You want something, Isabella?" His question burned her lips, and the way he growled her name was a whole new level of enchantment.

She panted into his face, lost her mind in the dark magnetism of his eyes. And her deepest, secret, wish spilled from her lips. "I want you to make me forget."

CHAPTER 3

NATE

Nate sucked in a jagged breath, but Isabella's whispered words seared through his mind. They'd been unexpected. Strangely vulnerable.

They were the hottest fucking words he'd ever heard.

"I'll make you forget your own damn name." If he didn't forget his own first. Roughly, he ripped open his pants, only one thought hammering through his lust-fueled brain.

Make her mine.

Still gripping her hair in his fist, he wrapped his other arm around her. Her flesh was warm and silky-smooth. As her lips parted in a soundless sigh and her lashes swept over her eyes, he swallowed a groan. There was no hope of him slowing things down and taking his time.

He needed her. Right now.

They had the rest of the night to take it slow.

He claimed her lips again as his cock teased her wet slit. She writhed, digging her nails into his shoulders and her legs tightened around his back. His grin was feral, and she smiled back, their teeth grazing in a kiss that blew his mind.

His blood thundered in his ears. All he could see was Isabella, naked except for her provocative crimson bra, and his last defenses crumbled. He thrust into her, and she was so hot and tight around him he couldn't remember which damn planet he was on, never mind his name.

She shuddered in his arms and he stilled, even though it nearly killed him. "You okay?"

"I will be." Her eyes were glazed with passion. "I can still remember my name, though."

He laughed and released her hair so he could trail his fingers along her flushed cheek.

"I'm not done, yet."

She mirrored his action, and her light caress tipped him over the edge. He sank into her, up to the hilt, and she dug her heels into his ass, anchoring them for an elusive, breathtaking eternity.

"Now," she breathed, and his last vestige of restraint unraveled. He hammered into her and she met every frenzied thrust, gripping him so damn tight the world threatened to shatter. And when she gasped his name as her orgasm splintered through her, he followed her into the rapture drenched vortex.

Harsh breaths rasped his chest as his forehead rested against hers. He couldn't move. Didn't want to. Remaining impaled within Isabella's sweet heat seemed like the best idea ever.

He closed his eyes and grappled to find remnants of control. But why the hurry? He could enjoy this for a few more bliss-filled moments.

Finally, she stirred, her palm sliding over the length of one of his locks. He raised his head just enough so he could look into her eyes.

She gave a soft, satisfied hum that vibrated through every cell in his body. "What's my name?"

"No idea." He grinned at her. "Who needs a name?"

"Not me." She lightly grasped his hair. "That was the best way I've celebrated a business deal in my life."

He'd forgotten about her businesses or the fact he was meant to be investigating the real power behind the *Inanna* clubs.

Losing sight of his main objective, no matter how pleasurable the distraction, was a novelty, but he wasn't going to stress about it. "Any time you want to celebrate, I'm happy to help."

"I'll keep that in mind." She was still smiling but she shifted on the desk, as though she was no longer comfortable. With more reluctance than he'd ever admit, he slowly withdrew from her.

Why the lingering desire not to end this moment? It wasn't as though he intended leaving her yet. There was plenty of time for another...

His lips twitched with amusement. For another *celebration*.

"Hold that thought." There was husky promise in her voice as she edged off the desk. As he shoved his cock back in his pants his gaze slid over her gorgeous body. Why was he still dressed? Next time, he was getting naked too.

"Consider it held." He took her hand and kissed her fingers. She gazed at him, apparently mesmerized, and a discordant thought skimmed across his mind.

Without a low-level glamour to obscure their so-called heavenly radiance, it was a fact that humans—most mortals, in general—tended to be spellbound when in the presence of archangels.

Frankly, it was a fucking pain in the ass.

It was an easy enough fix, and he barely even thought twice about throwing up a suitable glamour when needed. But although Isabella had seen through it, was it possible she'd still been dazzled by his archangelic heritage, rather than just by *him*?

What the hell was he even thinking? First, it didn't matter. Second, he *was* a fucking archangel, so the distinction didn't even exist.

Vaguely unnerved by the direction of his random analysis of a situation that *did not matter*, he eyed her ruined lingerie, that had slipped down to her ankles when she'd stood up. As though following his thought, she bent and picked up the torn scrap of lace.

"I owe you one," he said, as she dropped it onto the desk and pulled on her jeans.

"I'll hold you to that." There was laughter in her voice, and the knotted muscles in his shoulders relaxed. Besotted humans tended not to laugh when in the presence of archangels. They simply worshipped. She could see through his glamour, but only, thank fuck, partially.

He needed to get back on track. "Coffee?"

"Thought you'd forgotten the reason why I brought you up here."

"Some things are even better than coffee."

"Would those things be amazing?" She raised her eyebrows.

"You tell me." He washed his hands in the sink in the corner of her office and then busied himself with the machine. Soon the air was filled with the rich scent of coffee. When he turned around to hand her a cup, she was on the chaise longue, her legs tucked under her. Tendrils of hair had become loose from her ponytail and clung to her face, and her breasts were almost spilling out of that sinfully sexy bra.

"Amazing," she confirmed, as she accepted her coffee. He hadn't even asked how she wanted it. Just given it to her strong and black, the way he liked it. It was funny how caffeine gave him a hit in a way human produced alcohol never could. She took a sip and her lashes fluttered in evident approval.

He sat next to her, taking up most of the space, and gently clasped her bare foot. He needed to know why there were demonic traces in the nightclub, and Isabella might be able to help him.

She gave him a considering look through the steam rising from her cup. "Are you on a case?"

Unaccustomed guilt stabbed through his chest. Before he

could construct a convincing defense, she tapped his hand with one finger.

"You said you were a bounty hunter."

It was obvious she had her doubts about what he did for a living now, but at least it explained her question.

"I'm always on a case." He gave her foot a gentle squeeze. "But right now, I'm with you."

"How long are you staying in the area?" She took another sip of her coffee, but her eyes never left his.

"For a while. Haven't decided yet."

"So it depends how long it takes to collar your mark?"

He leaned into her space. "Now who's asking all the questions?"

She didn't even blink. "I've found it's a good way to uncover information."

"How about quid pro quo?"

He'd expected her to agree right away. They were just flirting. But her hesitation piqued his interest. Was she hiding something, after all?

"That could be dangerous." There was a thoughtful note in her voice, as if the notion was tempting rather than threatening. Not that he'd intended to threaten. "Should we set some ground rules first?"

"You can set any rules you like."

"Good. Because the truth doesn't always set you free. It can give you nightmares, too."

"You have no idea."

She smiled, but it looked kind of sad which for an unaccountable reason made him want to pull her into his arms. "Don't tell me you have a fucked-up family as well?"

He didn't have a family. He'd never had a family, even though his bitch of an Alpha Goddess had tried to create such a thing, millennia ago. "So fucked-up, you wouldn't believe it."

"You'd be surprised what I'd believe."

"Tell me something you don't believe in."

"Ooh, tricky." She contemplated the ceiling for a few moments. "Fairy tales."

"You don't believe in the big bad wolf?" He flashed her what he imagined was a wolfish smile and she laughed.

"Maybe. But I don't believe in happily-ever-afters."

"So cynical, for one so young."

"Watch it. I'm not as young as I look."

"That makes two of us."

She appeared about to answer him, when she suddenly straightened and thinned her lips. He frowned. What had just happened? She hitched in a sharp breath and flung him a bright smile.

"Phone." She pulled her phone from her jeans pocket and studied the screen. Maybe she had it on vibrate because he hadn't heard it go off.

She shoved the handset back in her pocket, and he had the weirdest conviction she'd just lied to him about the call. But why would she do that?

"I'm so sorry." She sounded quietly furious. "I've an unexpected meeting in an hour. I need to get ready."

He didn't move a muscle. "Is everything all right?"

She dragged in a long breath. "Yes. Just bloody awful timing. I'm *really* sorry to cut our evening short."

So was he. And not just because he wanted to have more sex with her. Huh. Fact was, he'd enjoyed talking with her. She was fun.

Even if she was a human.

Besides, he still needed to get information from her.

"We can pick this up another night."

"Yes, we could." She sounded surprised, as though that possibility hadn't occurred to her. "Might as well make the most of things while you're in town."

He wasn't exactly in town, but he could hardly tell her the

truth. That it didn't matter where his base was, since it only took him moments to get anywhere in the universe.

She wouldn't believe *that*.

"Tomorrow?" He tried to tell himself the only reason he needed to see her again was to extract information from her, but it wasn't very convincing.

"Sounds great. Do you want to do dinner?"

Did he? He'd been thinking more of another rendezvous here, in her office. But he could do dinner. Hell, why not?

"Sure. Give me your number, and I'll let you know where I make reservations."

"That's a sneaky way to get my number."

"Did it work?"

She rolled her eyes. "Yes, it did."

They exchanged numbers. He always kept a couple of human phones on him for emergencies. What now? He'd never been in this position before. His hook-ups in the past rarely led onto anything other than a parting of the ways.

She picked up her T-shirt and sweater and pulled them on. "I'll take you back to the club."

"I'm sure I can find my way back to the bar."

"Yes, but if I don't show a face, Yvette—my brilliant manager —will assume you murdered me."

He laughed. "Thanks."

"Don't take it personally. She has a suspicious nature."

"I'll bear that in mind." He stood and ignored the thread of reluctance that wound through his chest at leaving her. *Get a fucking grip.* They were seeing each other tomorrow night.

She pulled on her boots and they went back downstairs, but this time she held his hand. Once they were back in the club, she turned to him.

"Are you staying?"

He couldn't tear his gaze from her face. "No. Going to catch up on some work."

"See you tomorrow then." She went onto her toes and kissed him.

"Good luck with your meeting." It was harder than it should have been to release her hand and walk away. Even harder not to glance back at her.

He swallowed a groan. Why was he resisting it? He halted by the exit and turned around. She was standing where he'd left her, and her smile didn't just light up her face.

It lit up the whole damn club.

He raised his hand in farewell. *Until tomorrow.*

When he intended to have his shit together and not forget the main reason why he was seeing her again.

Dagan had infiltrated Isabella's club, and he needed to discover why.

CHAPTER 4

BELLA

*B*ella watched Nate stroll from the club, and the breath tangled in her throat. He really was spectacular.

Careful...

The warning floated through the back of her mind, dampening her mood. She knew she had to be careful. It wasn't as though she was going to do something stupid and fall for him. She couldn't afford to get that close to anyone.

Because in the end, everyone died.

Everyone but me.

Ice squeezed her heart and an old, familiar panic bloomed in her chest. Not now. She *wasn't* going to have one of her attacks right now. She hadn't succumbed for years. *I'm stronger than this.*

"Like I said," Yvette's voice speared through her and she sucked in a sharp breath, compressing all her nightmares back into their soulless boxes. "You tell me. Hot or not?"

It took her another couple of seconds to compose herself before she turned to Yvette with an expected smile. "You were right. Hot as sin. What's up with everyone here?"

"I was a tad concerned when I saw you go upstairs with him." Although Yvette wasn't yet forty, she labored under the delusion that she was so much older than Bella and therefore had the tendency to sometimes mother her.

Not that she usually minded. Yvette was lovely. She would've made a great mother. Far better than her own, that was for sure. She slammed the door on that memory. Not going there, not now, not ever again.

"Heat of the moment," she said drily, as they made their way back to the bar.

"That's not like you, though."

For most of the year that was true. But even she was allowed a night off.

Not that it was that big a deal. Unlike Yvette, she had the advantage of superhuman strength. There wasn't a man on Earth who could overpower her, never mind try and murder her.

"Well don't worry. I doubt it'll happen again." Sure, she was meeting him tomorrow. Maybe she'd hook up with him a few more times. But that was all. It would never—*could* never— be anything serious.

"I didn't mean it like that. It would be *great* if you met someone."

"Hey, I meet people all the time." She squeezed Yvette's hand. "Which reminds me. I have a meeting later tonight. Can you make sure no one disturbs me?"

"Of course."

Once she was back in her office, she locked the door. Not that she expected anyone would interrupt her, but she was nothing if not careful. Then she teleported home to have a quick shower.

As she dried her hair, she scrutinized her reflection. Did her lips really look swollen from Nate's kisses, or was it her imagination?

Illicit thrills collided between her thighs and she tried to drag her mind from Nate and focus on her upcoming meeting. Except she was still irrationally annoyed that her mentor had contacted her tonight of all nights. Sometimes she could go years without hearing from him, but it had only been six months.

His telepathic message had caught her completely off guard. She hoped Nate hadn't sensed anything suspicious, but why would he? Telepathy wasn't exactly a common human ability.

She puffed out an exasperated breath and scraped her hair back into its usual ponytail. Maybe she'd leave it down tomorrow night, for a change.

Hmm. Maybe she'd better stock up on some condoms, too. Not that she needed to protect herself the way a human woman would, since she'd never been sick in her life, but she didn't want Nate asking questions. Come to think of it, why hadn't *he* broached the subject?

Heat of the moment. Her comment to Yvette echoed in her head, giving her the answer. She tilted her head and smirked at her reflection. It was a good thing she *wasn't* fully human, otherwise she'd be freaking the shit out about possible repercussions right now.

Enough. She straightened. Although she'd told Nate her meeting was in an hour, her mentor always, without fail, arrived fifteen minutes earlier than he stated. It was time to return to *Inanna* and discover what the huge emergency was that had interrupted the best night she'd had in living memory.

She arrived back in her office with a minute to spare, and the first thing she saw were her ruined knickers. Hastily she scooped them up and shoved them in her desk drawer, just as her mentor materialized by the chaise.

"Bella," he said. His dark golden eyes glittered, and she had the uncomfortable conviction that he knew what she had been doing in here barely an hour ago. *None of his business.*

"Eblis." She only just prevented herself from bowing her head. He always made her feel somehow *less than*. Probably because he always confronted her with his incredible pearlescent wings slightly unfurled.

Or maybe it was because he was one of the oldest pureblood demons in existence, whose powers eclipsed any Earth-born demon blood descendant she'd ever encountered.

Plus, she owed him her life. When Eblis called, she always answered.

"There's been an unexpected development," he said. He rarely indulged in small talk. "A vampire was found in possession of an immortal forged sword. We need to find the rogue archangel responsible for its creation."

Although she'd never met a vampire, her friend Octavia worked with them every day. And by any reckoning, they were immortal when compared to humans.

But she'd long ago discovered that as far as Eblis was concerned, true immortals were confined to the fabled Alpha Pantheon of antiquity, who were the ancestors of the myriad gods and goddesses humans had worshipped over millennia, and pureblood demons.

And archangels.

Even those with mere traces of demon blood such as herself commanded a higher status than the so-called Undead in the immortal hierarchy.

"You think the rogue is known to the Watchers?" It was thanks to Eblis that she'd been accepted into the arcane network. And although he wasn't a member, and they shared an unspoken understanding that she never mentioned his name to anyone, they were all on the same side.

To unite descendants of demon kind. And bring the cursed archangels to justice.

"That's what we need to discover. Why would an archangel be in league with a bloodsucker?"

She knew his subtext. *What could a bloodsucker offer an archangel?*

"I'm going to the sacred mountains next week for the Equinox. I'll see what I can find out."

The Watchers met once a year, in their temple hidden deep within the mountains of what used to be ancient Mesopotamia. It was a chance for all the members to be among their own kind. To learn their history and draw pride from their suppressed heritage. But more than that, it was a chance to make lasting friendships. Something she'd never managed to do before. She doubted Eblis had any idea how much that meant to her.

"Good. The sword itself has disappeared, so I haven't been able to analyze it." Frustration threaded through his voice. "If it's in the possession of the Watchers, I need to know."

"Of course." Unease stirred. If the Watchers did, indeed, have the sword, she hoped he didn't expect her to steal it. Because that was a line she wasn't sure she was prepared to cross.

Her phone buzzed, and she pulled it from her pocket, intending to silence it. Except it was Nate. Anticipation sizzled through her, which was ridiculous but whatever.

"I need to take this," she said, and although Eblis didn't say a word or move a muscle, she knew she'd just seriously displeased him.

She angled away from him and took the call. "Hey, Nate."

"Isabella." His disembodied voice was sexier than ever and sent warm tingles running over her skin. She didn't know why she hadn't corrected him when he'd called her Isabella. She hadn't been called that for years. Not since she had lived with her mother, so long ago, when the sound of her name being called would cause dread to knot in her chest.

But Nate made each drawn out syllable sound infinitely seductive.

"Hope I caught you before your meeting started."

She didn't even glance at Eblis. "It's just about to. What's up?"

"Change of plan for tomorrow. I'm going to cook us dinner at my place."

She couldn't help smiling, even though she knew Eblis was watching and she preferred to keep her private life *private* when it came to him. Not that she had much of a private life when it came to relationships but that was beside the point.

"Sounds perfect. Unless you have an ulterior motive for not going to a restaurant?" Not that she cared if he did. The idea of him cooking for her was beyond charming, and if they were already at his place, there would be no delay between their pudding and sexual gratification.

Don't think about sex with Nate, while Eblis is standing next to me. It just felt wrong, somehow. But she couldn't help herself. There was something utterly irresistible about Nate, even when he wasn't present in all his gorgeous glory.

"Nothing ulterior about it." There was a laugh in his voice, as if he knew exactly what she meant and agreed with it. "Bring your toothbrush."

She laughed. "Subtle." *Wind up the conversation.* It was insane that she was keeping Eblis waiting but talking with Nate was just too much fun. From the corner of her eye she saw Eblis' wings flutter in silent censure and she sucked in a sharp breath. Fun over. "I have to go. Give me your address."

He told her and she barely managed to hide her surprise. He lived literally a couple of minutes down the road. "See you tomorrow," she promised, before hanging up.

She took longer than necessary pushing her phone back into her pocket. What was the matter with her? Yet she had the uncomfortable certainty that Eblis was judging her and finding her severely wanting. A prickle of resentment flared. There was nothing in their decades old agreement that said she couldn't have a sex life. In fact, one of the first things he'd shared with her was a demon made implant that prevented conception.

It was just awkward that he'd appeared as she was embarking on a rare, fleeting affair, even though it shouldn't be.

She gave up trying to analyze it and finally met his gaze.

He didn't say anything.

The pause grew and the silence became suffocating. She

fought the urge to fold her arms. It was a sign of insecurity, of weakness, and if there was one thing Eblis could not tolerate, it was weakness.

Finally, he uttered one, condemning word. "Nate."

Irritation bubbled through her veins. Yes, she owed Eblis everything. He'd discovered her at her lowest point and had literally brought her into the light. But that didn't mean he had the right to poke his nose into something entirely unconnected to their professional arrangement.

"I don't wish to discuss him."

It was the closest she'd ever come to defying him. Because there was no mistake. That one word had been a demand for more information.

His eyes glittered. She had the bizarre conviction that instead of condemning her insolence, he approved of her assertive retort.

"Have you ever wondered," he said, "why I took the time to nurture you?"

Taken aback at his sudden turn in the conversation, she stared at him. "Because I have demon blood."

His smile was almost pitying. What was *happening*? "I've met countless descendants of demons over millennia. On Earth, the bloodlines are diluted by untold generations. But you, Bella, are a rarity. You are a true half-blood demon."

Her heart slammed against her ribs. She'd never met anyone who could trace their immortal lineage with any accuracy, never mind pinpoint it to a parent. Since discovering her heritage, she'd imagined her unknown father was simply another nameless descendant of a demon who'd visited Earth countless years ago. Was Eblis trying to tell her...

"You're my father?" she whispered.

He cocked his head. "What? No. Why would you think that?" He sounded genuinely staggered by her question. Actually, he sounded faintly disgusted, but she'd let that go. Because if he *had* been her father and hadn't told her for all the years they'd known each other, she would've been furious.

After she'd recovered from the shock.

"Why wouldn't I think that?" she countered. "What are you getting at? Do you know who my father is?"

When she was a child, her mother had often told her she was the spawn of Satan himself.

A frown flickered over his face. "I've no idea. It's not important. The point is, you're far more powerful than you realize."

She wasn't sure how she felt about the revelation. Did it really change anything? She knew many others with demon blood, but no one really knew for sure just how much they possessed.

The baseline for acceptance into the network was an extended lifespan and the ability to heal from at least moderate injury.

To ascend into the ranks of the Elite, far more was demanded.

Most of the Elite were telepathic, and many could teleport. The ability to understand a multitude of spoken languages without first having to learn them was less common, and telekinesis was rare.

Yet Eblis had warned her not to let them know of the extent of her powers. They had no idea what she could do. When she'd queried it with him, his response had been enigmatic.

Never show your hand until you know you can win.

"And why are you telling me this now?"

"I'm telling you this now," Eblis said, barely concealed impatience in his voice, "because events are escalating. The existence of the sword on Earth is evidence of that. You've heard of the Archangel Nathanael."

It wasn't a question.

"Yes." After she'd passed the initiation ceremony for acceptance into the Watchers, she had learned of the hidden history of the world. And how, through millennia, one archangel had taken it upon himself to hunt down every descendant of demon kind.

But it wasn't only ancient history. As recently as one hundred years ago, before she'd joined the organization, he'd breached the Watchers' sacred temple and slaughtered all those who had tried to prevent him from destroying their archives. After a fierce battle, he'd finally been overpowered and thrown from the mountain. Since then, the Watchers had been vigilant in guarding against another invasion.

As far as she was concerned, there was a special circle in hell waiting for him. "You think *he's* the rogue responsible for bringing the sword to Earth?"

"Much as it pains me to defend Nate in any way, no. I don't believe he's responsible for that. But he wants that sword as much as I do. And believe me he'll go to any lengths to acquire it."

Her heart thudded an eerily slow tattoo against her ribs. Eblis had referred to Nathanael as *Nate*.

The archangel who hunted those with demon blood. The one who the Watchers had vilified for centuries.

Nate. The man she'd just had sex with, in this very room.

She drew in a long breath. It was a common name. There was no connection.

Except Eblis had dropped that name deliberately. There had been nothing random about his conversation at all.

There was nothing random in the silence that screamed between them now, either. He was waiting for her response.

"I hope you're not suggesting that the man I was speaking with on the phone *just so happens* to be the Archangel Nathanael?" It was hard to push out the words, she was so mad. Mad at Eblis for connecting the two and with herself for giving it a second thought.

"I sensed the taint of archangelic presence the moment I arrived. And then Nate calls you."

A thousand denials swarmed in her mind. She couldn't voice one of them. *It's not true.* She'd scanned his aura, the first and most basic safety precaution Eblis had taught her, and Nate was human.

With unidentified immortal traces in his heritage.

Why wouldn't a hunter of demons mask his true nature, the way she did?

"I—" She cleared her throat, an unpardonable show of self-doubt. She understood exactly what Eblis had yet to say. That Nate had seduced her solely because he'd known who she was.

The daughter of a full blood demon, whose connections might well have allowed him unchecked access to the Watchers.

Tonight hadn't been a casual hook-up. He'd stalked *Inanna*, waiting for her.

Waiting to make his move.

No wonder he'd asked her so many questions. And she had imagined it was because he was genuinely interested in her, as a person.

Nausea rolled through her. Had he bedazzled her? It would explain why she'd found him so fucking irresistible.

But it was more than that, and she knew it. If he'd tracked her down on any other night, she could have resisted him. *I have to believe that.*

Tonight, she'd been vulnerable. That was the only reason he'd succeeded in blindsiding her. Because her defenses were already fragile before he'd even set foot in her club.

Had he somehow *known*?

She had the mortifying urge to curl up on the chaise and hide from everything. From the piercing gaze of Eblis.

From the treacherous duplicity of Nate.

I'll cut my throat before I crumple. She pressed her lips together. She'd been fooled by an archangel, but he wouldn't reach his goal through her. They'd had one night together. That was it. It was fine to feel used. Because she had been. And she wouldn't give him the opportunity to do it again.

But it wasn't fine that her heart ached. Even if Nate had been human, and even if things had progressed beyond a few enjoyable dates, they'd never had a hope of anything more. She hadn't met a demon blood who interested her romantically and had long ago faced the fact it was easier to be on her own. She couldn't do relationships when she'd outlived everyone she'd ever cared about in the past.

It hurt too much.

How ironic. The Archangel Nathanael had lived for millennia. There was no chance of her outliving *him*.

Unless she destroyed him. And as much as she'd love to claim that victory, it would take more than a half-blood to accomplish it. Demons and archangels were as indestructible as the gods of antiquity.

But what if she found the immortal forged sword?

"How long ago did he find you?"

To her knowledge, he'd been searching for her for at least two weeks. "I don't know. I've been away, and only met him tonight."

"Good." Eblis folded his wings. "Only your pride is injured, then."

Her pride. Right. That's all this was, and she'd get over it. "You want me to find out everything he knows."

"You can try." Eblis didn't sound very concerned one way or the other. "He won't reveal anything to you. Your mission remains unchanged. Discover if the Watchers are in possession of the sword. As for Nate, he's obviously uncovered your heritage and hopes your powerful demon blood will help his quest. Be aware and don't fall."

"I'm in no danger of falling." She injected as much ice into her voice as she could. Did he think her completely stupid? It had been a long time since she'd been a gullible girl grateful for any scrap of kindness tossed her way. Yet with Nate, for a couple of delusional hours, she'd believed there had been something special between them.

"It's time to reveal more of your cards with the Watchers."

Brutally, she pulled herself back to the present. She had no idea what Eblis was talking about. "What?"

His eyes narrowed. "The common rank and file are no longer any use to us. You need to rise higher in the hierarchy. The only way to do that is for the Elite to acknowledge your superior bloodline. The ability to teleport is only rarely inherited and that alone will gain you access to the upper echelons."

"Understood."

"I hope you do, Bella." His smile didn't reach his eyes. "If we don't discover who gave the vampire the sword, Earth will become the battleground of ancient immortals."

CHAPTER 5

NATE

$\mathcal{N}$ate grinned as he finished his phone call with Isabella. After leaving *Inanna*, he'd found a furnished loft apartment within walking distance of the club. Within ten minutes he'd located and persuaded the estate agent to sign the lease over to him.

His powers of persuasion were very useful when it came to cutting through mortal-inspired red tape.

He strolled through the open plan living area into the bedroom, where a door led out onto a roof terrace. It was a disappointing view, with no trees in sight, just a sweep of other warehouse conversions. Still, he didn't plan on living here.

It was just a temporary base where he could bring Isabella.

And then a telepathic message cut through his lascivious plans on what he intended to do with Isabella the following night.

Nate. I'm done.

He hadn't expected to hear from Astrid yet. He'd taken the sword to her because her knowledge of weapons was legendary and if anyone could discover its origins, it was her.

On my way.

He teleported to her base, located on the far side of the Milky

Way. Unlike many of the archangels, who after the exodus from Earth had migrated to Andromeda, she'd chosen to stay in the backwaters of the universe.

Astrid was some distance from her beachside home, standing on the black sand as the local sun set beyond the ocean. She didn't turn at his approach.

He stood by her side and eyed the volcanic landscape. It possessed a stark beauty, enhanced by an underlying threat of imminent eruption, even though this section of the planet had been dormant for millennia.

Finally, Astrid turned to him. "The sword you brought me is the last one I crafted in Ama-gi."

It was of archangelic origin? He hadn't expected *that*. Somehow, it made the injuries the vampire had inflicted upon Az even more horrific. "You destroyed all your weapons in the aftermath."

After the archangels had escaped their vindictive Alpha Goddess, who had imprisoned them in the place of their creation while devastation swept the Earth.

"Yes." Astrid once again gazed at the tranquil ocean. "But this one was stolen before our goddess called us home."

He let out a harsh breath. He'd been so sure the sword was demon forged. It fit with his conviction that Dagan was involved. *I know he's involved.* "It must have been taken by an immortal, to get past your security. Any idea who it could have been?"

"I've always known who stole it."

A dark suspicion flared. "Who?"

"Your friend, Dagan." A hint of steel threaded through the words. She and Dagan had never seen eye to eye. "Except he wasn't a demigod, was he?"

Fuck. He was responsible for taking Dagan to Ama-gi, which meant it was his fault his friend Azrael was currently missing half a wing. On the other hand, it was the proof he needed that Dagan was the one who'd given the sword to the vampire.

The question was *why?* Although what reason did demons need to cause destruction and devastation in their wake?

For decades, he had counted Dagan among his closest friends. And in the end, he'd taken everything Nate had shared in confidence and betrayed the archangels' deepest secrets to their mutual goddess. And spilling those secrets had led to the destruction of the archangels' beloved children.

He'd never forgive Dagan or his cursed, treacherous race for that.

He'd never forgive himself, either.

Never trust a demon. It had become his mantra.

"No." Guilt dripped from the word. "How long did you know what he was?"

"A few years. Like you, I believed the lies he spewed."

Yeah, Dagan had been so very convincing.

"I'm going to find him, Astrid."

She inclined her head. "I can tell you where the sword has been. Its history has permeated the fabric of its soul."

He didn't believe a weapon could possess a soul. But Astrid had created it, forged it from the elements itself, and if anyone could discover its secrets, it was her.

"Tell me everything you've discovered." Nate barely suppressed a shudder, as the vision of Az's ruined wing, after he'd slain the vampire, flashed through his mind.

It was late morning when Nate woke. After leaving Astrid, he'd spent what was left of Earth's night in his new apartment, and sun streamed in through the window, sending a deceptively warm glow across the timber floorboards. Although the view was shit, the place compared favorably to many of the temporary bases he'd stayed in over the centuries.

He was in the kitchen, searching through the cupboards,

before he remembered he didn't have any coffee. Which reminded him. He didn't have *anything*, and he'd invited Isabella to dinner tonight.

The memory of her smile helped ease the bitter knot of guilt that had lodged in his chest since speaking with Astrid.

For millennia, he'd hunted dangerous demon kind as a form of penance for allowing Dagan's lies to blind him to the truth. He'd also harbored the hope one of them would have a solid lead that would give him a trail to Dagan. None of them had.

Now, finally, he had evidence that Dagan had not only been on Earth recently, but that he'd equipped a vampire with a weapon capable of destroying full blood immortals. The trail was no longer cold, and he intended to pursue it until the end.

But first, he needed coffee.

He left the building and walked along the grim looking back street, and within a couple of minutes saw *Inanna*. He headed into the nearest coffee shop.

Standing in front of him, queuing up at the counter, was Isabella. He grinned. What were the chances?

He lowered his head and growled into her ear. "Good morning."

She swung around so fast they almost smacked faces. He laughed. She didn't. In fact, she looked pissed off.

"Morning." She sounded as though the word killed her.

He frowned. Maybe her meeting last night had been a disaster. "Hey, are you okay? Anything you want to talk about?"

"No, I don't think so." She turned back and gave her order. To take away.

Fuck that. He leaned over her shoulder. "Make that two, to stay." Before she could take issue with him, he paid with one of his credit cards, took her arm, and ushered them to the only spare table in the place.

She sat opposite him without a word, but her eyes glittered

with fury. He shrugged and offered her another grin. Which she ignored.

"Come on, Isabella." He reached across the table and took her hand. She didn't unclench her fist. "Who's messed with you? Want me to sort them out?"

Her gaze was like a laser. "Tell me how you *sort out* your problems."

"Tell me what your problem is, and I'll construct an appropriate response."

She drew in a long breath. "It doesn't matter." Her gaze dropped to the table. "Let go of my hand."

Slowly, he released her fingers. "Are you pissed off with me?" He frowned. She'd been fine last night. And on the phone.

"Goodness. Why would I be pissed off with you?" Derision dripped from each word and he leaned back in his chair as his ego processed her retort.

Her reaction was... *interesting*.

"I don't know," he said, just as their coffees arrived. He waited until they were alone again. "You tell me."

She took a sip of coffee and appeared to be considering her answer. "All right." She placed her cup back on the table. "See if you can tell me the truth. Are you a bounty hunter, or not?"

Intrigued by the strange direction their conversation had taken, he shook his head. "You're the one who said I was a bounty hunter. I told you I hunted violators."

"Oh yes. Specifics." She made the word sound like a curse.

"The devil's in the details. Or so I've heard."

She didn't even crack a smile. What the fuck had happened in the few hours since they'd last spoken?

"Am I on your hit list?"

"What?" He stared at her, floored by her question. Where had it even come from?

"I know you've been stalking *Inanna* for the last two weeks. It doesn't take much to conclude you were waiting for me. Did you get all the information you needed? Am I expendable now?"

Well. Fuck. He wasn't often speechless, but he was now. Someone else at the club had noticed him, despite his glamour, and had found it suspicious enough to tell her. He sucked down his coffee and waited for the caffeine to hit. Isabella never took her accusing gaze from him.

If he wanted to see her again, and by the gods he certainly did, it seemed he'd have to tell her a version of the truth.

"First, you're not expendable. That's nonnegotiable." He paused but wasn't surprised when she didn't favor him with a smile. "Second, I have been watching *Inanna* although I wouldn't call it stalking. I can't go into all the details, but I've reason to believe something's going on that you're unaware of. And yes." He sighed. She'd never know how much it cost him to admit to making an error. "Before I met you, I did think you might be involved. Even I make mistakes on occasion."

Her eyes narrowed. It appeared she wasn't impressed by his concession to share the partial truth with her.

"There's nothing going on at *Inanna* that I'm unaware of."

"I'm referring to something that happened in the past."

"If it happened in the past, why are you investigating it now?"

She was *interrogating* him.

He was tempted to lower his glamour, just for a moment, to see her reaction. Except he didn't want her spellbound by his archangelic radiance. He wanted—hell, he craved—her unvarnished honesty.

"You've heard of cold cases?" He waited until she gave a reluctant nod. "Something happened to a friend of mine recently that gave me a new lead. Your club is connected."

She took another sip of her coffee, obviously processing his words. "What happened to your friend?"

Although suspicion still saturated every word, some of her antagonism had faded. He'd take that as a win.

Except then her question registered, and his wings, hidden beneath his glamour, rippled with primal dread. He'd never forget the sight of Az's severed feathers, or the river of blood across the floor.

He swallowed and shoved the memory to the back of his mind. "He was attacked."

"Is he okay?"

Define okay. "He'll live, if that's what you mean."

"And you think his attacker is connected to my club."

"The attacker was neutralized. But I need to find out who was behind the hit."

"It was an attempted assassination?" She sounded intrigued. He needed to shut up. The more he told her, the more potential danger she could be in.

"Classified." He leaned across the table. She didn't back away. "Anything you can tell me about the inner workings of *Inanna* could help."

"What kind of things do you want to know?"

"Do you have a silent partner?" *Who could be a demon?*

"No. The clubs are all mine."

"Anything unusual strike you about the previous owner?" He'd done all the research, but not everything was recorded into archives.

"I didn't meet the previous owner. All the properties I take on have been more or less abandoned and left to fall into disrepair. This was an executor sale."

He knew that, but the executor had been the son of the owner. Last week, he'd paid the man a visit and there hadn't been even the faintest hint of demon around him. But it was always possible there might have been something Isabella had noticed at the time.

Obviously not.

"It's okay. I'll figure it out."

"Don't you have any other questions?"

"Yeah." He took her hand again and this time she didn't protest. "What's your favorite food?"

She stared at him as though she thought he'd lost his mind. She wasn't far wrong. Because tonight couldn't come soon enough.

"Why?"

"Our date tonight." Had she forgotten? It was a good job his ego was the size of a small planet, otherwise he'd be feeling severely bruised right about now. He grinned, at both the image of his wounded ego and the startled expression on Isabella's face.

"Oh." She shifted in her chair, appeared to notice their clasped hands for the first time, and shot him a guarded glance. "Surprise me."

CHAPTER 6

BELLA

*Y*ou're *not seriously going on this date tonight.*

Bella had to agree with the voice in the back of her head. It was an insane idea. Walking into the enemy's lair, an immortal with power that eclipsed her own, was just asking to be murdered. Or worse.

Except a tiny niggle of doubt kept gnawing through her brain. *He doesn't know who I am.*

Or was she merely deluding herself? Archangels were, after all, the greatest of the deceivers. Nate had once failed to destroy the heart of the Watchers. It was logical he'd use any means he could to gain access to the temple, including forging a sham connection with her. Yet she couldn't shake the feeling that she was right.

Which made Eblis wrong.

"Challenge accepted," Nate said, and it was damn hard not to gaze into his deceptively gorgeous eyes and smile at him.

She was done smiling at him, so she picked up her coffee and finished it instead. But the underlying horror in his voice, and haunted expression on his face when he'd told her about his friend kept flashing through her mind.

There had been nothing fake about that, at least. He wanted revenge for his friend.

"Is there anything you definitely *don't* eat? Or are allergic to?"

She glanced at him over the rim of her cup. Was he for real? If he knew of her demon blood, he didn't even need to get her alone in order to destroy her. He certainly wouldn't go to the trouble of poisoning her, or even luring her to his lair in order to end her life.

"I've a cast iron stomach," she told him. "I can handle anything you throw at me."

"Interesting idea. But I'd planned on using plates tonight."

Archangels weren't supposed to have a sense of humor. And while rumors of their mesmeric beauty were common knowledge among members of the Watchers, she'd never imagined *she* might find one in the least bit gorgeous.

Even though her defenses *had* been compromised last night, it was mortifying she'd been so bewitched. And although it was conceivable she had been dazzled by Nate's radiance, Eblis' disclosure that she was a genuine, half-blood demon made that next to impossible.

"Plates it is, then." She placed her cup on the table and once again eyed the way Nate's large hand covered hers. His touch should be like acid eating into her skin, but instead he made her feel warm and protected.

Definitely delusional.

Archangels didn't protect. They destroyed. She needed to remember that, if she planned on seeing him again.

I've no intention of seeing him again.

To underscore her point, she stood, and a despicable sense of loss shivered through her as his hand slid from hers. But it lasted only a moment, as when he joined her, he threaded his fingers through hers as though he had the right.

She tried to ignore the flutters of need that burst into life at his touch, but her body clearly had no scruples when it came to base lust. Fine. Her body didn't rule her. She could hold his hand until they were outside and then she'd say goodbye and never see him again.

"I need to get to work."

He opened the door for her, and they stood facing each other outside the coffee shop. They were still holding hands. Surreptitiously, she caressed his knuckles with her thumb, and his fingers tightened.

Don't. You. Dare.

But she'd already decided. Because there was a raw, needy sliver of her soul that craved to know if everything he'd said to her was a lie. And the only way to find the truth hidden within his deceptions was if she spent more time in his company.

He didn't know who she really was. That gave her a shred of advantage, at least.

"Did you want to come back with me and look around the club while it's closed?"

"Are you sure you don't mind?" His eyes gleamed with humor. It was *really* hard not to respond with a mocking retort, the way she'd so easily done last night. But if he was playing her, she'd be damned if she'd give him the satisfaction of falling so easily for his charm.

"If I minded, I wouldn't have asked." *Stop gazing into his eyes.* Ruthlessly, she turned from him and focused on her club, just down the road. "It would help if you could give me a clue as to what you're searching for, though. I might be able to help."

He matched her stride as they crossed the road and she tried to ignore how crazily right it felt, holding hands with him.

An archangel.

Enough. She was only doing this because she needed to find out exactly what Nate was doing. And if it meant she had to play along with him for a while, then that's just the way it had to be.

"It's hard to be specific," he said, as she unlocked the door and they went inside. "The best way to explain it is I guess you could call it a sixth sense. I can pick up vibrations in the atmosphere. Feel free to laugh. I won't be offended."

His accompanying grin took her breath away. Even if she didn't know his true identity, she would have believed he was telling the truth.

"I'm not laughing. I've been called a psychic before."

And the first time had been by her mother, when she'd been five years old. Except the word used hadn't been *psychic* and she'd been locked in the dusty attic for a week as punishment.

All because she had repeated out loud what her mother had just thought.

"Really?" He turned to face her, and if she didn't know better, she would have sworn genuine interest etched his features. But then, maybe he was genuinely interested? Or maybe he still suspected her heritage, and this was another ploy to get her to reveal herself?

She couldn't afford to assume anything when it came to Nate.

"Yes. It's not always as great as it's cracked up to be."

"I'll concede some abilities are worse than others."

She led him up the main stairs that, unlike the staff only ones behind the bar, were open to the public on special occasions. His arm brushed against hers, and ripples raced along her skin. Why was she still holding his hand?

Because I want to learn all I can about my enemy.

And obviously, holding hands was vital to her mission.

Right.

"What abilities are we talking about here, specifically?" They reached the landing, where the elegant rooms could be hired out for private parties. "Is your clairsentience good or bad, in your opinion?"

"It has its moments." His voice was dry, as though in reality his ability to sense energy signatures wasn't that great. Not that she'd know, since it wasn't an ability she possessed. "What's your special power?"

He wouldn't catch her out that easily. "I read the cards."

Not a lie. In the past, reading the cards had enabled her to earn enough money to keep a roof over her head. At least she'd never had to kill anyone for a gold coin or two.

She unlocked a staff only door, and as they climbed the second staircase that led to the converted attics, he gave her an accessing glance. "Are you any good at it?"

"I've never had any complaints." Not that she read them anymore. There was no need. Although… "Do you want me to read yours?"

This time his smile looked a little grim. "Not sure it's a good idea for you to learn all of my secrets."

"We never did play a game of quid pro quo."

What the *fuck* was she saying? Last night, it had just been a bit of fun. For her, anyway. Who knew what it had been for Nate? But today was different. She saw hidden meanings in every word he said, even though in her gut she was sure he was ignorant of her demon blood.

Trying to find out more about him was one thing. Playing dangerous games was something else. Then again, how else would she discover anything?

A slow smile curved his deliciously decadent lips.

Stop *right* there. She wasn't going to recall all the things she'd imagined his mouth doing to her last night, when she'd been unable to sleep. All his mouth was capable of was lying to her.

Which made the prospect of uncovering anything useful from him damn near impossible. So why was she indulging her frustrating need to spend more time in his company?

"Do you have a list of ground rules?"

It took her a second to figure out what he meant. "We're both adults here. If you tell me you've done something illegal, I don't have to respond in kind."

He laughed. "Have you done anything illegal, Isabella?"

"Wouldn't you like to know."

They were in her office and he made no attempt to release her hand. Mentally, she gritted her teeth and pulled free. There. That wasn't so hard, was it?

"There's a lot about you I'd like to know," he said, his gaze never leaving hers. A despicable flutter ignited deep inside at his provocative promise. Or was it a threat? The worst thing was, she didn't even care which it was.

"Likewise." She wasn't flirting. She was digging for information. To underscore that reminder, she took off her coat, and draped it over the chaise. The image of Nate caressing her foot last night flashed across her mind, and unwanted warmth licked through her treacherous blood. *Focus.* She inhaled a long breath, in the vain hope that might smother her overexcited libido and turned to face him. "Okay, I'll start. I was born in London, the only child of my mother, and none of her relatives would acknowledge me."

"Why not?"

"What?" He was supposed to give her something in response, not question her statement. "Because—" She swallowed her retort before she dug an even bigger hole for herself. Why had she even mentioned her mother's relatives? It had no place in this exchange with Nate. Besides, she had long ago stopped craving the love of her grandmother and aunt who had always tried to deny her existence.

Nate was still waiting for her answer. She offered him a brittle smile. "Because I was born out of wedlock."

Let him make what he liked of that. It was a despicable reason, yet it was the truth. They had only tolerated her presence when she was a child because they'd mistakenly believed she was the offspring of her mother's wealthy protector.

"That makes two of us."

Brutally, she throttled the memories that threatened to spill from the dungeon she usually kept buried deep inside her mind. Why did she keep thinking of her past when she was with Nate?

It was the second time she'd spoken of her family, and she'd only met him last night. It would be so much easier on her pride to suspect he was using his corrupted abilities to force her to confide in him, but she knew the truth.

It was the way he focused on her, as though he was genuinely interested in everything she said. The sexy gleam in his eyes, and irresistible smile, that melted her defenses and overruled her caution.

He was just too bloody easy to talk to.

But he wasn't wriggling off the hook this lightly.

"I need more than that."

"Fair enough." He frowned at the ceiling, as though contemplating his answer. Her mouth dried. Was he striking that spectacular pose on purpose, or did he have no idea just how breathtaking he looked?

Except all he was doing was standing there. Thinking. And she couldn't drag her eyes from him.

"Okay." Finally, he caught her gaze, and the mysterious, dark depths of his irises ignited all her good resolutions into liquid flame. "This is going to sound like I'm shitting you, but it's the truth. Many of those I share possible DNA with wish I'd never been created. Luckily, we never cross paths."

"Created?" It would've been so easy for him to say *born*, because that was the accepted term, and she could have quietly despised him for lying. But, in this at least, he'd told her the truth. She knew the history of how the Alpha Goddess had first created her beloved demons, before casting them out in favor of her archangels.

He gave her a cynical grin. "It fits."

It fit perfectly. If only he *had* lied. It would give her something solid to hold against him other than what she'd heard about him. It was a struggle to maintain an icy grip on reality when he could charm her so damn easily. She hauled her besotted senses back in line before she did something unforgiveable. Such as kiss him.

She took a hasty step back, as a precaution. "*Possible* DNA?"

Gods, why was her voice so husky?

"At best, you could say my parentage is questionable."

Despicable warmth fluttered through her chest at his confession. She sucked in a sharp breath to help clear the sex infused fog beguiling her mind. It didn't help. He was telling her the truth of his origins and didn't even realize how much he was truly revealing.

"And at worst?"

"My parentage would be confirmed."

"Wow. I didn't expect that." She had the contemptible urge to smile at him. "Most people want to know their parentage." The way she'd always wanted to know who her father was? And now she knew he was a full blood demon, what real difference did it make?

"I'm not most people."

"You can say that again." Okay. Stop flirting *right now*.

"Was that a compliment? Because I feel there was some condemnation lurking in there somewhere."

Despite her best intentions, her smile escaped. Damn it. "I think you have an ego problem."

"I think you could be right."

She was having far too much fun. He wasn't just some random archangel. He was the one who not only hunted those with demon blood for sport but had almost destroyed the only sanctuary her kind had on Earth. The one who had a special circle in hell waiting for him. Just because it was hard to reconcile the reviled hunter with the irresistible immortal standing before her, was no excuse to lose sight of her objectives.

With more reluctance than she'd ever admit, she tore herself from his magnetic presence and made her way to her desk. She didn't have to be looking at him to know he never took his hot gaze from her.

Enough. She needed to get back to business. "How do you want to do this? Go through the offices one by one?"

Could he sense the lingering presence of Eblis, the way Eblis had detected Nate?

"Yes, that'd be good." His phone buzzed and he frowned as he checked the screen. "I need to take this."

"Sure." She logged onto the Internet, but her attention was centered on Nate.

"Hey, Nic," he said. "What's the problem?"

She tapped a couple of keys, in case he correctly guessed she was attempting to eavesdrop. Annoyingly, even with her acute hearing, she couldn't pick up anything Nic said.

"Uh-huh." Nate glanced her way. She pretended not to notice. "I can be there within the hour."

He pushed his phone back into his jeans pocket before strolling over to her. It had been a mistake to sit down. Because now he towered over her desk, like a living mountain, and the oxygen evaporated.

Breathe.

"A new lead on your case?" Somehow, she managed to sound casual.

"Could be." He gave a frustrated sigh. "We still on for dinner tonight?"

"Why not?" The words were out before she could stop them. But it was fine. She knew the dangers and had no intention of doing anything stupid. It was possible, in his lair, he'd open up even more to her. Finding out everything he knew was, of course, the *only* reason she intended seeing him again.

"Seven?"

"Sounds good."

He planted his hands on her desk and leaned closer. Her heart stuttered and breath stalled. He was going to kiss her. It was no big deal. She could do this. His lips brushed hers, tender, questioning, and her resolve to remain motionless melted.

Her fingers teased his jaw, his stubble grazing her in a seductive caress. A deep groan vibrated through him, sending shivers of need dancing across her flesh. Slowly he straightened, raw lust glowing in his eyes.

"You better believe it," he growled, and his smoldering gaze left her in no doubt he wasn't thinking about the dinner he'd promised her.

And she couldn't wait.

CHAPTER 7

BELLA

It had been an hour since Nate had left, and Bella still couldn't concentrate. It was ridiculous. And annoying. She pressed her lips together—they still tingled from his touch—and narrowed her eyes.

For the last forty minutes she'd been on NightRaven, aka the deep net. It was a little like the demon version of humanity's dark net, except it was impossible to access without explicit invite from the Watchers' Elite. It was a place where her kind could stay in touch with others from their hidden world, as well as share information, rumors and speculation.

She had slipped into the feeds of several of her most reliable sources, looking for information on the powerful sword. She'd always found it amazing how easily others were willing to spill things online, but so far, she'd come up blank.

She let out an impatient sigh as she scrolled through yet another watercooler where members seemed to do nothing but bitch about humans, and how it was time for the long overdue demon uprising.

Whingeing demon bloods got on her nerves. Instead of

complaining, why didn't they get off their arses and do something constructive, like enter politics?

There was nothing in any of the public access areas. She went deeper, using AI that Eblis had shared with her, that allowed her to enter private sites. The Elite would freak the fuck out if they knew she possessed such technology and hadn't shared it with them.

Finally, she hit pay dirt.

There's a big cover up going on in Romania.

I don't give a shit what the vampires are doing.

Nah, word has it, an archangel was almost destroyed.

Her breath stilled and mind whirled. Octavia was in Romania. A few days ago, she'd met the archangel responsible for the Great Massacre of dhampirs.

Nate had told her his friend had recently been attacked. And Eblis had dismissed the possibility that Nate might be the archangel behind bringing the immortal forged sword to Earth. But he'd been clear about one thing.

"He'll go to any lengths to acquire it."

There were a thousand reasons why Nate might want that sword. But once again, the barely disguised horror in his voice as he'd spoken of the attack echoed through her mind.

It must have been an extraordinary injury, to have shocked an archangel. She doubted he'd care if the victim had been a mere mortal, which pointed one way. His friend was another archangel. Was the weapon used the same one Eblis sought?

And was Nate's friend the same archangel that Octavia had met?

She owed Eblis so much. He wanted that sword, and this was a possible lead.

There was only one thing for it. She needed to go to Romania.

Nate

Nate teleported to the medieval castle in Romania, where only days ago he'd fought dhampirs and vampires side-by-side with Azrael and Nic. It was early afternoon and raining as he marched across the forecourt to the castle's massive double doors. The timing of Nic's call fucking sucked, no pun intended, but at least he was seeing Isabella tonight.

He let out a long breath. She intrigued him, and he was going to enjoy every moment until their inevitable parting. But before then, he intended to discover every secret she kept.

She was hiding something he needed to know. Yet the more he learned about her, the less he understood.

It was why he was still so utterly charmed by her.

As Nic strolled out of the castle, he forcibly dragged his mind from her tempting lips, addictive scent, and mesmeric eyes. He'd never had trouble focusing on work before.

First time for everything.

"What have you discovered?" he said by way of greeting. In general, archangels and vampires didn't get on but he and Nic went back centuries. The vampire, who had no problem with sunlight, was one of his closest friends and the founder of an ancient order of immortals, the Strigoi Echelon.

"Octavia is still analyzing the unidentified sample we found in Sakarbaal's lab." Nic's lips thinned at the mention of the ancient vampire that Azrael had slain. The vampire who had raised a dhampir army with the apparent intention of conquering the planet.

Among other things.

They entered the castle. There was no sign in the great hall of the battle they'd waged or blood that had been spilled. It was scrubbed clean and the faint smell of disinfectant hung in the air. "But you think it's connected to his attack on Az?"

"Possibly. We need you to question him and see if he knows anything about it."

"Sure." They had reached the lab, located in the dungeons, and he nodded a greeting to Octavia who was supervising her team. Against his better judgment, his gaze slid to the flagstone floor, but no trace of Azrael's blood remained.

"Hey, Nate," Octavia said when they reached her side. "Have you ever seen anything like this before?" She handed him a small phial half-filled by a strange, liquid smoke.

Eerie shudders of revulsion chased over his fingers. Evil exuded from whatever the phial contained, and he crushed his instinctive reaction to drop the glass cylinder onto the floor.

"No." His voice was rough. He couldn't help it. What the fuck was this stuff? "How much of this did Sakarbaal have?"

"You're holding about a quarter of what we've found. So far, we've not identified any of its elements."

It burned through the phial into his skin, and nausea churned. "It's not from Earth, then."

"I doubt it's from this universe," she responded.

Well, fuck. "What the hell was that twisted piece of shit up to?"

"That's irrelevant," Octavia said. "I'm interested in what this is, and where it came from."

"And what it's capable of doing." Nic picked up a cylindrical case and handed it to him. Obviously, Nate hadn't hidden his reaction as well as he thought he had. Relief clawed through him as he slid the phial into the case, muting the alien malevolence. "From the way you handle the phial, it appears the substance affects your physiology in a way that it doesn't ours."

The implication drilled through his skull. There were many things that could adversely affect mortals and even vampires that didn't have any impact on archangels. This was the first time the opposite held true.

"That's fucked up." He'd visit Azrael, but he'd also take a sample to Astrid. With her knowledge of elemental forces, it was possible she'd come across this substance before.

"This whole thing is fucked up." Nic swept his condemning gaze around the lab.

"I agree," Octavia said. "But his science is fascinating."

"I'll get back to you as soon as I have any news," Nate said, as Octavia's phone rang. He and Nic left the lab and Nate glanced at the antique furniture and priceless artwork that gave the castle a deceptively cultured air. "Are you moving your base here?"

Nic flashed his fangs in a humorless smile. "Only temporarily, and only because I don't have your advantage of long-distance teleportation. There's a great deal of work to be done here. It's easier than transporting everything to London."

"Do you mind if I take a look around?"

"Be my guest." Sarcasm dripped from each word. Nate was fully aware of how much Nic despised everything about Sakarbaal, including his cursed castle. He grasped his friend's shoulder, before making his way to the stairs. The last and only other time he'd been here all he'd seen of the place was the great hall and the lab.

The opulence continued in every room and passageway, with the image of the phoenix interwoven in tapestries and furnishing. Considering how the bastard had tortured his captive bird, it was fucking obscene.

Dhampirs who worked for the Echelon were scattered throughout the castle, as well as several vampires who didn't need to hide from the sun. He entered a circular room in a tower, that besides being unusually sparse, also afforded a breathtaking aerial view of the surrounding countryside. From his vantage point at the window, he could see the edge of the forest to his right, and in the distance to his left, beyond rolling meadows of snowdrops, was the nearest village.

A lone figure approached the earthen ramparts of the castle. He knew the castle was visible to mortals, but Sakarbaal had cloaked it in a protective glamour that caused humans to subconsciously avoid the area. The vampire's demise hadn't destroyed the protection.

This human didn't skirt the perimeter. *This* human appeared to know exactly where they were going.

He leaned forward, narrowing his eyes. A tall woman, her hair hidden beneath a beret, hurried across the grass. No way. He was so fucking obsessed by Isabella, now he was seeing her in random strangers. It would be funny, if it wasn't slightly alarming.

But he couldn't drag his fascinated gaze away. Because she *was* Isabella. Or her doppelganger.

"Fucking losing it," he muttered, before he teleported beyond the ramparts. It was still raining, and the figure was some distance ahead of him. Without warning, she stopped dead and swung around. His heart slammed against his ribs. There was no mistake.

It was her.

Her eyes widened in obvious shock as she caught his gaze. For endless seconds the world stilled as raindrops glittered on her eyelashes.

He let out a harsh breath and broke the spell. "Isabella?"

For an incredulous moment he had the certainty she was going to deny her identity. But then she blinked, shook her head, and stepped forward. "Nate. What are you doing here?"

He could ask her the same thing. Fuck it, he *would* ask her the same thing.

"How did you get here?" Okay, not exactly the same. But he'd been with her in London barely three hours ago. How the fuck had she traveled across Europe so quickly?

"The same way you did, I should think."

Yeah, he doubted that. Belatedly, his scrambled brain righted itself. Just because he'd never flown in a plane was no reason to forget that was how mortals navigated their planet. "You didn't say anything about going to Romania." What the hell? Now he sounded as though he expected her to confide her every move to him. Which he didn't.

"Neither did you," she countered.

Fair enough, except he could visit the Andromeda Galaxy and still be back on Earth in time for their dinner date.

Stop thinking about that fucking date.

It was an effort, but he managed to drag his gaze from her and cast a deceptively casual glance at the castle. "A minor emergency came up. I needed to visit a friend."

When she didn't answer right away, he gave into his need to look at her again. Tendrils of blonde hair had escaped her beret and clung against her rain streaked cheeks. Was he imagining that wary expression in her eyes?

She cleared her throat. "You're not going to believe this. But me too."

She was right. He didn't. But what other explanation could there be for her unexpected appearance?

"Your friend lives in the village?"

"Uh, no." She shifted, as though his question made her uncomfortable. Or maybe she was just uncomfortable from standing in the rain. "She's working at the castle."

But there were no humans in the castle. Did she know that?

It didn't seem likely. Humans weren't the most accepting of races. She probably had no idea her friend wasn't human. Although considering the operation currently being undertaken there, he doubted Nic wanted any oblivious visitors. Who was she meeting?

"Are you going inside? Or waiting for your friend out here?"

"Out here. What about you?"

He shrugged. "I'm done. Want some company until she arrives?"

"If you don't mind getting any wetter." She pushed her hands into the pockets of her coat and looked adorably bedraggled. *Did I really just think that?* "Is your friend also in the castle?"

It hardly mattered if he told her the truth, considering they were standing right outside it. "Yes."

"And is the reason you're here connected to my club?"

Since he'd already told her *Inanna* was on his radar, he figured there was no harm in once again telling her the truth. "Possibly."

She shivered in the chilly breeze and he wrapped his arm around her shoulders. If he couldn't teleport them both somewhere out of the rain, the least he could do was share his body heat. She didn't melt into him, but she didn't shove him away, either. It seemed she still hadn't completely forgiven him for having *stalked* her club before meeting her.

They walked across the forecourt. She might not be allowed inside, but she could at least be sheltered from the weather in the entrance.

"I wish I knew what you were *really* doing." She glanced up at him.

"I haven't lied to you." He pulled her closer and this time her tense muscles relaxed. "But if I told you the whole truth, I'd have to kill you." He grinned at her and was rewarded with a clearly reluctant smile.

"Okay. Now *that* I believe."

He laughed. "Sometimes I think you have a very low opinion of me."

"You have no idea."

"You have a great way with words. Anyone ever told you that?"

"It's one of my superpowers." Her voice was dry, but another smile tugged at her lips. Why did she seem so unwilling to share a laugh with him? It was a bit extreme if she was still pissed off that he'd been casing out her club for a couple of weeks. "You bring out the worst in me."

They reached the doors where they were finally protected from the weather, and he backed her up against the stone wall. "I noticed. Are you staying overnight in the village?"

Confusion flashed across her face. "What?"

"I'm guessing you're not flying back to England tonight. We could have our date here, instead."

"Oh." She appeared to be thinking it through. This woman would end up crushing his ego to the size of a walnut. He snorted with laughter at the incongruous image, and she narrowed her eyes at him. He shrugged, feigning innocence, and she let out a sigh. "Okay. Why not?"

"Don't sound too excited. I might get ideas."

"You're so—" She bit off her words, gazed at him for a moment and then shook her head, almost in wonder. "*Weird.*"

One of the doors opened before he could ask for clarification because what the hell did she mean by weird? She sounded as though he contradicted everything she expected, which pointed to the possibility that whoever had told her he'd been checking out *Inanna* had also shared some unsavory personal details.

Nobody knew his personal details to share.

He'd ask her later.

A sharp intake of breath caused him to look over his shoulder, where an all too familiar dhampir was standing, her deep auburn hair pulled into its usual French plait. "Octavia?"

"Nate." Her startled glance darted from him to Isabella. With reluctance, he pulled back.

"Isabella, this is Octavia."

Silence greeted his introduction. Realization dawned.

They knew each other. He'd assumed Isabella's friend was a regular dhampir, one nearer her own age that she could have met anywhere and who passed herself off as a human. Dhampirs, after all, blended into the mortal population without any problems. But he hadn't expected her to know one so high in the hierarchy, or one of the Echelon's most eminent scientists.

It reinforced his conviction that he needed to uncover the secrets she seemed so keen to keep.

CHAPTER 8

BELLA

*B*ella hitched in a shallow breath as awareness pummeled through her mind.

Nate and Octavia knew each other.

Did Octavia want to acknowledge their friendship or not in front of him? She wouldn't do anything to put her friend in an awkward position, but they couldn't remain in this stalemate for much longer without Nate getting suspicious.

She took a chance. "Hello."

It was a neutral response, and Octavia could take it in any direction she needed to.

"Hi." Octavia's voice gave nothing away. Heat swarmed through Bella's body and as Nate folded his arms and transferred his gaze between them, she knew he hadn't been fooled for a second.

Once again, an excruciating silence descended. She half wished she'd stayed in London and just spoken to Octavia on the phone. But there were some things that could only be shared face to face. Which was why she'd arranged to meet her here.

"Right," Nate said at last, breaking the deadlock. "I'll catch up with you later."

"

For endless seconds his intense gaze burned into her, as though he could read all her secret thoughts. Or maybe he was simply debating whether or not to kiss her.

Did she want him to kiss her?

Hell yes.

Despicable regret surged through her when he merely gave her an enigmatic smile and walked away.

Don't watch him go.

It was harder than it should have been to tear her besotted gaze from his retreating back and face Octavia. She could pretend all she liked, but the truth was she relished her interactions with Nate. If that wasn't a sign of a warped obsession, she didn't know what was.

Concern etched her friend's face. "How long have you known Nate, Bella?"

Was it really only yesterday they'd met? It seemed he had been a part of her life for so much longer. In any case, she was fully aware of what Octavia was really asking.

"I know what he is."

Shock flashed across Octavia's face. "I had no idea you knew any archangels, let alone…" Her voice trailed away before her gaze sharpened. "That you were in a relationship with one."

"I wouldn't call it a relationship."

"Even *so*." Octavia grabbed her arm and pulled her into the castle. "I thought you despised them all."

"I do." She sighed, because how hypocritical did she sound? "Obviously, I didn't know what he was when we met. Otherwise I never would have got involved with him."

"No wonder you wanted to see me."

Oh yes, about that. She'd almost forgotten the reason why she'd contacted Octavia. "No, he's not the reason I called you. I didn't even know you knew him."

"Hmm." Octavia frowned. "I don't know him that well, but

he's been around the Echelon for years. He's one of Nico's oldest friends."

Great. Soon after befriending Octavia, when they'd discovered each other's immortality, Bella had learned her friend worked with an ancient vampire who had founded a powerful Order. She'd had no idea the vampire hung out with archangels.

Nico was the *Nic* that Nate had spoken to on the phone earlier today in her office.

"Is there somewhere private we can talk?" Because what she was about to tell Octavia, wasn't something she could do in public.

"Sure." Octavia gave her a curious glance before leading her across the hall. Bella couldn't help herself as she ran a critical eye over the great hall. What was with the obsession with phoenixes? Their images were carved into the ornate wooden furniture and woven into breathtaking tapestries that hung on the walls. Sure, the mythical bird was fabulous but, in this castle, it also seemed somehow ominous.

She trailed her fingers over the stone wall as they went up the spiral staircase, but no flashes of insight came to her. Had Nate picked up any vibrations in here?

Gods, she'd almost died when he had called her name.

But it confirmed one of her suspicions. She was on the right track when it came to connecting the vampire, the sword, and the attempted assassination of an archangel.

And Nate still wants to go out to dinner with me tonight.

"This castle has had many additions over the centuries," Octavia said as they emerged into daylight once again. "It's like a labyrinth. Anyway, we have our rooms on this floor."

She pulled her attention back to the present. Even if she did go out with Nate tonight, it was only so she could find out more information. Despite Eblis' conviction, Nate didn't appear to mind sharing things with her. Sure, they weren't immortalized secrets, and she supposed he hadn't really told her anything of vital importance, but when he *had* shared personal insights—he hadn't lied.

I don't care about his personal insights.

Except a contemptible part of her did.

Octavia opened a door to a bedroom that could have come straight from a five-star hotel. Bella shut the door behind her and took a deep breath. She wasn't looking forward to this, but if she wanted Octavia to break confidences, then she had to break some of her own.

"What's this all about?" Octavia tucked her hands into the pockets of her white lab coat. Bella pulled off her beret and unwrapped her scarf, but she couldn't procrastinate forever.

"We both know there are sides of our lives that we've never shared before."

Octavia's expression didn't flicker. "Yes."

"You've probably guessed I've met a lot of demon bloods over the years."

"It makes sense. Why wouldn't you? I know scores of dhampirs."

"That's different. Your race hasn't been vilified throughout history."

"I don't think humans would be accepting of dhampirs, if they knew we walked among them."

Maybe not, but Bella still didn't think it was the same. Dhampirs had always known where they belonged, but until Eblis had found her, and until she'd joined the Watchers, she'd been alone. Thinking she was a horrifying freak of nature.

But that wasn't the discussion she needed to have right now.

"Before I say anything else, I need your word that it stays between us."

"You have it."

"And the reason I'm telling you now, is because I think our investigations intersect."

Octavia was silent for a moment. "You believe if we share information, we can help each other?"

Now came the tricky part. "I'm not sure I have any information that might help you. But I'll tell you something of my life, and then it's down to you whether you can share anything with me."

"Okay." Although Octavia's voice was neutral, intrigue gleamed in her eyes. "I'm not promising anything, though."

"I possess more powers than you know. I can teleport."

"Ah, I wondered about that. And it does explain how you appeared at the castle so soon after your phone call."

Well, shit. She'd been all hyped up, ready to give a demonstration, and Octavia wasn't even phased by the revelation. It wasn't a good start.

"Not that it matters, but teleportation is a rare ability for demon bloods to inherit."

Fuck. Now she sounded defensive.

"Is it?" Octavia appeared fascinated by that. "You know, there's hardly anything in the histories about demons. Even Nico hasn't met one. I'm certain he'd like to meet you, if you're willing."

By the way things were going, revealing her heritage to the leader of the Strigoi Echelon might be the only way she'd get any answers. But that would be a last resort, since she was sure Nico would want a lot more information than she was willing—or able —to give.

She had to get back on track. "I'm a member of an underground organization that seeks out descendants of demons. I haven't shared this with you before because its existence is a closely guarded secret. The Elite plug any leaks by destroying not only the source, but also anyone connected to that source."

"But?" Octavia prompted.

"*But,*" Bella repeated, "I suspect the vampire who recently attempted to assassinate an archangel used a sword that could now be in this organization's possession."

"Ah."

"I won't ask you anything. But if you can confirm any of my suspicions, that would be helpful."

Octavia was silent. Bella held her breath. Finally, her friend spoke.

"This castle belonged to Sakarbaal. He arose at least three thousand years ago in ancient Phoenicia. I'm here working to unravel the —" she hesitated, as if unsure whether to confide or not, "distasteful experiments he undertook. I'm not investigating the attack on Azrael when he and Nate fought the vampire, or the whereabouts of a sword that was able to sever the wing from an archangel."

A shiver skated over her arms at the graphic image that flashed through her mind. The friend Nate had told her about. No wonder he'd sounded so horrorstruck.

No. She couldn't afford to extend him any measure of empathy. Azrael was the slayer of dhampirs, and Nate would destroy her without a second thought if he discovered who she really was.

Would he, though?

She dug her nails into her palms to focus her thoughts. The Archangel Nathanael was a hunter of demon kind. He'd already tried to crush the Watchers once. She couldn't afford to forget it, even if every time she was in his company she *did.*

And then the rest of Octavia's words penetrated.

When he and Nate fought the vampire.

Nate had been here when Azrael was attacked. He may have been one of the last to see the sword. Did he know where it was?

Did he take it?

Octavia was still waiting for her response. She reeled her spinning thoughts back into line, unwilling to plunge her friend into an untried conspiracy theory. "I don't know how the sword could disappear from here and end up in my organization's possession."

"What makes you so sure that's where it is?"

It was what Eblis suspected. But if he'd been aware of Nate's involvement in the destruction of Sakarbaal, would Eblis still suspect the Watchers?

"I've heard rumors," she said, not wanting to share Eblis' connection or her own suspicions.

Octavia regarded her. "Does Nate know who you are?"

"That would be a no."

"And you're not *involved*?"

"I'm not in any danger of falling for him, if that's what you mean." First Eblis, and now Octavia. Did she have a sign over her head, proclaiming her to be a complete idiot?

"I've never seen him look at anyone the way he was looking at you downstairs."

"*What?*"

Octavia shrugged. "He's hooked up with a couple of our warriors in the past. And he's never—" she hesitated, clearly trying to find the right words. Bella could think of a few choice ones. "This sounds ludicrous even inside my own head. But he had a definite protective air about him. Almost possessive."

She had the scary urge to laugh. Except this wasn't funny. "You're right. That's ludicrous."

"I'm saying you need to be careful, Bella. If he suspects you've been playing him, he could dispose of you without a second thought."

"Thanks for that. But I'd already worked that one out."

Worry shrouded Octavia's face. "Be careful."

She had every intention of being careful. And emerging from the other side of this assignment intact.

And that included her heart.

CHAPTER 9

BELLA

This was absolutely one of the worst ideas she'd ever had.

A date with an archangel was one thing. But going on the date with the sole aim of getting Nate to admit to stealing the sword was bordering on certifiable.

But his involvement in the fight with Sakarbaal wasn't the only thing she'd learned from Octavia. Unlike the impression Eblis had given her, not every "true immortal" considered all vampires to be nothing more than bloodsuckers at the bottom of the hierarchy.

Nate and Nico were friends. And while she was sure there was an element of professional give and take in their relationship, it seemed to be built on mutual trust.

It didn't matter how much she wished otherwise. Nate was an enigma. Despite what she knew about him, he continually made her question everything.

And now here she was, in a gorgeous fifteenth century guesthouse, with a room that boasted a view of a secluded market square, just so that Nate wouldn't become suspicious of her travel arrangements.

This afternoon she'd arrived in Romania with the intention of going back to London after speaking with Octavia, but meeting Nate had thrown that plan out of the window. Especially when he'd asked her out again. So she'd tracked down this guesthouse, and after she'd secured the room, she'd teleported home, so she could pick up some clothes and essentials.

The kind of things a regular human would take with her for an overnight business trip.

She pulled on her coat, then hesitated over her beret. She'd been completely ridiculous and had spent ages curling her hair and didn't want to spoil the effect.

Seriously. She was concerned about messing up her hair? Anyone would think she cared what Nate thought about her appearance.

She left her beret on the bed and went downstairs. A Gothic arch led to the small reception room with its faded, reproduction, eighteenth century sofas and standing by the door, taking up most of the space and all her oxygen, was Nate.

His slow smile when he caught sight of her caused liquid flame to unfurl between her thighs. Mentally, she gritted her teeth. If there was one thing she was sure about, it was that there would be *no* sex happening tonight.

Why did you bring condoms in your luggage, then?

Her libido ignored her good advice, and prickles of awareness danced over her skin as Nate strolled across the room to her. His shirt was opened at the throat, revealing a tantalizing glimpse of bronzed flesh, and his long winter coat gave him a seductively dangerous appearance.

Her eyes focused on his boots as he stood before her. "Hey," he said, his husky tone a blatant invitation to sin.

Her mouth dried and she dragged her besotted gaze to his face. It should be illegal for an archangel to be so breathtakingly gorgeous. He'd pulled his hair into a loose knot at the back of his head and his dark eyes ensnared her, promising to fulfil every wicked fantasy she'd ever imagined.

And then some.

Breathe.

She sucked in air, which didn't help mobilize her brain since the subtle scent of cedar, patchouli and spicy saffron scrambled her senses. She had the debasing desire to fling her arms around his powerful shoulders and to hell with the rest of the world.

"Hi." She sounded breathless, needy, and desperate for his touch. But at least she'd managed to speak, which was a minor miracle in itself. "You look tasty."

No. Wait. Had she actually said that *out loud?*

"So do you." He caressed the end of one of her curls between his finger and thumb and yet again her lungs forgot their primary function. "Like a vision from Ama-gi."

"Ama-gi?" She'd never heard the word before, and couldn't immediately place what language it was, but it rippled through her, somehow familiar. As though understanding shimmered on a long-lost forgotten horizon.

This time there was an indefinable hint of sadness in his smile. It was utterly bewitching. "A place I knew a long time ago." He released her hair and wrapped his arm around her shoulders. She really shouldn't be enjoying this so much. "I found a great little restaurant just down the road."

They left the guesthouse and walked along the narrow, cobblestone street. Thankfully, it had stopped raining so at least her hair wouldn't be ruined. *Stop obsessing about my bloody hair.*

Against her better judgment, she stole a sideways glance at his face. His profile was harshly beautiful, the perfect visage of an immortal warrior, and his earring glinted in the silver light from the moon.

"Verdict?" He didn't look at her, but his lips quirked with amusement.

She was behaving like a starstruck mortal. The oddest thing was, she didn't care that he'd caught her admiring him.

Don't forget...

Yeah, she wasn't likely to forget who he was. It didn't mean she couldn't appreciate his physical attributes.

"Still tasty," she said, as they turned into a side alley, where a covered stairway tunneled up the hill.

"If you want to skip dinner, I'm fine with that."

"I've not eaten all day. I might pass out."

"In that case, we've arrived." They emerged from the stairway. From this vantage point, the village lights glittered at the foot of the hill, and in the distance, she could just about see the black silhouette of Sakarbaal's castle.

Nate pushed open the door to a restaurant, and the aroma that wafted out made her stomach rumble. They found a table by one of the windows and moonlight cast a sinister glow across the distant castle. Had Nate picked this table by design?

He helped her with her coat, which was ridiculously charming, and she draped it over the back of her chair.

A teenage girl ambled over, ready to take their order.

"Could we have a few moments, please?" Bella smiled at her, before picking up the menu.

"Your Romanian is perfect." Nate sounded impressed.

"It's a gift." Her voice was dry.

"How many languages do you speak?"

"How many are there?" Whoa, what was she doing? She never drew attention to her abilities.

"Current or archaic?"

"I'm not that gifted."

He leaned back in his chair, and belatedly she realized they'd just spoken in Mandarin. Well, fine. It wasn't a crime to be a polyglot. She offered him a sweet smile and switched to Russian. "You're quite gifted yourself, I see."

"You fascinate me, Isabella." He reverted to English, and his dark eyes glowed with admiration. Sensual awareness rippled through her, warm like molten honey, and twice as tempting. It was an effort to keep the smile on her face, when she desperately needed to suck air into her deprived lungs. "I've never met anyone like you before."

Coming from an archangel, that was really saying something. And he probably wasn't wrong, either.

"Likewise." And wasn't *that* the truth, too.

They were interrupted by the arrival of the girl again, and after they gave their order, she couldn't help glancing at the castle. It perched there, on a nearby hill, like a physical manifestation of the secrets and half-lies that lay between Nate and her.

An odd pain squeezed her chest. It was bad enough that he was an archangel. But why did he have to be the *worst* one?

"How long have you known Octavia?"

She couldn't tell him the truth. Her ageing process had frozen when she was twenty-eight, but she'd known her friend for decades. He'd think she was either lying or come dangerously close to guessing her secret. "Years."

"I was surprised to see you at the castle. It's all top-secret shit over there."

He hadn't asked her an outright question, but it was there, under the surface. She could pretend ignorance. He probably thought she had no idea what was going on. But just how much would he share with her, if he thought she was a completely oblivious human?

She wouldn't betray Octavia's confidences. But what would happen if she let him know she was aware of the other world that existed, right in front of humanity's unseeing senses?

It was a gamble. She might lose a lot more than she stood to gain. But it was a calculated risk she was prepared to take. Besides, she didn't have a choice if she wanted to find out what he knew about the sword.

"I don't know what's going on at the castle. But I know I'm not of the same race as Octavia."

His intense gaze was mesmeric. She struggled not to fall beneath his spell. *Remember your goal.*

"What race might that be?" His voice was low, hypnotic. Inviting her to lay bare her soul.

How easy that would be. She was almost tempted. Somehow, she managed to claw back a sliver of common sense before she spilled out her heart and signed her death warrant.

She leaned over the table and watched, entranced, as he did the same. Their breath mingled and his eyes were black with desire. Her voice came out in a husky whisper. "A race that humans would fear if they knew it was more than a myth."

It was safer that he imagined she was speaking of Octavia. Even if she was referring to herself.

"You told me you don't believe in fairy tales. Yet you know of the true stories behind them."

"Yes. But those aren't the stories that are told, are they?"

"How did you discover the truth?"

It was an effort to break the spellbinding web he was so easily spinning around her. If she didn't keep a grasp on reality, she'd end up telling him everything she shouldn't. "It's my turn to ask a question. How long have *you* known supernatural races live on Earth?"

His eyes crinkled as he smiled.

"I've always known. But I haven't met many—" He bit off his words, as though reconsidering what he'd been about to say. "Others who do."

Humans. That was what he'd almost said. And while he hadn't, obviously, told her the whole truth, he still hadn't lied.

If only he had. It would make it much easier for her to despise him. Heat rushed through her. What was she thinking?

I should hate him.

Not only because of the way he'd hunted demon bloods

throughout history, although that was bad enough. It was more personal than that.

There was only one place where she and others of her mixed-race heritage could find the answers to their past. Where they could discover they weren't freaks or slowly losing their minds. Somewhere they could speak freely of their immortal lineage with others who understood.

Sure, there were radicals who wanted to overthrow humans, and the unifying doctrine of the Watchers was a loathing of archangels. But ancient ritual and history aside, countless friendships were formed between the members. Connections that helped them to survive in a world unaware of their existence.

And if Nate could once more gain entry to the temple of the Watchers, he'd destroy it without a second thought.

It was a massive relief when their food arrived, and she didn't need to answer him straight away. Or look at him. But when they were once again alone, there was no excuse not to meet his curious gaze.

He was clearly still waiting for her response.

"Hmm." She hoped she sounded convincingly neutral. Unfortunately, he appeared to require more. "It's not something you can talk about with just anyone."

"Is that the reason your relatives treated you so badly? Because you tried talking to them about things they didn't understand?"

She really needed to be more careful what she said to him. Not that it mattered. And he was right.

In a way.

"Something like that." Except the only supernatural race had been *her*. "I was fourteen when they disowned me."

"That's rough." He was no longer smiling. "Just because you can see things they can't?"

There had been more to it than that. After her mother's protector had died, his legitimate heir had evicted them from the only home she'd ever known. They'd gone to live with her grand-mother and aunt and when they'd tried to pimp her out, to earn her keep, she'd destroyed everything in their house in a wave of telekinetic terror.

Probably best not to share that with Nate.

"They were very old-fashioned." A euphemism, if ever she'd heard one. And only if compared to those living in the twenty-first century. None of her relatives' contemporaries would have found anything terrible about flinging a brat of Satan into the gutter.

"They were total pieces of shit," he said. She blinked. He sounded mad. On her behalf. "No one should turn their back on their own kid."

"It happens all the time."

"Doesn't make it right."

She took a forkful of her rich stew to keep her mouth occu-pied. An archangel was the last person she'd expect to care about such issues as parenting. The Watchers' histories documented archangels' efforts in that area, and they weren't a great role model when it came to their own offspring. After all, when Earth had reset her celestial clock millennia ago during the Great Cleansing, they'd fled the planet, leaving their children behind to perish.

She took a sip of the full-blooded, red wine they'd ordered and cast Nate a surreptitious glance. He had a brooding expres-sion on his face.

Don't ask. But she couldn't help herself. "Do you have any chil-dren, Nate?"

"Gods, no." He sounded both taken aback by her question and horrified by the possibility. "That's never going to happen."

Now *that* attitude was more like the history she knew. Unlike demons, archangels had rarely reproduced during their occupa-tion on Earth, and certainly not afterwards.

Also unlike demons. Their numerous descendants, who knew

nothing of their demonic bloodline until they were brought into the fold, was testament to that.

Not for the first time, unease slithered through her as she considered that fact. The Watchers pushed that distinction between the two races of immortals as being more proof of demon superiority, but she'd never seen what was so great about demons spreading their seed and then ignoring the outcome.

How different would her own life have been, if her father hadn't vanished after seducing her mother?

"How about you?"

His question thrust her back to the present. Once upon a time, she'd longed for a family of her own. But as she'd told Nate, she no longer believed in fairy tales. She had a different kind of family now, with her friends in the Watchers. "No. I'm committed to my career."

"Your nightclubs."

It wasn't a question, and yet she got the distinct feeling he was asking her one.

"Yes." She sure as hell wasn't going to tell him about her role in the Watchers.

"And Octavia could help you with your minor emergency?"

She'd forgotten that was what she'd told him earlier today. Although to be fair, it wasn't a lie. "She helped clarify something for me."

"About *Inanna*." Again, it wasn't a question. And yet, it was.

She resisted the temptation to fidget beneath his scrutiny. She didn't owe him anything. Not even the truth. She didn't usually have such a hard time avoiding awkward conversations. Long ago, her survival had depended on her learning to lie with conviction.

If she didn't uncover the truth, Eblis believed Earth would become the battleground for ancient immortals. She needed to discover what Nate knew about the sword.

He'd never share, not even with a human who knew dhampirs

walked the Earth. She had to give him more. She had to tell him she was aware of the existence of that weapon.

It's too dangerous.

Yes, it was. She was insane to even consider it. But just being with Nate was a form of madness, anyway.

"*Inanna* isn't my only passion. I also adore antiques and sometimes Octavia can help me source certain items." Let him think she relied on Octavia's expertise because she was an immortal and had an impressive network. "But unfortunately, she couldn't this time." No way would she put her friend in danger.

"You came to Romania to ask Octavia about an antique?" There was a faint trace of bafflement in his voice. She couldn't blame him. It did sound absurd. Who would fly across Europe to ask that kind of question?

Unless the antique in question was not of this world.

Was she sure about this? There was still time to change her mind. But once the words were out, there was no turning back.

Go for it. All she had to lose was her life.

"Not just an antique." And Nate wasn't just an archangel. She was playing with fire, all but daring him to question every aspect of her carefully constructed life. The prospect should horrify her, not send illicit thrills of forbidden anticipation colliding through her blood. Against all the rules of circumspection that she'd lived with for so long, she said the words that could seal her fate. "I believe it's an immortal forged sword."

CHAPTER 10

NATE

Nate stared at the woman opposite him as her careless remark thundered through his brain. Yes, he'd intended to discover why she had come to Romania, and how she knew Octavia. But he'd never expected Isabella to so casually confirm that she knew of the existence of dhampirs, and he sure as hell hadn't anticipated her tossing *an immortal forged sword* into the conversation.

He swallowed the contents of his glass, but the alcohol didn't help shove his reflexes into gear.

Her gaze didn't waver from his as she waited for his response. Her hair tumbled over her shoulders in a distracting riot of curls, and her royal blue dress clung to her like a seductive, second skin.

He took a measured breath and hauled his focus back into line. It was unlikely the sword she spoke of was the one he'd taken from the castle. It was simply coincidence.

Another one. They seemed to flourish around Isabella. Despite how he didn't even believe in them.

"What makes you think this sword was forged by an immortal?"

For a fleeting second surprise flared in her eyes, as though his reaction wasn't what she'd expected. "Rumors and speculation, mainly."

Right. Some of the tension in his muscles relaxed. The universe was full of rumors and speculation and very little of it meant anything.

"Nothing tangible, then."

"I can't prove its existence." She sounded reluctant to admit that. "But it was allegedly used in an assassination attempt on an archangel."

What the *fuck*? Where had she found her information? The attack on Azrael was known by only a handful of immortals.

Nic had a spy in his midst.

He had to reply to her, but he was damned if he knew where to start. "An archangel?"

"I know. Pretty unbelievable, but that's the word on the street."

On the *street*? Which fucking street did she hang out on?

To give himself a few seconds to analyze her comments, he picked up the wine bottle and refilled both their glasses. Unfortunately, it wasn't long enough for his brain to figure it out.

He gave up.

"Who told you this?"

She shrugged, as though she hadn't a clue that she'd just knocked his world view off its axis. *That's because she doesn't have a clue.* "I picked up bits and pieces here and there. You know how it is."

"The Internet?" If so, he needed to check it out. He'd had no idea Earth's Internet had evolved to such a degree.

"You haven't heard anything about this, then?" Her beautiful eyes were guileless. Her ignorance of the danger she would be in if she pursued her curiosity was terrifying.

"Why are you interested in it? This isn't simply a coveted antique to add to your collection."

"So you believe me?"

He resisted the urge to tug at his collar. It was already undone but damn, it was hot in here. He had the surreal sensation Isabella was leading him into a rabbit hole of his own making. But for some warped reason, he couldn't lie outright to her. "Yes. But that doesn't mean it's true."

Even though it was.

"Will you help me search for it?"

He already knew where it was. And he suspected Astrid had every intention of destroying it. But even if she didn't, there was no way it would ever return to Earth.

There was something Isabella wasn't telling him. It drifted in the air between them, an intangible awareness just beyond his grasp. What was she hiding from him? More to the point, why?

They'd already established he wasn't freaked out by the so-called supernatural.

He could discover the truth easily enough by invading her mind. But that was a tactic he reserved for enemies. Was she being used by Dagan as a human front to hunt down the sword? Whatever the reason, he wasn't leaving her side until he had Dagan. And the truth.

Under the guise of searching for this elusive sword.

"Okay."

Her eyes widened. Had she expected him to refuse?

"You will? That's... great."

"Why did you ask me, if you were so sure I'd say no?"

She tucked a long curl behind her ear. A striking red and carnelian lion hung from her earlobe. Another symbol of the goddess, Inanna.

"I hoped you'd say yes, but I wasn't counting on it. I'm still trying to wrap my head around the fact you don't think I'm crazy."

"How many other races do you know?"

"How many do you?"

He grinned. "Like that, is it?"

She returned his smile, and it took his breath away. It was the same smile she'd given him last night. He hadn't realized just how guarded she'd been with him today. But now, it seemed she'd finally forgiven him for staking out her club.

"How many other races *are* there?"

Even he didn't know the answer to that. Not if she wanted him to include the entire universe. But here on Earth?

"Fuck knows."

She laughed, and shook her head, almost in wonder. "You're funny."

"I'm funny and weird. Not the look I was aiming for."

"What were you aiming for?"

"Irresistible?"

"I wondered where your ego had gone."

The young human who had taken their order came over and took their plates. He waited until they were alone again before leaning across the table. "My ego doesn't stand a chance around you."

She blinked, her long lashes hiding her eyes for a fleeting moment, and her smile faltered. Her gaze turned oddly wary. What the hell had just happened?

"Where do you think we should start?" Although her eyes were still dark with desire, and voice temptingly husky, he knew she wasn't talking about sex.

He wrapped his fingers around her hand. She didn't protest. "At your club."

She stiffened. "Why do you think it would be there?"

"I don't, but I think someone who had it was there. Is that a problem?"

"I guess not." She hitched in a jagged breath. "Do you want pudding?"

There was only one thing he needed right now. "I want you."

Bella

"Let's get out of here." Her voice was hoarse. If she had any sense, she'd be mortified by how easily Nate could charm his way into her bed. Clearly, her good sense had taken a hike. She hoped it didn't reappear until morning.

He held her coat for her, and as she concentrated on fastening the buttons, his thumbs grazed her neck in a sensuous caress. She swallowed, relieved he couldn't see her face. Sex was one thing, but the truth was brutal. It was more than that. If it was *just sex*, she could handle it. But it was so much harder to ignore the rush of warmth deep inside whenever he did or said something unexpected.

Like being pissed off by how her family had treated her. Or the enchanting way he poked fun at himself. Archangels weren't meant to even know the meaning of self-deprecation. Nate was a revelation in so many ways, and it was killing her that she had to keep reminding herself of his true nature.

Before she had time to find her card, he had already paid. That made twice in a row. "Next time I'm paying," she said, as he held open the door for her.

"Deal." He slung his arm around her shoulders and pulled her close. Before she could stop herself, she slid her arm around him. Damn it, he felt so good.

The temperature had dropped, and the breeze was chilly, but she wasn't cold. The stars glittered in the frosty night sky and she snuggled closer to Nate as they descended the hill through the covered stairway.

She pressed her cheek against his shoulder, and his woolen coat was like a soft caress. Tonight, she wouldn't think of all the reasons why he was the last one on Earth she should be with. Or reflect on all the ways she should be planning to destroy him.

Tonight, in this beautiful, fairytale village, was for her.

The village that was in the shadow of a vampire's castle. A

looming reminder, in case she had forgotten, that she didn't believe in fairytales.

As they walked along the road to the guesthouse, a group of drunken youths staggered their way. They were loud and made obnoxious comments, clearly oblivious that both she and Nate understood their language.

It didn't bother her. She'd faced far worse than lewd jeers in her time.

Tension vibrated through Nate's body and she glanced at his face. His expression was lethal. Before she could stop him, his arm shot out and he grabbed the nearest youth by his coat, hiking him into the air. The guy's toes dangled an inch above the ground and none of his friends appeared inclined to intervene.

"What did you say?" Nate's voice was low, but menace radiated from him. Warmth bloomed deep in Bella's chest. No one had ever defended her honor before. It was strangely touching.

"Nothing," the unfortunate human gasped, as he attempted to loosen Nate's fingers from his coat.

"Apologize."

She didn't think he was going to comply. The words were clearly lodged in his throat. But then Nate gave him a little shake and the rest of the guy's bravado vanished.

"I'm sorry." His eyes practically rolled back into his head with fear and his friends edged back, apparently mesmerized by how badly their night was going.

Nate dropped him and the guy landed on his hands and knees, before scrambling to his feet.

"Get out of here." Nate swept his gaze across them, and without fail, each one shuddered, before turning tail and disappearing down the road. His arm tightened around her. "Are you okay?"

He sounded concerned. She guessed if she was a regular human woman, she might've been shaken up by the encounter. Especially if she'd been on her own. But in the past, she'd broken more than a few bones of misogynistic shitheads who'd thought she was fair game to attack.

Nate didn't know that, though. And although his chivalrous behavior shouldn't give her the warm and fuzzies, she couldn't help it.

"I'm fine," she assured him. "It's not spoiled the evening."

They entered the guesthouse and she held his hand as she led him up the stairs. Once in her room she turned to face him, their fingers still interlocked. She should pounce on him, pin him to the bed. Fill her mind with nothing but hot, sweaty sex. Because that was safer than these unwanted, ethereal *feelings* that craved a connection with him that could never be.

His gaze was quizzical. "You can tell me if there's a problem. It's not like we're strangers anymore."

Why was he so frustratingly observant? She needed to up her game if she wanted to hide her innermost thoughts from him.

If I want to survive.

She had to focus on facts, and not fantasy. "True. I don't tell most people I meet that my best friend is a dhampir."

With infinite care, he unwrapped her scarf and draped it on a chair. Should that feel so seductive? When he proceeded to leisurely unbutton her coat, it was all she could manage not to shiver with heady anticipation.

"Some time you'll have to tell me how you and Octavia met." He slid her coat from her shoulders before dropping a teasing kiss against her neck. Heat washed through her and her eyes drifted shut as she melted into his arms. His teeth grazed her flesh and she could imagine his wicked smile as he left a trail of kisses along her jaw.

He tossed her coat onto the chair and wound his powerful arms around her. She sank against his rock-hard chest and rested her head against his shoulder as his lips teased the tender skin behind her ear. Why had she never known how irresistibly erotic that was?

"I will," she whispered. "If you tell me how you met Nico."

His fingers skimmed over her hips and waist, sending ripples of need cascading through her sensitized body.

"You'd never believe me." His voice rumbled against her ear, amusement and lust vying for dominance. It was enchanting, even though it should be anything but.

"Try me." Gods, why was it so easy to flirt with him?

A silent laugh shook his big body. "I take it back. You would believe me."

Her hungry gaze roamed over his face, searching for a hint of the monster she knew lurked beneath. But all she could see was Nate's admiring eyes, focused on her, and the chiseled perfection of every autocratic feature.

She curled her hand around his neck and pulled him closer until their lips all but touched. "Has anyone ever told you that you talk too much?"

"Frequently." His husky voice was more potent than any aphrodisiac. "It's one of my better qualities."

"You intrigue me." *No.* Stop speaking.

"Makes two of us. You captivate me, Isabella." His fingers tangled in her hair, pulling her head back. Tension spiked the air, electrifying her senses. "There's something about you I can't... fathom."

And the day he did, would be her last. It should terrify her. And maybe in the morning it would.

She dragged her fingers along his jaw, his stubble grazing her palms. "If you knew all my secrets, you wouldn't be standing here with me now."

"Then keep your secrets." He brushed a fleeting kiss across her lips. "For a little longer."

She'd keep her secrets for the rest of her life.

CHAPTER 11

NATE

Nate unzipped Isabella's dress, and she pulled back to allow the soft silk to glide from her body and pool on the floor. He sucked in a sharp breath and feasted his gaze on her matching royal blue lingerie that sculpted her curves with delicate ribbons of lace.

He'd never seen anything so utterly bewitching in his life.

You captivate me. He'd told her the truth. But when he uncovered the secrets that made her so alluring, she would no longer fill his mind or cloud his reason.

"Stop thinking." She breathed the command against his lips, as she tugged his coat down his arms. "There's nothing to analyze."

He laughed, couldn't help it. "What makes you think I was analyzing anything?"

She draped his coat over hers, before running her palms over his biceps. "It was written all over your face."

Right, that wasn't so funny. He didn't think he was that easy to read. "Is this another one of your superpowers?"

"No. It's called being human." She tilted her head and gave him a smoldering look from beneath her lashes. "I'm not looking for anything serious, Nate."

He wasn't sure why her comment struck a discordant note. After all, it mirrored his own sentiments. But something just seemed... off. And it had nothing to do with the fact humans never called the shots because he'd already accepted she wasn't affected by his archangelic presence.

It was why she was so irresistible.

He gave her a slow smile and allowed a sliver of immortal radiance to escape. She didn't even bat an eyelash. Instead of diminishing, his fascination for her dug deeper into his psyche.

He cupped her face, his thumbs stroking her cheeks. "That's fine by me."

Her eyes darkened with desire. Even though he had witnessed the phenomenon countless times before meeting Isabella, it had never been this bewitching. "I still want your help in tracking down the sword."

"You have it." His fingers slid into her hair and she gave a delicate shudder.

Her hands clenched on his biceps. "Why are you still dressed? I want you naked."

"That works for me."

She groaned in mock exasperation and proceeded to unbutton his shirt. "I hope you remembered the condoms this time."

His fingers froze in her hair. Fuck. That hadn't even entered his mind. Was *that* the real reason she had been so icy with him all day? Because he'd forgotten a basic hook-up rule when it came to mortals?

Truth was, he couldn't recall the last time he'd taken a woman who wasn't at least part immortal herself and was fully aware of who he was.

It was pointless telling her she had nothing to worry about when it came to health and conception. She knew of dhampirs and vampires, but she'd sounded distinctly disbelieving of the existence of archangels. There was no reason to tell her who he truly was. It was warped, but he liked the fact she was ignorant of his true heritage. Besides, he had the feeling the time for such a confession had passed. And there was no way he wanted a discussion of his race's reproductive shortcomings.

"Isabella," he began, although he had no idea what he was going to say, but she cut him off with a smile designed to incinerate every star in the galaxy.

"Relax. I've got some in my bag."

Relief surged through him that she obviously didn't intend lambasting him for his oversight last night. He tore off his shirt and dropped it onto the floor. Her lips parted in a silent sigh as her gaze roved over his chest as though she'd never beheld such a vision before.

He grinned. Despites his joking, she did great things for his ego.

"You're like a warrior from the dawn of time." There was a wondering note in her voice he found crazily alluring.

"And you're a goddess of temptation." He meant to make her laugh, to shatter this mystifying spell, but instead she gave him a strangely enigmatic smile.

"From Ama-gi?"

What had possessed him, when he'd told her of Ama-gi? It wasn't a word he spoke of lightly. Then again, what the hell. "Yes."

She went onto her toes, pressing her curves against his chest, and tugged at the band around his hair. The lace of her bra caressed his naked flesh and her erect nipples sent sparks of lightning blazing through his blood. He cradled her butt, and her uneven breath dusted his jaw as she concentrated on her task.

"Do you need any help?" His voice was rough, but damn she was driving him out of his mind.

"Got it." With one final tug, she released his hair and admiration glowed in her eyes. "You're nothing like I imagined."

"Neither are you." He had the uncanny feeling she hadn't meant to say that aloud, and he didn't know what she meant by it, but it was only sex talk and when did that ever make sense? He forced his mind back to practicalities, so he didn't need to think about it later. "Condoms?"

Gods, he couldn't believe he'd just asked that. He'd never used such a thing before.

She blinked, almost as though she had no idea what he was talking about. But since she was the one who'd brought it up, his lust was clearly giving him hallucinations.

"Oh. Yes." She cleared her throat before unzipping a side pocket on her luggage that was on the floor by the chest of drawers. She tossed a packet onto the bed. "I got you the triple X size." Her grin was pure evil. "Didn't want you having any problems with your blood supply."

It sounded horrendous. He managed not to shudder. "Good call."

Without taking her eyes from his, she unbuckled his belt before skimming her fingernails over his erection. Even through his pants her touch was like fire. Why was she taking so long? The suspense was killing him.

With infinite care, she eased his pants over his hips and down his thighs until she kneeled on the floor at his feet. Unlike last night, this time he'd gone commando. Her gaze devoured his cock and the tip of her tongue peeked between her lips, an erotic invitation. With a growl of frustration, he toed off his boots, transfixed by her rapt expression.

"Magnificent," she whispered, and glided the tip of her finger along his length.

He hauled her to her feet. As much as he wanted her gorgeous mouth around his cock, he had plans for making tonight one she would never forget.

"Later." He backed her up against the bed and she wound her arms around his neck, her fingers teasing his hair. As if that was going to stop him. Within a second, she was flat on her back, and he climbed on the bed after her, bracketing her hips with his knees. "Questions?"

She scraped her nails over his pecs and circled his nipples. His cock jerked in appreciation. "Hundreds," she breathed. He had no idea what she was talking about. Her fingers were instruments of mind-altering pleasure. "Everything you do throws up another dozen. But they can wait for another time."

"Has anyone ever told *you* that you talk too much?"

Her smile caused his gut to clench with need. "Only if they had a death wish."

He laughed. "Spare me. At least until the morning."

Her smile faltered, and somewhere in the back of his mind, through the swirling heat of lust, unformed doubt stirred. *Why does she do that?*

And then she dug her fingers through his hair, gripped his head and pulled him down. Her kiss was sweet, exploring, and his disquiet at her strange glimpses of melancholy vanished.

He cradled her face, her silken curls cascading over his fingers as he took everything she offered. It was only a kiss, but it was so much more, a fleeting touch of something insubstantial that was buried deep inside his chest.

Panting, he pulled back. Her eyes were glazed with passion and a hint of her evocative vanilla perfume scented the air. For endless moments it seemed time had suspended, and then she gave a soft smile and pressed the tip of one finger to his forehead.

"Stop thinking."

"You want me to stop thinking you're the most beautiful woman I've ever encountered?" Well, fuck. Really?

Yes, really.

"Is that what you were thinking?" She didn't sound as though she believed him, despite her smile.

He captured her lips. "Yeah." He nibbled kisses along her throat, and she gave a breathy sigh. He'd known goddesses and vampires and had met countless females from advanced civilizations across the universe. But they all faded besides Isabella.

He buried his face in her scented cleavage, and she clasped his head. Within a moment he'd unhooked her bra, and with seeming reluctance she loosened her grip so he could peel it from her.

But his gaze remained locked with hers. Her eyes were hypnotic, the swirls of blues an invitation to drown in their mysterious depths. He swallowed a groan of defeat. She was right. He needed to stop thinking when he was with her because it was driving him crazy.

Slowly, he inched down her lush body, lavishing attention on her beautiful breasts. He sucked on her nipples, cradling her breasts in his palms, and her sighs of pleasure were the sexiest sounds he'd ever heard. His tongue swirled and she gripped his hair, her body arching into him with provocative delight.

"You're slaying me," she groaned, and he grinned, his teeth grazing her flesh.

"You've uncovered my nefarious plan." He glanced up at her, and her grip on his hair tightened in mock warning. "You'll be screaming for mercy before I've finished with you."

She let out a choked laugh. "You wish."

"Is that a challenge?"

"I don't scream for anyone."

He teased her nipple with the tip of his tongue, and she writhed beneath him. Satisfied, he trailed kisses over the curve of her waist. "Challenge accepted."

His fingers glided over her soft skin, before sliding beneath the lacy band of her knickers and inching them over her thighs and along her legs. Gods, she was exquisite. He pressed his lips against her slit, and she tasted of…

Ama-gi.

"Not screaming," she slurred, as her nails dug into his head.

"Not finished," he countered, before circling her clit with his tongue. Her muffled moans filled his mind and her scent weaved an exotic spell around them both. He tongue-fucked her, his hands exploring her hips and waist and finally her luscious breasts as she bucked helplessly.

Blood pounded, blurring reality. Her breath rasped and he knew she was so close. But she was fighting it. Primal need surged through him, and as he sucked her sweet clit, he pinched her erect nipple.

She shattered, gripping his head as she came inside his mouth. He barely heard her scream his name above the thunder of his heart. Only one imperative thudded through him.

Make her mine.

He rose onto his knees, his cock nudging her silken heat. She wrapped her legs around his hips, and dark desire glowed in her eyes. He raked his fingers through her hair, and from nowhere, a warning hit him.

Shit. He had almost forgotten. *Again.*

It fucking hurt to pull back, but he gritted his teeth and without tearing his gaze from her, he grabbed the packet she'd tossed onto the bed. Her eyes widened in apparent amazement as she watched him grapple with the packet, before he conceded defeat and glared at the damn thing so he could see what he was doing.

He ripped open the box and frustration clawed through him like a feral lion. He'd faced down countless packs of bloodthirsty demon spawn in his time. A condom wouldn't beat him.

"It's okay," Isabella gasped, flapping a hand at him. "You don't need to…" Her voice trailed off as he triumphantly ripped his prize from its wrapping and rolled it on. It wasn't a great fit, but neither was it as horrific as he'd feared.

"Ha." He grinned at her and she gave a disbelieving laugh as though the fact he'd remembered staggered her. His fingers tangled in her hair and she wrapped her arms around his shoulders, pulling him close. His kiss was savage, branding her, and it was crazy and primitive, but he was beyond caring. With demeaning lack of finesse, he thrust into her and lost what was left of his mind.

She clasped his length in a silken embrace of molten fire. Nothing existed but this moment, with the scent of lust and sex filling the air, the sound of harsh breaths and pleasure echoing around the room, and Isabella's face the only anchor in the universe.

And as her climax claimed her, cascading over his buried cock, he let go, following her over the edge into a starburst oblivion.

CHAPTER 12

NATE

Nate stirred, and reluctantly opened his eyes. Early morning sunlight slid through the gap in the curtains, creating a golden halo of light around Isabella's tangled hair, as she slept on the bed beside him. The sheet had slid down during the night and her exposed shoulder was devastatingly enticing. Stealthily, he sat up and trailed kisses along her bare flesh until she rolled onto her back.

He gazed, entranced, as her long, dark, eyelashes flickered, and she gave a sleepy sigh. His cock thickened and he swallowed a groan. Maybe he should have told her of his heritage and the reason why there was no need for precautions. But he'd made the choice. He had to suffer it.

They'd used up all the condoms during the night.

"Morning, Isabella." He murmured the greeting against her lips and felt her smile in response.

"Morning." Her voice was husky, and he pressed his forehead against hers in an effort to stem the primitive need to take her right here, right now. She didn't help his resolve when she wound her arm around his shoulder. "I thought you might've disappeared before I woke up."

"Why would I do that?"

She shrugged. "No strings." She sounded vague, as though that wasn't what she really meant at all. "No more condoms."

"You think the only reason I'm sticking around is for the sex?" He gave her a mock frown, and twined strands of her hair around his fingers, even though a warning thudded in the back of his mind.

He did want more sex. But he shouldn't. The primary reason he should be *sticking around* was to discover what secrets Isabella was keeping and to protect her from possible danger.

"Hmm. Well, I'm not complaining." She wrapped her hand around one of his locks. "Last night was reasonably spectacular."

He laughed. "Reasonably?"

"Okay. *Totally.*"

"Lucky you had a pocket full of protection."

"I didn't want us to be caught out like the other night."

The memory of both nights melded, a hot and erotic fantasy fusion. Frustrated need pounded through his blood. But he had to commend her foresight. It sure as hell had flown over his head.

And then her words penetrated the fog of lust and he frowned. "You didn't know I was going to be here, so why did you have condoms?"

She blinked up at him, and he could have sworn alarm flashed in her eyes for an eternal second. *What am I accusing her of?* She could have bought the damn things in the village. Except Sakarbaal's influence had prevented it from becoming an international tourist attraction and its few shops tended to close early on Saturday afternoons. Isabella hadn't even left the castle by then.

"A girl has to be prepared."

"Okay." He wasn't accusing her of anything. So what if she traveled abroad with a handy supply in her luggage. He sure as hell wasn't insinuating that she shouldn't be even *thinking* of sleeping with anyone but him, because that was fucking mad.

"I got you the triple X size." Her teasing words from last night

jarred his brain. What the fuck was going on? He had serious shit to focus on. He didn't have time to pick apart inconsequential inconsistencies in Isabella's conversations with him.

"I got them in London," she said, almost as though she could read his mind. Except that wasn't possible, even if she'd belonged to a telepathic race. Nobody could penetrate an archangel's mind without their permission. "I don't know why I packed them. Good job I did, though."

He forcibly buried the questions gnawing through his mind. There was no mystery, here. With difficulty, he released her hair. He needed to get back on track. "What time's your flight?"

Her smile turned quizzical, as though she had no idea what he was talking about. "Oh." She pulled the sheet around her and sat up. "Soon. I'd better… pack."

"Right." He guessed this was his cue to leave. "Want me to give you a lift to the airport?" It would be easy enough to hire a car for the purpose. It would be even easier if he could just teleport them both to London.

"What time's *your* flight? Or are you staying here for a little longer?"

Fuck. How many flights to London were there from here on a Sunday? He had no idea. He hoped Isabella didn't, either. "Later today."

"Well, it's a bit much expecting you to drive me all the way to the airport and then hang around for hours." She gave his wrist a gentle squeeze. "Thanks for the offer. I'll get a taxi."

"Sure." He leaned back against the headboard and watched her leave the bed. His mouth dried at the sight of her gorgeous ass and long legs. Any delusion that last night had tempered his lust for her evaporated like snow in the path of a volcano. She pulled on a sweater before turning to face him.

"So, anyway." She folded her arms. Was she nervous? The prospect jolted him. What had changed between them? "I should probably tell you that I've a business trip on Tuesday. So I won't be around for a few days."

He ignored the flare of disappointment that burned through him. Because, *seriously*. "No problem. It'll give me some time to research that sword you're after."

Or, rather, to find out how such information had leaked into the human interwebs.

"Yes." There was an oddly doubtful note in her voice. "Thanks. I'll call you when I get back home."

"Here's an idea." *Do not fucking say it*. Yet again, he ignored the voice of reason. "I could come with you."

She gazed at him, and he couldn't figure out the expression on her face. A strange combination of bafflement and wistful hope. "I'd actually love that." She cleared her throat and shook her head, as though waking from a daze. "But these people are…" she hesitated, and a frown creased her brow. "It wouldn't go down well." She sighed. "It's an intense, confidential thing. I can't even really talk about it."

Interesting. What part of her business could be that secretive? It wasn't as though he'd planned on attending the meetings with her. "In that case, we'll catch up when you get back."

She turned away from him, and her hair fell across her face as she bent to retrieve her dress from the floor. The rich blue looked so damn good against her skin and he shifted on the bed, in a vain attempt to ease the pressure between his thighs.

It didn't work. He had the feeling he was going to be fantasizing about Isabella wearing that provocative dress all week.

She straightened and caught his hot gaze. "You're very distracting."

"Not as distracting as you."

"Are you sure we're going to be able to work together without wanting to jump into bed every five minutes?"

"Only every five minutes?"

She shook her head. "This is going to end so badly."

"No, it won't." An uneasy possibility crawled through his mind. Not unless she fell for him. But what were the chances of that, when his archangelic radiance had no effect on her?

"Not everything always goes to plan." She avoided looking at him, instead draping her dress onto the end of the bed. "Are you any closer to finding the one who attacked your friend?"

She stroked her hand over the royal blue material. It was an innocent gesture, but he found it way too sensuous as he recalled how the soft silk had felt beneath his fingers, and the way it had hugged her beautiful body.

An unformed sense of unease flickered. It was an odd choice to pack for an overnight trip when she had only flown to Romania to see Octavia.

What was he thinking? It had nothing to do with him. She could wear whatever she liked. Except something seemed off kilter. That dress was the kind of thing a woman wore when she had seduction on her mind.

"Nate?" She tilted her head. "Are you okay?"

No, he wasn't. The longer he spent in her company, the more fried his brain became. There was no way he'd tell her *that*.

He flung back the bedcover and left the bed. Her glance dropped to his far from disinterested cock, and she swallowed.

"I'm fine." His voice was a low growl, and he captured her face between his hands before kissing her tempting lips. Her palms caressed his biceps and shoulders, and her cashmere sweater was an erotic whisper across his skin. It physically hurt to pull back.

His breath rasped, burning his chest. She clung onto him as though she didn't want him to leave, but if he didn't go now, he'd pull her back onto the bed and there was no way she'd catch her flight.

Altruism be damned. It had nothing to do with her missing her flight. He had to walk out. To prove that he could.

Her hands slid down his arms and she stepped back. There was an enigmatic smile on her face, as though she knew of the battle that raged within him. He grabbed his clothes and the incongruity of an archangel fighting the attraction for a mere human rattled his senses.

It was almost funny.

A reluctant grin twisted his lips. It *was* funny. But that didn't mean he had to let it rule him. As he pulled on his shirt, he forced his mind to more mundane matters. "I'll be in touch before you leave. To let you know how things are progressing."

Discovering why Dagan was using *Inanna* as a base was his number one priority. Until he did, Isabella was in danger. He'd pledged to protect her, and he didn't break his word.

AN HOUR LATER, Nate teleported to a country lane in Cornwall, and ran his gaze over the large stone house. It was a short distance from the nearest village, set in its own uncultivated grounds with several magnificent magnolia trees in full bloom of white and pink. Since the attack, Azrael hadn't been able to teleport, and had declined Nate's offer to take him back home to an obscure planet in Andromeda III. He'd wanted to stay on Earth and was recuperating in the country.

With the dhampir who had stolen his heart. Rowan.

He wasn't looking forward to meeting her again. He'd misjudged her, believing that she was Sakarbaal's spy, sent to bring Az down. When in fact, she'd been just as much of a victim of the vampire as Az.

Hey Az. You at home in that country house?

Not that Az would be anywhere else. He'd temporarily lost the ability to cloak his wings in a glamour, so he could hardly go out for a stroll around the village. At least, Nate assumed it was only temporary. But this was the address Az had given him, in case of emergency.

And this was an emergency.

Yes. Azrael's reply was cautious. *What's up?*

Nate strode up the path to the front door and rapped on it. It was one thing teleporting directly into another archangel's residence when they were alone. But not when they'd found their soulmate.

Strange. In Ama-gi, many archangels had fallen in love. But that was so long ago, and he'd severed contact with so many. Of those he still saw with any frequency, not one had fallen in millennia.

Most of them had learned their lesson, back then. It wasn't worth the heartache.

Not that Az had ever fallen. Nate was still processing the fact that he had, now.

The door swung open.

Holy fucking goddess. It wasn't Az standing there. Was that…

"Gabe?"

"Long time, Nate." The Archangel Gabriel shrugged.

That was an understatement. They hadn't seen each other since Ama-gi had been destroyed and Gabe had rampaged through the devastated Earth, searching for his beloved and their child.

Yet there was something different about Gabe. It had nothing to do with the passage of time. It was fundamental, something elusive, just beyond the reach of his senses. And he could hardly ask, considering how long it had been since they'd last spoken. Although it seemed that Az had kept in contact, throughout millennia, since he was staying here.

"You live on Earth?"

"I do." There was a wary note in Gabe's voice that sent a shiver of presentiment along his spine. "You might as well hear it from me. I'm no longer immortal."

Nate froze. *No longer immortal?* But that made no sense. Archangels were immortal. There was no getting around that fact. At least, not that he'd ever discovered. Yet it explained the strange sense of *otherness* he'd felt from him. What the hell had Gabe done?

Before he could get his scrambled brain into gear to question Gabe, Azrael entered the hall and walked over to them.

Nate only just managed not to flinch at the sight of Az's damaged wing. At least it wasn't still gushing blood.

"I didn't expect you to turn up here." Az sounded wary. Was it because he knew Nate hadn't seen Gabe in so long? But they had never fallen out, not the way he had with some of the other archangels in the aftermath. He and Gabe had simply drifted apart.

"There's been a development." He glanced at Gabe. How much did he know? *How the fuck did he lose his immortality?*

"I can leave, if you want me to." There was a sardonic note in Gabe's voice.

"If you're talking about what happened in Sakarbaal's castle, I've told Gabe everything."

Nate guessed that was inevitable, considering the state of Az's wing. He and Gabe were obviously good friends. It was just odd Az had never mentioned it to him. He'd assumed that, like him, there were many archangels Az was no longer in contact with, but his assumption was wrong.

"Either way," Gabe said. "Come in so I can shut the door."

This was so fucking weird. Gingerly, he stepped over the threshold and Gabe pushed the door shut behind him. He glanced around the large, square hall, with its flagstone floor and central staircase.

It all felt very human.

"We can talk in my office." Gabe led the way across the hall and into a room with French doors that looked out into the back garden. The walls were lined with books and there were a couple of desks with laptops that definitely did *not* look human made.

Az gave him a probing look. "Have you discovered how Sakarbaal got hold of an immortal forged sword?"

"Not yet. Although I have my suspicions." He wasn't going to divulge the sword had been created by Astrid. Not yet, anyway. "Octavia's team found something in his lab. She's analyzing it, but she's never come across anything like it before. Nic wants to know if you have."

Instinctively, he braced himself as he retrieved the cylindrical case from his coat pocket. Even through the steel, his fingertips reacted to the malevolence within. He almost thrust the thing at Az, so he didn't have to touch it anymore, but instead he gritted his teeth and twisted off the lid.

As he tipped the phial onto his palm, both Az and Gabe sucked in harsh breaths. And not just of repugnance.

They both recognized this substance.

He should have worn a glove. Since neither Az nor Gabe appeared inclined to take the phial from him, he placed it on the end of one of the desks and flexed his numb fingers.

"How much more of this fucking stuff is here?" Gabe demanded. "It doesn't belong in our universe."

Right. That had been Octavia's reaction, too. "What is it?"

Gabe glared at him. Ancient horror glowed in his eyes, and a chill soaked through Nate's soul. What the fuck had happened?

"It's from the atmosphere in the Guardians' Voids."

"The Guardians?" Nate double checked, because the Guardians were freakish little shits that existed in the Dark Matter between galaxies. As far as he knew, they didn't live on any of the planets in the universe although they did have an abhorrent habit of abducting random mortals for reasons that could only be guessed at.

Az took a clearly reluctant step closer to the desk, his eyes fixed on the phial. "Sakarbaal ordered Rowan to inject me with this poison, to incapacitate me so he could strike a killing blow." His gaze caught Nate's, and there was the same remnant of horror that had haunted Gabe's eyes. "How much of this did they find at the castle?"

"Not much." Although, by the sound of it, more than enough. "What have you done with the stuff Rowan had?"

Az and Gabe exchanged a look. "Aurora's analyzing it."

Who the fuck was Aurora?

"But she's not getting far." Gabe heaved a frustrated sigh. "The Guardians' atmosphere is alien to our universe. We don't know what the components are."

"Which means we're waiting to hear back from Mephisto."

This just kept on getting better. Mephisto was the first archangel their Alpha Goddess had created and undisputedly her favorite. He'd not heard that name in millennia. And he didn't want to hear it now.

Except he didn't have a choice.

"Mephisto's working on this with you?"

"We passed it onto him a couple of days ago." Az said. "According to Gabe, Mephisto negotiates with the Guardians. Whatever the fuck that means."

He could believe anything of Mephisto, after the way he'd betrayed them all to their goddess, in those last days in Ama-gi.

His jaw tightened. He couldn't think of that now. He tried not to think of it at all, but the memory flashed across his mind, regardless.

In the aftermath of the great destruction, while Earth burned, he'd witnessed the apocalyptic meeting between their goddess and Mephisto. The pair of them standing together, as though everything was fine.

It was the last time he had seen either of them. And later, when Mephisto had attempted contact, he'd blocked the bastard.

Whatever the hell was going on, it was serious.

CHAPTER 13

BELLA

It was mid-morning when Bella teleported home to Richmond upon Thames. After checking out of the guesthouse in Romania she'd found a deserted alley. It was easier to vanish from a small village rather than go to the inconvenience of getting a taxi to the airport, when she had no intention of catching a plane back to England.

In her bedroom, she hung her coat in the antique mahogany wardrobe that matched her dressing table with its satinwood banded decoration. She'd spent three years searching markets, online, and antique shops for a perfect match and her bedroom was exactly the way she'd envisioned it from the moment she had first seen the house. From its stripped floorboards to the meticulously restored fireplace, it was Edwardian elegance at its finest.

It was her home. And unlike when she was a child, and her security had been ripped out from beneath her feet, no one was going to take *this* from her.

She sighed, forked her fingers through her hair and peered at her reflection in her dressing table's oval beveled mirror. If she wanted to continuing enjoying the life she'd carved out for herself, why was she getting involved with Nate?

She should have severed all contact as soon as she found out who he was.

A groan escaped. She was in such deep shit. Last night, it had seemed like a great idea to see how far she could go in letting Nate know she wasn't as ignorant of the world as he supposed.

But where had it really got her? He hadn't divulged any secrets. All she'd done was sink deeper within his irresistible web.

Although he hadn't admitted to taking the immortal forged sword—not that she'd expected him too—he had promised to help her find it. Which was intriguing since not for a second did she imagine he'd ever let her get her hands on *that*.

Enough. She had work to do. One of the jobs she undertook for the Watchers was overseeing the progress of potential new members, from when they were first introduced to their new world until they were formally accepted into the fold. With the annual convention in a couple of days, she could guarantee her Watchers email was overflowing with messages from new recruits, anxious about all the arrangements.

She hauled out her laptop and logged in. Honestly, if the new members just took the time to read their introductory package that she'd put together for them, most of their questions were answered. They didn't need to worry about airport security. For the forty-eight hours during which members arrived, everything was taken care of. Including monitoring all CCTV coverage so any problems could be erased from the digital records. No one would be stopped, searched, have their passports questioned, or luggage confiscated.

It was an impressive operation which involved a combination of demon blood abilities and having strategic members situated in positions of power.

A couple of hours later, after dealing with the last frantic enquiry, she went downstairs and into the kitchen. A cast iron range cooker, that she'd salvaged from a tip and spent a fortune restoring to its former glory, stood against one wall, and although the rest of the kitchen was modern, it had all been hand made to her specific requirements for an uncluttered, sleek feel.

She loved it.

As she made herself some lunch, her phone rang. For a crazy second, she imagined it was Nate calling her.

It wasn't.

"Hey, Octavia."

"Still alive, then." It wasn't a question.

Since the door they had kept close by mutual, unspoken agreement throughout their friendship had been well and truly blown open, she might as well ask the question. "Do you know any other archangels?"

"No. Like I told you before, Nate's been around for ages, but he doesn't often visit the Echelon. I only met Azrael last week, but that was mainly because of Rowan."

Bella frowned. "I don't know who Rowan is."

"She's a dhampir." There was a reluctant note in Octavia's voice. "That information isn't classified, but I can't tell you anything else."

She took a sip of her chamomile tea while she processed that. Was Octavia inferring that Azrael, slayer of dhampirs, was now involved with one?

It didn't seem likely.

"Okay. Well, thanks for checking up on me." She was joking, but a dark undercurrent slithered through her mind. Because, like it or not, her friend was right to be concerned. Archangels answered to no one. If Nate decided to terminate her, he could erase all evidence of her entire existence.

IT WAS LATE MONDAY MORNING, and Bella was packing for her trip to the Watchers temple, hidden deep within the sacred

Zagros mountains, the following day. But for the first time, she wasn't flying there. Eblis wanted the Watchers to know of her powers, so she planned on teleporting.

Although how the Elite were going to react to the fact she possessed as many, if not more, powers than they did, she had no idea. Not when for the last several decades she'd passed herself off as a lower caste immortal with a diluted demonic bloodline.

To be fair, that's exactly what she'd always thought she was, until Eblis' unexpected revelation the other night.

Maybe she shouldn't reveal everything. The Elite possessively guarded their inner sanctums, and she was sure they'd put her through a grueling evaluation before allowing her entrance to their elevated ranks. Eblis had, after all, only mentioned revealing her ability to teleport, and that alone was enough.

Her phone rang. Surely Octavia wasn't checking up on her again? With an exasperated sigh, she glanced at her screen.

Nate.

Her heart did a completely unnecessary leap in her chest.

She took a deep breath and let it ring again before answering. He'd promised to let her know how things were progressing before she left the country, and he was following through. That was all.

"Isabella." His sinful voice was dark and rich, and rolled over her skin like every forbidden vice she'd ever imagined. "I promised you something and didn't deliver. What's your address?"

She sank onto an antique grandmother chair by the window. It was either that or suffer the indignity of her knees wobbling.

"I don't remember you not delivering on your promises." And how. She forcibly stopped herself from indulging in a visceral flashback to their night in Romania. Also, thank the gods her voice didn't betray just how much she enjoyed hearing from him. This wasn't a game. She had to focus on the fact that the Archangel Nathanael was dangerous.

His sexy laugh was like molten honey flowing through her veins. Briefly, she closed her eyes in disgust at her body's treacherous responses, but it didn't stop a small smile from escaping.

"I'm referring to your scandalous lingerie."

She couldn't seem to wipe the despicable smile from her face, so she gave up. "Lingerie? What am I missing?"

"A pair of knickers." Amusement threaded through every word, and she could imagine the irresistible amber flecks glittering in his eyes as he spoke the words.

Stop it. She shook her head, as though that might help jog her brains back into their proper place. "Oh right. Your Neanderthal display the other night." Then his comment penetrated. "Wait, you've bought me another pair of knickers?"

Surely not. Then again, why not? Everything he did was so alien to all her preconceived notions of archangels as beings of incalculable arrogance, and their legendary disregard of any creature besides themselves.

It's only underwear. There was no need for hyperbole.

"I did," Nate said, intruding into her attempt to push him back into a box in her brain marked *Deadliest Enemy.* "When are you free? I'm up for a special delivery."

She pressed her thighs together and ignored the primal tug of need that flared at his barely disguised promise. Not that she was going to metaphorically fall at his feet.

"A platonic delivery only, I presume?" Did she sound coolly amused? She hoped he couldn't guess how much of an effort it had taken her.

"Totally. I don't want your lasting memory of me to be of a lingerie ripping asshole," he said then groaned. "That didn't come out the way I planned."

She laughed. "It really didn't. I hope."

"Your address?"

He was being very persistent. Or was she being overly sensitive? Except she never gave out her home address to anyone but her closest friends. Nate wasn't—and could never be—a friend.

And she had to face it. If things turned nasty, it wouldn't take him five minutes to find out where she lived.

She gave him her address.

"Be there in half an hour," he said, before ending the call.

Either he wasn't ready to see her yet, or he was continuing the farce that he needed time to travel across London. Brooding, she gazed at the screen of her phone, as the question she kept ignoring finally pushed its way to the front of her mind.

How is this going to end?

EXACTLY THIRTY MINUTES LATER, there was a knock, and she could see Nate's outline through the decorative stained-glass panels. She counted to ten before going to open the door. No way did she want him to think she'd been waiting down the hall for him.

His hair was pulled back from his face and black gems glittered in his earlobes and nose. Even when he greeted her with a devastating smile, it didn't dispel the aura of formidable warrior that clung to him.

He would be lethal in battle.

A shiver skittered along her arms. He was her enemy, but she hoped she never had to witness him in action.

"As promised." He held up a bag from an exclusive London lingerie boutique, and her sense of danger melted, the way it always did when she was in his company. He stepped into her house without being invited and she closed the door behind him. Because she had already invited him in when she'd given him her address.

"Thank you." She took his gift but didn't open it right away. Truth was, she couldn't drag her fascinated gaze from his face.

Although he still dazzled her with a half-smile, she got the impression he wasn't used to doing this kind of thing.

She steeled her nerves against his charm, but warmth seeped through her chest regardless.

With a silent sigh, she led him into the drawing room. Her pièce de résistance. It was like stepping back in time with the inlaid rosewood sofas, lamp tables, and cast-iron fireplace. Unlike her kitchen, there was nothing modern in the room.

Well, except for twenty-first century electricity, obviously. There was no way she was going back to relying on gaslight.

"Nice place." Nate swept a keen glance around the room.

"Thanks. This house was virtually derelict before I moved in, but I had to buy it. I loved the Edwardian era." Shit. Had she said *loved*? Luckily, Nate hadn't appeared to notice the slip of her tongue.

"You renovated from scratch?" He seemed genuinely interested.

"Yes. My next project is the main bathroom. I've already sourced an original claw foot bath, it's in my garden shed at the moment."

There was an enigmatic half-smile on his face, as though he found her enthusiasm when it came to restoration amusing. Sometimes she *did* get carried away by her passion.

She placed the bag on one of the sofas and pulled out the large gift box. She glanced at Nate, who was taking up all the space by the door. "It's a big box. Are you passing comment on the size of my bottom?"

"Your bottom is perfect."

She tried not to laugh and failed. "That's not a very platonic thing to say."

"I wasn't speaking from a platonic viewpoint."

"I know." It didn't matter how many pep talks she gave herself when she was alone. As soon as she saw Nate again, all her good resolutions flew out of the window.

She took the lid off the box and a gasp caught in her throat. Delicate cornflower blue knickers, bra, and exquisite corset nestled in pale blue tissue paper. With infinite care she placed each gorgeous item on her sofa. Nate came up behind her, and although they weren't touching, she could feel his heat envelope her in a sensual caress.

"You like?" His voice was husky.

"Yes." She dragged in a ragged breath. "They're beautiful."

"No chance of modeling them for me? In a purely platonic manner?"

She gave a small *huh* of laughter. "There's no way we'd keep things out of the bedroom if I wore these for you."

"Who says we need the bedroom?"

She let out a long breath and turned to face him. He was standing way too close for comfort, yet not nearly close enough to satisfy her craving. It was a toss-up between flinging her arms around him or backing away.

She folded her arms. This was her turf and she wasn't retreating.

"You enchant me, Isabella." He was flirting, she knew that, but woven through his words was a sense of genuine bafflement. "I know it's safer for us not to be involved but every time I see you, I lose my mind."

Why did he always say the most captivating things? And then his comment penetrated the delusional rose petals that threatened to turn her brain into pulp. "Safer?"

She knew damn well it was safer for her to keep away from him. But what did *he* mean by it?

His face darkened, and it was like thunderclouds obscuring the sun. *I'm so screwed...*

"I've come across some ruthless—" he paused for a split second, considering. "People in my time. They wouldn't hesitate to harm someone I cared about, just for the hell of it."

Something strange and sharp twisted deep inside her breast. "You care about me?"

"It's hard not to." He gave her a sardonic smile, but she wasn't fooled. He wasn't messing around.

There was no other reason for him to say such a thing unless he meant it. She was under no illusion that if it suited his purpose he'd kill her, but right now that was a secondary concern.

He wasn't supposed to be getting under her skin like this. Even before she'd known who he was, their one night together was meant to be just that.

But the more she saw him, the more complicated it all became. She was literally speechless.

He gave her ponytail a gentle tug. "I'm no expert, but isn't this where you say you care for me, too?"

"I—" The words lodged in her throat. Not that she was sure what those words even were, but she had to say something. *I'm the daughter of a demon.* Or maybe *I despise all archangels and everything they stand for.* How about *I don't even know who I am anymore when I'm with you.* She dragged her frantic mind back in line. Some truths could never be revealed. "I'm not an expert in this, either."

"Hey." His big hand cradled her face. "Don't worry. I'm not going to let anything happen to you, okay?"

He thought she was afraid of being hurt. And she was, but not in the way he imagined. There was no point denying it any longer. She *did* care about him. And their inevitable parting, even if it wasn't acrimonious, would haunt her for far too long afterwards.

She threaded her fingers through his, pressing his palm more securely against her cheek. "I can take care of myself, Nate. I'm pretty good at it, actually."

His jaw flexed, as though he waged an internal battle as to whether he should share more with her, or not. When he sighed, it was clear caution had prevailed. "Okay. Just promise me you'll be careful."

"I'll promise. If you will, too."

He cocked his head. "Me?"

"Yes. Hunting violators has got to be dangerous, right?"

He gave a crooked smile that did something completely illegal to the pit of her stomach. "Are you worried about me?"

"Is that a crime?" *Yes, it is.*

"I guess not." His gaze roved over her face. It was insane how arousing she found it. "But you'd be the first."

Something squeezed deep in her chest. It definitely *wasn't* her heart because that was physiologically impossible. "I find that hard to believe."

"Why?"

He sounded sincere, but while myths abounded on the callousness of archangels and how they were incapable of love, there were also plenty of stories in the archives of how humans had fallen for them since the beginning of their creation. Nothing would convince her that Nate hadn't experienced his share of mortal adoration during his long life.

"Are you telling me you've never had any serious relationships in the past?" Then again, that depended on what she meant by *serious relationships*. A mortal could love an archangel without any promise being made between them. Did that count? Now she'd thought about it, she wasn't so sure.

"I'm not what you'd call relationship material." There was a dry note in his voice. "The women I hook up with only want one thing."

"That's..." she hesitated. How could she even think of saying such a thing to the immortal warrior in her arms? But she couldn't stop herself, because so many times in the past she'd known a man only wanted to get close to her for *one thing*. "That's kind of sad, Nate."

"I'm not complaining."

She wished she could say the same thing. But if not for her demon powers, how many times would she have been taken advantage of, when she was a young girl trying to survive on the streets of London?

"It *is* sad. And I think you're wrong, anyway. I'm sure some of your conquests genuinely felt a lot more for you than you're aware."

He wound his arm around her waist and tugged her a little closer. "The only conquest I'm interested in is you."

"What makes you think you've conquered me?"

"Have I?"

His dark gaze was mesmeric. If she didn't know who—*what*—he really was, she could so easily fall under his magnetic spell.

If I hadn't already...

No. She was aware of the risks. It was her only protection and she wasn't going to jeopardize her heart for anyone, least of all an archangel. She could enjoy these moments with him if she held onto the truth. Even if that truth was a lone, flickering flame in the farthest corner of her sane mind.

"Define *conquered*."

"Hmm." His thumb caressed her cheek while his arm tightened around her. "The way you look at me."

"With my eyes, you mean?"

"Yeah. Your eyes look at me, and I know."

She laughed. "What else?"

He drew in a deep breath. She had no idea why that was so incredibly alluring. "Your scent." His voice dropped to a growl and she gave a delicate shiver. "Elusive and sexy. Binding me to you. Even when we're apart."

She tugged her hand free from his and wound her arms around his neck. Not just because she wanted to feel his hard, gorgeous body pressed against hers. But because his words sank into her blood, like the finest champagne, a heady maelstrom that caused her limbs to tremble like a sacrificial virgin.

Sanity struggled to reassert itself. "That sounds as though *I've* conquered *you*."

"I'm not keeping score."

"So we've vanquished each other."

He trailed his fingers up her back before grasping her hair in his fist. "You put such a negative spin on things."

She mirrored his actions, wrapping his thick locks around her knuckles. "I'm a realist."

His breath singed her lips. "That's right. You don't believe in fairy tales."

"Let's put the platonic thing on hold."

His smile was surely forged from the mythical pit of Hades itself. "I can work with that."

Warning bells clanged in the back of her mind, but it was too late for that. Why did she crave to create another memory of how easily her enemy could penetrate her defenses? What was *wrong* with her?

Whatever. She didn't care. She wasn't a fragile piece of porcelain that would shatter when—*if*—the truth ever came to light.

With infinite care she unbuttoned his shirt, revealing his magnificent bronzed pecs. His musculature was so breathtakingly defined, as though he'd been lovingly sculptured from living marble, and his harsh sigh as she scraped her nails over him was electrifying.

She pressed her lips against his flesh, savoring the taste of him on her tongue. His grip on her hair was brutal, sending sharp pinpricks of awareness flooding through her skull, and she loved it.

As she eased his pants down his rock-hard thighs, she nibbled teasing kisses across his abs. Although he had the physique of a warrior, and she was certain he'd fought countless battles, not a single scar marred his skin.

But then, none of her scars showed, either.

She sank onto her knees and hastily shoved his pants to his

ankles, unable to tear her bewitched gaze from his mouthwatering cock.

"The way you're looking at me now," he choked out.

She didn't pretend to misunderstand. "Totally conquered." She breathed the words against him, before teasing his swollen head with the tip of her tongue. His groan filled her mind, along with the addictive essence that was all Nate. Somehow, she managed to find her voice again. "Vanquished together."

"Never." It was a feral growl, intoxicating. She wrapped her hand around his thick length and took him into her mouth. His sharp intake of breath reverberated through his body, sending sparks of lightning cascading across her skin. She cupped his heavy balls in the palm of her hand, relishing how he filled her mouth, so hard and unyielding.

In my power.

The knowledge swam through her, ephemeral, unimportant. Because all that mattered was now, this moment, and the man whose slightest touch could make her forget every rule of survival.

One fist grasped her hair and his other hand anchored the back of her head. It was primitive, savage, an age-old display of machismo, and for the first time the notion didn't fuel her ire.

Because this was Nate. And this was what she wanted.

With a muffled curse, he pulled back and ripped off his pants, leaving her panting. He joined her on the floor, a wild gleam in his eyes, before he tore her jeans from her and pinned her beneath him.

"Do you realize what you've just given up?" She wrapped her legs around him, needing to feel his strength against every inch of her body.

"Later." It was a harsh response. "I'm not giving up anything." Then agony flashed across his face, and bracing his weight on one hand, he grabbed his discarded pants. "Fucking condom." He pulled a packet from his pocket, and a perilous wave of tenderness flooded her. She couldn't afford to get sentimental. But she'd unpick that later. Right now, his concern for her overrode everything.

"You were pretty sure about getting lucky today, then?" She flattened her palm against his jaw.

"I wanted to be prepared." His grin lit up the whole damn room. She made the decision without even considering it.

"It's okay. We don't need to. It's safe."

For a moment, indecision battled in his eyes. He was an archangel. She knew he was immune from infections that plagued mortals. The only thing that worried him was her peace of mind.

And then his mouth covered hers, and his kiss stole whatever was left of her reason. His hands slid beneath her sweater, exploring, caressing, and she writhed, desperate for all of him. The solid length of his erection burned her thigh, but still he took his time, gliding his fingers over every particle of her sensitized flesh.

"Nate, please." Had she begged? She didn't care. He dipped inside her, teasing, pushing her to the very edge of the known universe. "*Now.*"

"Your wish is my command," he ground between his teeth, his eyes a hypnotic swirl of midnight and madness. He thrust into her, filling her so completely that she couldn't breathe, couldn't move, and she clung onto his hair as her only anchor in the sea of sensation.

He rode her hard, giving her everything she needed. Sensation flooded through her, a thrilling whirlpool of starbursts and rainbows, incredible, *crazy*, but she was beyond rational thought. And when he groaned her name in ecstasy, she discarded Earth and fell with him into the celestial maelstrom.

CHAPTER 14

BELLA

Nate rolled onto his back, taking her with him, and she snuggled against his hard body as he idly traced circles with his fingers along her spine. His evocative cologne weaved a sensual web around her, a fantasy cocoon where nothing but this moment in time existed.

She'd take it. Real life would intrude way too soon.

Finally, he spoke. "This platonic thing is overrated."

She laughed and propped her chin on her hand so she could see his face. "What platonic thing? That idea lasted less than five minutes."

He sighed and stroked her bottom. Renewed desire rippled through her and she shifted restlessly. "You're just so irresistible."

"Are you blaming me for your lack of restraint?"

"There was no blame attached. Trust me."

She dropped a gentle kiss on the tip of his nose. "Trust doesn't come easily to me." And even if it did, how could she ever truly trust *him*?

It was illogical to mourn that irrefutable fact. So why was she?

"Same." There was a pensive note in his voice. His hold on her tightened, became possessive. "Who hurt you, Isabella? Is it because of your childhood?"

She shouldn't confide in him. But in his arms, sated and still psychically humming from their joining, his question didn't seem that intrusive. What did it matter, if she shared a little more of her life with him?

"I lived on the streets for a couple of years. You tend not to trust anyone, if you want to survive." At least she'd had it easier than most. With her abilities, she'd managed to eat and find shelter, while avoiding the worst degradations that were so common for orphans in the slums.

Technically, she hadn't been an orphan as her mother was still alive, back then. But as far as Bella was concerned, her mother had been dead to her from the moment she threw Bella into the gutter.

The same anger she'd witnessed the last time she'd spoken of her family, flared in his eyes. Why did his concern ignite a flame deep inside? Maybe this hadn't been such a good idea, after all.

"Two years." He made it sound like a curse. Enchanted, she gazed at him. "Did your long-lost relatives find you when you were sixteen?"

She tilted her head, and the end of her ponytail brushed against his shoulder. She couldn't imagine what he was referring to. "What?"

His frown intensified. "Just guessing. When did the relative who left you their legacy discover your whereabouts?"

Her quizzical smile froze, and she frantically clawed through her mind. When had she told him such a thing? Except she already knew the answer.

She hadn't. Why would she? There was no such relative.

"Sorry." A frown slashed his brow. "I read it somewhere before I met you." And then he gave her one of his irresistible grins. "Does that make me a stalker?"

She exhaled a shaky breath through her mouth, willing her

panicky heartbeat to slow. If she didn't pull herself together, he'd guess she was hiding something big. And although the truth might come out later, she'd deal with it then. But she sure as hell didn't want to deal with it now.

Didn't want to spoil this moment in his arms, when his concern for her shitty adolescence had touched a deeply buried crack in her heart.

But how could she answer him without lying? Before the advent of mid-twentieth century technology, it had been easier to flit through society without leaving a traceable footprint.

But the world changed and to escape detection, she'd had to adapt.

First Eblis, and then the Elite in the Watchers had instructed her on how to shield her longevity from mortals. And so, for human bureaucratic purposes, twice during the last seventy years she'd reinvented herself and fabricated an elderly relative who had died and left her an inheritance, in case anyone went digging into her background. But each time the "relative" had been *her*.

It was the reason she didn't have any personal social media accounts. The less information out there about her, the safer she was.

How ironic Nate was confronting her with the very history she used to protect herself.

His gaze turned watchful. Or was she imagining it?

Say something. She didn't usually find it hard to obfuscate when faced with a potential threat. But Nate was different. She couldn't lie to him. Didn't *want* to, which was terrifying when she considered the implications.

"It's a long story." She offered him what she hoped was a resigned smile. "And very boring."

There was no mistake this time. His gaze definitely sharpened. "It won't bore me."

Any time someone—say, an official—became too persistent in demanding information, it was a simple thing to subliminally hypnotize them into compliance. That wouldn't work with Nate, even if she wanted to do such a thing.

She compromised. She was doing a lot of that since meeting him. "It's hard for me to talk about."

He cradled her head so tenderly that an unwarranted streak of guilt at her deception burned through her. If only he'd try to invade her mind to find the answers he sought. He wouldn't succeed. She'd know right away what he was doing. But at least it would prove that the Archangel Nathanael was a dick.

"Okay," he said, and there wasn't even a hint of him trying to violate her privacy. "Just tell me you avenged the wrongs inflicted on you by your family."

That made her laugh. "Vindictive, much?"

"I prefer to call it justified vengeance."

Of course he would. He was known, after all, as the Archangel of Vengeance. The reality of her situation raised its ugly head, and her amusement died. "Do you ever forgive, Nate?"

"Sure." The warmth in his eyes assured her that he had no idea how serious she was. "Except for one thing. I never forgive betrayal."

Nate

Isabella's beautiful eyes clouded. He wished he knew what her fleeting moments of sorrow were really concealing. Logically, it had to be connected to when she lived on the streets and yet there was something about the tightness of her mouth that told him it was more.

But what could be more traumatic for a young human girl than having to survive in such a manner? He could only imagine the things she'd endured.

Another acidic wave of fury at her family's treatment consumed him. It was better that Isabella told him nothing of them. If she did, he might be tempted to hunt them down and exact retribution.

Maybe he'd hunt them down anyway, a side project after this current mission was finished.

She shivered, and with reluctance he rolled onto his side and withdrew from her. She gave him a faint smile before pulling on her jeans. "If I'd known we were going to get so friendly, I would've put the heating on."

"Next time," he said, watching as she loosened her hair from its band, before finger combing the tangled tresses and pulling her hair back into her usual ponytail. His response gnawed into his brain.

Isabella was like a drug that had invaded his blood and he couldn't get her out of his head.

"Not just the heating." She rested her hand on his chest, above his heart. "I'll wear the lingerie, too."

He groaned at the prospect. "Torturer."

She patted his chest. That was a form of torture, too. "You can think on that for the rest of the week."

Too right he would.

Hey, Nate.

Nate gritted his teeth as Azrael's voice filled his mind. Of all the times to get in touch. He could ignore it. But since Az might have news about the substance that had been discovered at Sakarbaal's castle, he was obligated to reply.

I'll get back to you.

"Everything okay?" There was a questioning expression on Isabella's face.

"Yeah, great." He wrapped his hand around her head and pulled her close for a lingering kiss. She tasted so good. He didn't want to leave. Vaguely unnerved, he released her and retrieved his pants. "Just some work-related shit I've got to sort out."

"How's that going?"

"More slowly than I'd like."

"Any new leads that connect to my club?"

"Nah." He paused in the process of pulling on his boots and looked at her. "Out of interest, what made you decide to call your clubs *Inanna*?"

She was still sitting on the floor, with her arms wrapped around her knees. She didn't appear fazed by his question. "The goddess has always fascinated me. She's such a powerful feminine force. I like to think she'll return, one day." She paused for a heartbeat. "If she was real, I mean."

Yeah, he couldn't see that happening. Inanna was no longer a great fan of humans from Earth, and currently she owned a very lucrative string of clubs in the Andromeda Galaxy. But Isabella didn't need to know that.

He took her hands and pulled her to her feet. "Give me a call when you get back."

"Will do." She went onto her toes and brushed a gentle kiss across his lips. "Be good while I'm gone."

AFTER LEAVING ISABELLA'S HOUSE, Nate teleported back to the apartment and took a quick shower. Should he have told her the one he hunted wasn't human? He'd wanted to warn her, but he hadn't wanted to terrify her. Although she hadn't seemed especially worried that his mark might want to harm her.

Fuck it. He wasn't used to second guessing every decision he made. But since meeting Isabella, he'd done nothing but.

It was disconcerting.

He pulled on fresh clothes and went outside onto the roof terrace and gripped the handrail. The dark clouds merged into the grayness of the warehouses. It wasn't an inspiring view. He sucked in a deep breath and contacted Az.

What's up?

Azrael responded immediately. *Mephisto wants to meet.*

Nate's lip curled. When Mephisto had discovered Nate had known all along that Dagan was a demon, he'd ripped Nate a new one.

Mephisto's wrath had been justified, yet he hadn't shared that knowledge with anyone else.

Whatever Mephisto might think, that wasn't the reason why Nate had blocked the oldest archangel of all when they'd deserted the ruined Earth. It was because of his blatant hypocrisy.

What's he discovered?

You know Mephisto. Frustration threaded through Az's words. *He wouldn't tell me anything.*

Great. Nate narrowed his eyes. It appeared Mephisto wasn't leaving him with a choice. *Tell him I'll meet him in Zega.*

He had no doubt Mephisto knew the place. It was the most exclusive club on one of the most expensive pleasure planets in the Andromeda Galaxy. Not that he'd picked the club for Mephisto's benefit. The club was owned by Inanna, and besides the fact it would be good to catch up with her again, she'd never put up with any of Mephisto's shit.

Fuck it, Nate. Can't you lower your block and tell him yourself?

Yes, he could. And no, he wasn't going to. It had taken decades of working on his mental blockades before they'd been powerful enough to seal that particular telepathic link.

I'll be in Zega if he wants to meet.

Az cursed in the language of the ancients and Nate gave a grim smile. The other archangel was clearly recovering if he could swear so eloquently.

Now? Az asked.

Sure.

He waited another twenty minutes before teleporting into the elegant grounds outside *Zega*. The sky was blue and indigo, with splashes of pink. It was the perfect backdrop for the club, which bore more than a passing resemblance to the magnificent Temples of the Universe that had once graced Ama-gi.

As an elite immortal, with DNA harvested direct from the original, Alpha Immortals of antiquity, Nate could have easily bypassed the stringent security measures and teleported directly inside the club. In other places, on other planets, he often did, if he wanted to cause a wave of awe or panic among the congregated mortals. But when it wasn't necessary, he preferred the more subtle approach.

From the cultivated grounds, he strolled into the front courtyard, where statues of the divine goddess in all her guises were strategically placed. Except they were more than just statues, they formed part of the security web. He gave a wry smile as she materialized before him.

"Hey, Inanna."

She was one of the few goddesses he trusted, and after she'd rubbed his nose in the fact that she'd warned him about the demon and he hadn't listened, they had fallen back into their pre-Dagan friendship.

It was an odd word to use between their races, when the majority of the gods tended to look down on archangels, but it fit.

"Hmm." She swept her critical gaze over him. "You know I don't like business being conducted within my domains without my permission."

"Who says I'm here for business?"

"Your recently activated pheromones suggest you're not in need of the kind of pleasure *Zega* offers."

"My recently released *what*? No, don't answer that." He held up a hand. Inanna had an uncanny ability to uncover things that were best left hidden. The fewer who knew about his connection to Isabella, the better. "I'm meeting Mephisto."

"Wonderful." Irony dripped from each syllable. "I can expect mass hysteria to erupt any second, then."

An ethereal ripple distorted the atmosphere, causing the hair on his arms to stand on end. Inanna had impressive alert mechanisms installed. She rolled her eyes and beckoned for him to follow her. "Your Alpha's favorite has arrived."

Inanna led him through the club, its soaring columns and elaborate arches that were so reminiscent of those ancient temples they'd both known in their youth. When they reached one of the main party rooms, Nate threw up a low-level glamour to disguise his archangelic radiance. Judging by how many mortals were clinging onto each other or collapsed onto the floor, Mephisto hadn't deigned to put such a precaution in place.

Still the same arrogant bastard as he'd always been.

Nate folded his arms as Mephisto strutted across the room to them, his midnight wings partially extended, apparently oblivious to the chaos in his wake. It had been eleven thousand years since they'd last seen each other, and he looked exactly the same.

He glanced at Inanna, who appeared exasperated, but not furious. In fact, there was a familiar gleam of admiration in her eyes.

In Ama-gi, many of the younger gods and goddesses had indulged in whirlwind affairs with Mephisto but he'd always assumed Inanna was immune to his charm.

Looked like he was wrong.

"Cloak it." Inanna waved a finger in the general direction of Mephisto's wings.

"You're no fun," Mephisto said, but his wings instantly vanished, and the mortals stopped reeling. For the first time, he looked directly at Nate. "I appreciate you seeing me."

He hadn't expected that. Mephisto sounded sincere. Not that it meant anything. Mephisto was a pro when it came to disarming his opposition.

"If you're going to fight, take it off planet," Inanna said. It appeared she was also skeptical of Mephisto's true motives. "I'll be seriously pissed off if you destroy my flagship."

"I'm not here to fight."

Inanna transferred her laser gaze to Nate. He shrugged. "All I want is information."

"Do I need to adjudicate?"

"No." But maybe she needed to be warned. The poison hadn't appeared to affect vampires or dhampirs, but the DNA of archangels and the minor gods came, one way or the other, direct from the Alphas. The gods might be just as vulnerable to the alien shit as archangels. "I'll keep you in the loop."

"Fine." Inanna didn't sound fine about it, but she stepped back. "I'll leave you to whisper your secrets to each other." With that, she teleported.

"It's been a long time, Nate."

He wasn't in the mood for small talk with Mephisto. "Not long enough, but Azrael tells me you're already working on this crap from the Guardians."

"There's something I need to discuss with you."

"Go ahead." Why was he making such a big deal of things? Oh yeah. Because he was Mephisto. To underline the point, the smug archangel threw up a top-level glamour which ensured that even Inanna's enhanced security would be unable to penetrate and hear their conversation.

"Are you aware of any archangel who fell for a demigoddess in Ama-gi?"

"What?" Nate glared at Mephisto. Because what the *fuck* did that have to do with anything? "Don't piss me around, Mephisto. You know why I agreed to meet with you."

"Two Nephilim have been discovered. One is a four-year-old child."

Nate's caustic response died in his throat. All Nephilim, the beloved children of archangels, had perished in the great devastation that had swept Earth. They all knew this. It was why so many of them had forsaken the planet.

Just because Mephisto said something, didn't make it true.

"If any Nephilim had survived, we would know."

"Yeah." Mephisto's lip curled in barely suppressed rage. Nate had the surreal conviction it wasn't directed at him. "These Nephilim were found on an obscure planet in Andromeda. Their ancestor was a demigoddess who had been on Earth and they had no fucking clue they're also descended from an archangel."

Nephilim had only ever been born in Ama-gi. And they had all died there. He had never had a child of his own, but their loss had haunted him through millennia.

But some had survived. *In Andromeda?*

He sucked in a harsh breath, but it didn't help clear his head. Fundamental beliefs that had been a part of him for too long threatened to shatter.

"You found them?" His voice was hoarse, accusing.

"I've met them. There's no mistake. They're ours."

Nate swung away and raked his gaze across the oblivious crowd. But he didn't see them. All he could see in his mind's eye was the ravaged Earth, after they'd escaped their goddess' gilded prison.

But they hadn't been the only ones to escape the planet.

Mephisto's revelation sank further into his brain, unfolding threadlike tentacles, and discordance stirred. How could the Nephilim be descended from a demigoddess?

Archangels only conceived with their beloved. And while many of the gods had been more than eager to take archangels as their lovers, the affairs were never serious. Because most of the gods believed, at their core, that archangels were anomalies of nature.

Slowly, he turned back to Mephisto, whose black gaze continued to bore into him.

"Demigoddess?" He double checked.

"I need to find the archangel, Nate. He should know of his descendants."

Well, sure. He agreed. It was of paramount importance that

the Nephilim were brought back into the fold, to be loved and protected as they had been in Ama-gi.

"No idea who the demigoddess is?"

"She died. Giving birth."

"Shit." What the fuck had happened? Demigoddesses didn't usually perish in such a mortal manner.

"You're still in contact with many archangels who broke ranks." It wasn't a question. Nate's feathers bristled at the not so subtle censure. But there were no ranks to break. There never had been. Mephisto had simply enjoyed being the number one. Their goddess' favorite.

He was right about one thing, though. Nate had remained in contact with a great many of the archangels who had turned their backs on Mephisto.

After a frigid silence, Mephisto exhaled a long breath. "Will you pass the word? The archangel responsible needs to contact me."

"Very well." He'd do it for the Nephilim, and for the archangel who knew nothing of his bloodline.

"How much longer are you going to keep this grudge going?"

Typical Mephisto. Total gaslighter. If not for the fact he still needed information, he wouldn't even deign to answer.

But if Mephisto was going to be an asshole, then maybe it was time to let him know the truth.

"Fine. I'll tell you. I returned to the shattered remains of Nibiru." He paused and rubbed his brow. Nibiru, the home world where their goddess had created her beloved archangels. The planet where she had incarcerated them when the devastation had struck Earth.

The place they had decimated in order to escape.

No flicker of emotion distorted Mephisto's basalt expression. Did he even remember meeting their cursed goddess after her unforgiveable betrayal?

"I saw you," he clarified. "With *Her*." Even now, the thought of uttering her name choked him.

Crimson flashed in Mephisto's eyes but was gone in a second. "And?"

"And nothing." It was all he'd expected, after all. Because the other archangel had no excuse to offer. "Tell me what you've discovered about the alien substance."

"It's an extraction from the Guardians' atmosphere. The elements are unidentifiable."

Gabe had already told him that. "Anything else?"

"No. How much of it do the vampires have?"

It was a valid question. "As far as I'm aware, not a lot."

"Can you get hold of it?"

"I doubt it."

"Did you hold any back from Azrael?"

What was this, a fucking inquisition?

"No." He ground the word between his teeth. He hadn't wanted to keep any of that shit, and the only reason Az had, with great reluctance, taken it was because he planned on handing it over to Mephisto. The fact he *had* withheld a minuscule sample to pass onto Astrid was none of Mephisto's concern.

"Just the vampires, then."

Was he being paranoid, or did that sound like a veiled threat?

"Their scientists are working on it. Az said you have information for me." Mephisto had wanted to see him. Surely he had more data to share?

"I told Az I needed to speak with you. And I've shared that information. As for the Guardians' shit—I'm dealing with that. Stay in touch." He gave a mirthless grin and vanished.

CHAPTER 15

BELLA

It was time to go to the Zagros mountains.

Bella eyed her luggage that sat at the end of her bed. Usually when she went to the Vernal Equinox celebration, she caught a flight and was picked up at the airport by a member of the Watchers who would then drive her, and any others who had recently arrived, to their hotel.

A couple of days ago, she'd cancelled her flight. But she hadn't yet informed the Elite of her new travel arrangements. It had been easy to agree to Eblis' order to reveal more of her powers to them, but now it came down to it, she didn't have a clue as to how she was going to handle it. How could she satisfactorily explain why she hadn't told them before now? More to the point, how would they react to her revelation?

She'd soon find out.

She pulled out her phone and called Zane, who was one of the officials who organized the annual gathering. He was also one of the few higher-ranking Elites who didn't exude an air of menacing superiority.

"Hey, Bella," he said. "No last-minute problems, I hope?"

"No, everything's fine. Where are you?"

"At work." There was a thread of amusement in his voice.

Bella sighed. "Can you get to Inanna's Eye? It's important."

"Now?" Suspicion had replaced the amusement.

"Alone," she added. "I'll explain when you get there."

"If you know of a security breach, then spit it out. Don't fuck around."

"It's not a security breach." Well, not technically, although she imagined some of the Elite might consider her one very shortly.

"Going now."

She picked up her luggage. She trusted Zane to go alone to the plateau near the summit of the sacred mountain, which had been called Inanna's Eye for countless centuries, due to the staggering views of the surrounding snow peaked mountains and fertile valleys.

What would Nate have made of it, if she'd told him the other reason why she'd named her clubs after the great goddess? It was a hidden link to the Watchers and therefore her heritage, buried within the cradle of Inanna's cult from antiquity.

Less than a heartbeat later, she arrived at her destination. The plateau was a massive slice of rock where in ages past, priestesses of the goddess had conducted awe-inspiring ceremonies.

Not that the Watchers were interested in collecting any of those mist-shrouded slivers of history for their archives. But she'd done her own research because, even though historically the gods had never been friends of demons, Inanna fascinated her.

Zane was standing at the mouth of what appeared, to the untrained eye, to be nothing more than a cave. He swung around, his phone in his hand, his green tourmaline ring, which signified his Elite status, flashing in the sunlight. His blistering glare wasn't encouraging. There was only one way to reach this plateau, and that was from the chamber beyond the cave entrance, that led to a ceremonial atrium situated near the peak of the cavernous mountain itself.

Unless you could teleport.

He took two strides her way before coming to an abrupt halt. "Is this a newly acquired ability?"

"No."

"Why?"

She didn't pretend to misunderstand his question. "I heard rumors on NightRaven that an archangel had been damaged while on Earth. I decided it was time to step up."

It was almost the truth.

What else can you do?

She kept her face blank. Zane hadn't merely fired a telepathic question at her. He'd spoken in Basque. She wasn't about to let him know she possessed all three of the most coveted powers. Especially when the majority of the Elites had only inherited two.

His expression gave nothing away. She kept her gaze fixed on his.

Never show fear.

"I can't guarantee everyone will understand why you kept this from us," Zane said out loud, reverting to English. "But we're always in need of stronger bloodlines. Welcome, Bella."

ZANE TOOK her to a room deep within the mountain. It seemed now she was on the brink of elevating through the ranks, she was entitled to stay within the sacred temple, rather than a local hotel. She wasn't fooled by the so-called privilege of her own room, though. They wanted her where they could keep an eye on her.

"This is yours." He opened the door, and while she obviously hadn't expected a window, a carpet on the rock floor would've been nice. "The Elite are gathering in the atrium in twenty minutes. Don't be late."

She had no intention of being late. Although she wasn't

looking forward to the interrogation from the Elite, passing their scrutiny was the only way she'd be allowed to ascend into their ranks. And possessing that honor was the only way she could gain access to restricted sections of the temple.

"I'll be there." She kept her voice cool. Although Zane had been outwardly fine since her revelation, she doubted he was as accepting of her newly shared ability as he appeared. She wouldn't, if their roles were reversed.

He smiled, but for the first time when it had been directed her way, it didn't reach his eyes, before he turned and strode away.

She closed the door and took a deep breath. At some point in the distant past—long before demon bloods had taken the mountain for their own—the interior had been painstakingly hollowed out, to create an inverse temple. The first time she'd seen the breathtaking structure, she'd been spellbound by its stark beauty.

She wasn't looking forward to the interrogation by the Elite and the sudden, inexplicable urge to contact Nate washed through her, stalling the breath in her throat. She had to stop thinking about him at such odd, random moments. He was the last person she could talk to about this secret part of her life.

For so long, she'd never been able to share anything that really mattered with anyone. After her family disowned her, she'd fought for survival and, as the years slid by, she'd had no option but to learn there was no one she could rely on but herself.

Things had changed after she'd joined the Watchers, even though it had taken her decades before she'd lowered her barriers enough to make friends. And of course, there was Octavia.

But that wasn't what she meant. She sat on the bed and glared up at the smooth, rock ceiling. There was an uneven, fluttery sensation in her chest, and she was afraid—more than afraid—to probe what it meant. What it could mean for her survival.

Long ago, she'd locked her heart away in a mythical fortress deep inside her psyche. She'd imagined it was impenetrable, hung with thick cobwebs, impervious to anything the world might throw her way.

It hadn't been a great way to navigate her existence, but it had worked. Until she'd met Nate.

Even knowing who he was, she'd confided more in him than anyone. And now, when she desperately needed someone to talk to, it wasn't Octavia she thought of. Would it be such a bad thing? Over the last few days, she'd seen the other side of an archangel firsthand.

She could trust him. *Unless she couldn't.*

She fell back onto the bed and squeezed her eyes shut. If she didn't get her shit together and focus on priorities, her head would explode.

SHE ENTERED the atrium with five minutes to spare, but already a couple of dozen of the Elite were seated. Shit. She hadn't wanted to keep them waiting. Many of them were centuries old, and despite how long she'd been a member, there were several she hadn't even spoken to yet. Unlike Zane and a few others, they liked to distance themselves from the general members.

The four magnificent columns, that punctuated each corner of the raised platform in the center of the atrium, soared into the sky, their fluted marble surfaces glowing violet and indigo.

Nijah, the eldest of them all and leader of the Elite, was standing on the platform. Rumors had always swirled around Nijah, that she had been born during the height of the Ottoman Empire and been instrumental in the untimely death of the previous leader of the Watchers more than two hundred years ago. She never attempted to suppress or address them which made Bella think they were true. Nijah indicated that Bella should stand before her, so everyone could see.

"We understand you have been concealing the true extent of

your abilities from us." Her tone was neutral, but it was an accusation, nevertheless.

"Not with malice. When I joined the Watchers, I wasn't ready to enter the hallowed ranks of the Elite." Her voice was strong, and she kept her gaze locked with Nijah's. It wasn't a complete lie. She'd been a mess when she'd first been welcomed into the fold. She hadn't been mentally equipped to become an Elite.

But if not for her promise to Eblis, she would have been more than prepared to ascend within a few years of discovering her immortal bloodline.

"And now you are ready to be tested?"

"I am."

Many of the Elite, although not all, could teleport. Several of them were telepathic and/or telekinetic. A handful were natural polyglots. To her knowledge, only Nijah and Zane, besides herself, possessed the coveted trinity.

She'd psyched herself up for the ordeal to come, but it was even more brutal than she'd imagined.

Every one of the Elite tested her.

Not just demanding to view her teleportation prowess, which included lightning fast visits to Antarctica and Tokyo and a score more places besides, which was no problem, but several psychic invasions.

Which were.

If not for the years of Eblis' training she'd had at developing her mental shields, they would have clawed every secret from her mind. By the time the last one finished raking through the superficial memories Bella had allowed them to access, her brain throbbed, and body ached, as though she'd been plugged into an electrical storm.

But the fact she could leave the atrium proved she had passed their criteria. Now she was one of the privileged few, permitted to attend Elite-only gatherings and access classified information.

She'd been right to hold back the full extent of her abilities, though. Envy from those who hadn't inherited that power, and simmering anger from others at how she'd concealed it for so long, tainted the air.

It was a chilling warning that she'd need to watch her back.

Nate

Nate opened his eyes and squinted as sunlight flooded his bedroom. Why had he stayed here last night? He didn't even like the view from the window.

It sure as hell had nothing to do with the fact it was closer to Isabella than staying in one of his other impersonal dwelling places spread across Andromeda's more civilized planets.

Damn, he'd got it bad. Worse, he didn't really care. They had no future together, but he couldn't let her go.

She's mortal.

Fucking great. He swung around, trying to ignore the echoey thud of his heart, that filled his head and squeezed his lungs. Curse the goddess, what was happening to him?

Mortals died. It was their fate. In Ama-gi he had witnessed many humans he'd called friends grow old and die. Their passing had caused his heart to ache but in the great stream of his existence, it had been fleeting.

He'd never fallen, the way some of his fellow archangels had. When their beloved had died, their grief had been terrible to behold.

A hoarse laugh flayed his throat. Isabella wasn't his beloved. She was a woman who fascinated him beyond measure, sure. He'd concede that point.

She was always an ethereal presence haunting his mind, no matter what he was doing. That wasn't fucking normal, but it didn't mean anything more than he had yet to get her out of his system.

Unnerved, he glared at his reflection in the bathroom mirror.

If not for the fact she was somehow tied up with his hunt for Dagan, he'd never see her again.

Liar.

"Shut the fuck up."

And now he was talking to himself.

He swore in the language of the ancients, which usually improved his mood, but it didn't this time. It was just as well he didn't know where she was going. He might've been tempted to follow her, just to prove to himself he could *see* her without having to *speak* to her.

He took a shower, forcing his mind to clear. It was harder than it should have been.

With biting economy, he dried off and pulled on a pair of jeans.

Barefoot, he strode across the apartment to the table and opened his laptop. It wasn't Earth-made but it would be easy enough to connect it to the local Net.

He needed to discover how Isabella had known an immortal forged sword had been used in an assassination attempt on an archangel. Had someone leaked it online?

Half an hour later, he was still searching. But he'd found nothing. At least, nothing credible that Isabella would take notice of. *So how did she know?*

He switched to the interstellar equivalent, the supercharged highway that connected the technologically advanced planets in the Andromeda Galaxy. But it was halfhearted, since there was no way she'd be able to access it from the primitive connection on Earth.

Frustrated, he leaned back in his chair and narrowed his eyes at the screen.

There was another way he could try. The telepathically advanced civilization where he'd acquired this laptop had installed additional technology that could only be accessed by a genetic mind print.

He went into telepathic mode, and the crystal globe that ostensibly served as a mouse blazed into rainbow bright life. Seemingly random images and texts scrolled over the screen, but there was a pattern, if it could just be found.

There was always a pattern.

A single word caught his eye and he froze the stream. *Inanna.*

Frowning, he scanned the archaic article. It told him nothing he didn't already know about Inanna and the glorious cult she'd inspired and once enjoyed on Earth. Many of the minor gods and goddesses had returned to the planet, when humankind had crawled from the remnants after the great devastation. They'd enjoyed a golden age of worship from the primitive mortals.

Moments later, a dozen images flashed over the screen. Mountains and valleys, and great cities that had fallen into ruin.

What the hell. It was a potted history of Mesopotamia. Where Inanna's cult had once thrived.

And where, Astrid had told him, her immortal forged sword had spent the last millennium.

Hell.

A couple of centuries ago he'd discovered a group of demon spawn styling themselves as the Watchers who had appropriated Inanna's ancient temple within the Zagros mountains. Since *watching* was basically all they did, he'd left them alone. After all, demon spawn who possessed the kind of power to destabilize world governments and cause untold chaos would hardly hang around with a horde of such diluted bloods.

But what if he'd been wrong?

About one hundred years ago he'd tried to enter the mountain, to see what they were up to. He'd been greeted by a group of demon spawn who could obviously see right through his glamour and had no intention of allowing him access.

He could've taken them on, no problem. But since he'd wanted to check out the place without drawing attention, the plan failed at the first hurdle.

And so he'd kept them in his peripheral. But as the years went by with no ripples, he'd all but forgotten about them. He hunted half-blood zealots, who possessed the power to obliterate civilizations if left unchecked, not a bunch of randoms whose greatest ability appeared to be seeing through a glamour.

Yet all along, the sword that Dagan had stolen from Astrid had been buried in the Zagros mountains where demon spawn now worshipped with their blood-soaked rites.

The germ of a plan stirred.

Astrid, are you at home?

She didn't answer right away, so he dug deeper into the shadowy sect. There wasn't much online, which threw up a massive red flag in his brain. The internet was overflowing with conspiracy theories and alleged supernatural abilities. But when it came to this particular group, it was as though they didn't exist. He doubted they didn't have an online presence, which meant they communicated outside of the regular Net.

Shit.

He sifted through buried memories. He'd first become aware of them during the Vernal Equinox.

And the Equinox was tomorrow. That meant they'd be there. Question was, would Dagan be joining them?

His half-formed plan solidified. But it was useless without Astrid's assistance.

Finally, she responded.

Yes

He teleported to her beach. Even if she couldn't help him, he still needed to see her, so he could give her the phial that contained a wisp of the Guardians' atmosphere. She stood at the entrance to her home and watched him stride across the black sand to her. He hoped he wasn't too late.

"Have you destroyed the sword yet?"

"Why?"

"It might be the only way to gain entry to a demon spawn lair."

"You've discovered the whereabouts of Dagan?"

"I may have."

"Tell me what you know."

He gave her a brief overview of the Watchers. And then took a chance. "You told me the sword's history has permeated the fabric of its soul. Can you extract that essence and use it to camouflage my presence? Corrupt it somehow, so I pass as a demon?"

She was silent, her wings rippling in a nonexistent breeze, as she contemplated his request. "You appear certain the sword is still intact."

"Am I wrong?"

Astrid exhaled a deep sigh. "No. But I believe there's a better way to ensure you remain undetected."

CHAPTER 16

BELLA

The atrium was a magnificent structure, situated above the temple but still protected on all sides by the outer shell of the mountain. It was here, before the rest of the Watchers, the new recruits proved their worthiness to join their ranks.

Tonight, beneath the star-studded sky, they weren't the only ones on trial. To prove her commitment to the Elite, she had been assigned to preside over the initiation ceremony. If she fucked up, the Elite wouldn't let her forget it.

She had no intention of fucking up.

The atrium was fashioned like a small amphitheater with the five thousand members seated around the circular platform. She stepped up to the altar, and a hush settled. Centuries ago, an eight-pointed star had been seared into the stone at her feet, and thick candles in ornate holders sat on the altar, throwing flickering light across the marble slab.

Nijah stepped forward to address the crowd. Her long ebony hair cascaded to her waist, and rubies glittered on her delicate golden snood and the jewelry at her ears, throat and wrists. Together with her red figure-hugging outfit and flowing gold robe, she exuded power, wealth, and uncrushable pride.

"Welcome." Her voice echoed around the atrium. "Once again we gather in the sacred mountain to celebrate our lineage and fortify our resolutions. For millennia we have been vilified, but our day is coming. We will rise again and avenge our unjust Fall from Grace."

Cheers erupted, and Bella surreptitiously glanced at the new recruits sitting in the front row. Their eyes blazed with passion. Even after all these years, she remembered the first time she'd sat in this atrium and listened to the same speech. For the first time, she'd been with her people. She hadn't been an outsider, a freak of nature, or a creature to be feared. Nijah's words had never failed to inspire her with pride for her heritage, no matter how many times she heard them.

Except tonight a sense of foreboding twisted through her chest. It wasn't because of the ceremony she had to perform. It was deeper than that.

It was a questioning of everything the Watchers had proclaimed. Meeting Nate had shown her that there was more to archangels than they'd been told. What else were they hiding?

"When the veil falls between the worlds, we shall claim justice for the wrongs inflicted upon our ancestors!" Nijah's hair rippled and the rubies sparkled like drops of blood. Bella kept her face impassive but treacherous thoughts spilled through her mind.

They'd spoken of rebellion and victory for untold years. But they never *did* anything. For most of the members, just knowing there were others like themselves made the organization invaluable, but Nijah always gave the impression that was a minor, secondary, benefit. What was the purpose of the Watchers, really?

What does Eblis know that I don't?

A shiver skated over her bare arms. To her knowledge, no full blood demon had ever graced the Watchers annual gathering with their presence, never mind one of the originals who'd been created by the Alpha Goddess of antiquity.

Maybe the history she'd learned was true. That the Watchers

was for only those who'd been born on Earth, and when their ranks reached an elusive, unspecified peak, the original demons would return and vindication would be theirs.

Or maybe not.

"Each one of us here is connected by our immortal bloodline." Nijah swept her gaze around her captive audience before settling on the new recruits. "Some of you are more polluted by human stock than others but know this. If you're accepted into our ranks tonight, you will forever be protected by our network."

Once again cheers erupted, and only when the applause finally died down did she turn to face Bella. Nijah smiled at her, but there was no warmth in it, or in her flawlessly beautiful face.

"This is a great honor." Nijah's voice was low, for her ears only. "I hope you're up to the challenge, Bella."

"I am."

"Good. Then our esteemed guest will not be disappointed." She handed Bella the ceremonial athame. "Enjoy." There was a thread of chilly amusement in her voice this time.

The metal hilt was warm against her palm as Nijah took her place by her side. Zane strode onto the platform and stood beside Bella, but as the first recruit was brought onto the platform, her mind whirled in a different direction.

What esteemed guest was Nijah talking about?

There was no time to cast a hurried glance across the crowd. She needed all her concentration for this. Zane stepped forward, power radiating from him, and fear flashed across the newbie's face.

She almost felt sorry for him, except it was never acceptable to show fear. Whoever had discovered him should have made that crystal clear. Another thought struck her. Gods, she hoped her first one survived the initiation. Occasionally, a weak link slipped through, and the result was devastating. Because anyone who failed this ultimate test was not only denied membership.

They forfeited their life.

"Do you trust in the powers of your forebears?" Zane's voice was low but echoed around the atrium.

"Yes," the newbie whispered. Zane placed a ceremonial bowl on the altar, a useless piece of theater she'd never understood, and led the man to her.

He swallowed, before turning his back on her. For a second, she fought against the irrational urge to flee. If she didn't go through with this, the Elite who wanted to dispose of her would have the perfect excuse.

This was merely a rite of passage they all undertook. There was no danger unless a new recruit's abilities had been fatally misjudged. Although she'd never done this before, she'd witnessed it countless times. All she needed was a steady hand and cool precision.

She took a deep breath, gripped his hair, and pulled his head back.

Cut the veins, not the windpipe.

Because if she messed this up, it wouldn't just be the newbie who would forfeit their life. She'd be on the chopping block too.

Nate

Nate teleported a short distance from the Zagros mountains where, centuries ago, Inanna's cult had flourished. There was nothing to distinguish this particular mountain from the rest in the magnificent range that divided the land for almost a thousand miles. A mortal could live their entire life in the surrounding valleys without the faintest idea an infestation of demon spawn had stolen a goddess' temple for their own uses.

It was late evening and starlight speckled the cloudless sky. He strode to the base of the mountain. Its entrance was concealed by a glamour, but since it was a relatively low level one it only worked on mortals. Stone columns flanked the reinforced steel doorway and a couple of demon spawn were on guard.

He halted some distance before them. Unlike the last time he'd tried to gain access, these guards didn't immediately confront him with aggression and threats. Probably because this time he hadn't thrown up a low-level glamour that rendered him all but unnoticeable to mortals but which they'd immediately seen through. They appeared not to know what to make of his appearance and he didn't miss the quick glance they threw each other.

Clearly, they were communicating by telepathy. He curled his lip, a threatening gesture they didn't miss. Astrid had been right. She hadn't needed to extract anything from the sword.

Just having it at his hip was enough to distort his archangelic radiance into demonic darkness.

His hunch had been right. The sword had spent untold centuries within the goddess' temple. The question was— had Dagan given the sword to Sakarbaal, or had the vampire somehow stolen it?

"Name," one of them said.

Nate made his eyes glow crimson and unfurled his wings. It was a cheap trick, but it worked. The guard backed up, clearly unnerved. Like archangels, only full blood demons possessed wings, a unique genetic gift created by their cursed goddess. Nate took another step toward them.

"I'm from the Demonic High Council." He had no idea if they'd even heard of the Council, and it didn't matter since the term was self-explanatory. "Checking shit out. Finally got around to Earth." He swept his gaze over them. "Hope you didn't send a message to anyone inside." It was a blatant threat.

"No." There was a hint of wariness in his tone as though Nate's comment didn't quite make sense. Not that he had time to question it.

Never trust a demon.

"Keep it that way, and you'll keep your heads."

The guards retreated and the door swung open. As he strode inside, the guard added, "Nijah's expecting you."

Interesting. He didn't deign to answer as he swept his glance around the temple. Curved columns had been carved out of the stone, and arched doorways led to various parts of the structure. Light flooded the interior, but there was nothing as primitive as candles or torches in sconces. Clearly, they'd set up a generator to power the electricity.

"They're in the atrium," the guard called. "The elevator's to your right."

The *elevator*? While not all demon spawn could teleport, why did the guard think *he'd* need to use such a thing? Then again, although he wasn't hiding his presence, he didn't want to land in the middle of their Equinox ceremony. A measure of discretion wasn't a bad idea. He was here to observe, after all.

He changed direction and found the elevator, an iron construction with several buttons on the interior wall for the various levels. He hit the top one. So far, this wasn't living up to his expectations of a demon spawn lair. Although it did prove his longstanding suspicion that the Watchers posed no real danger in the great scheme of things.

Except Nijah, who had been their leader a century ago when he'd first uncovered their existence and still appeared to be their leader now, was expecting him.

Obviously, not *him*. She was expecting a full blood demon.

Dagan.

Anticipation flooded through his blood as the door opened to an amphitheater that was barely half full of spectators. Their attention was riveted on the central circular platform, where three demon spawn stood. From this angle he could only see their backs, but he recognized Nijah when she turned her head to speak to the one beside her.

A frisson of unease electrified his senses as he frowned at the female standing in the middle. She wore a blood red dress that clung to her curves and fell to her feet and glittered in the flickering glow of the ceremonial candles. An elaborate headdress covered her hair and half of her back, concealing any glimpse of her face.

Eyes narrowed, he watched her pull back the head of a woman and slit her throat. Blood spurted, and the woman collapsed to her knees as a deathly hush fell across the crowd. After a moment, the woman stood, her injury healed. She raised her arms in victory, and cheers erupted.

An effective, if primitive, way of ensuring no mortals attempted to infiltrate their ranks.

He cast a steely glance around. The air was oppressive with the scent of demon spawn. He couldn't tell if Dagan was here, mingling in the crowd.

His gaze returned to the high-ranking female who was undertaking the initiations.

She lifted the knife, exposing a slim wrist. The motion was familiar and he frowned. It almost reminded him of Isabella.

Irritation seared through him. There was no fucking way a demon spawn reminded him of Isabella. He swung away and made his way back to the elevator.

He needed to find the heart of the temple, where the Watchers kept their archives. There was a link between the demon, and the demonic traces he'd sensed at Isabella's club. And tonight he was going to unearth it.

CHAPTER 17

BELLA

The headdress was killing her. Bella focused on the far wall of the atrium, but the blood splattered across the floor and the altar burned into her brain, regardless.

Thank all the damn gods the initiations were over. She could blame the heavy, ceremonial headdress all she liked, but the reason why her head throbbed, and eyes ached had nothing to do with the archaic outfit Nijah had insisted she wear.

Her fingers clenched around the athame, and she carefully placed it on the altar before she did something unforgiveable, such as drop it. The stench of spilled blood and the cloying incense from the candles filled her nose, and dizziness swum through her. So far, she'd managed to keep her face blank and back rigid, but if she didn't get out of here soon, she was going to fucking scream.

"Excellent work," Zane murmured in her ear. "Consider your promotion into the Elite approved."

At least this ordeal hadn't been in vain. "Good."

"One day you must share your reasoning for keeping this a secret for so long."

She wasn't sure if that was a request or a thinly veiled

demand. And it didn't really matter, since she was just as powerful as Zane even though he didn't know it.

"Maybe," she conceded. "But right now, I could do with a stiff whiskey."

"You know the drill." Faint amusement threaded through his voice. "The rest of the night is filled with expensive booze and decadent debauchery."

Sure, some of the members enjoyed the drink and orgies, but it had never been her thing. And she was far from alone in that. Although it seemed the new recruits she'd initiated were already both half drunk and half naked.

She turned away from the scene and looked at Zane. "That's a hard pass."

"Thought it might be. Nijah." He glanced over Bella's shoulder, and Nijah strolled to his side. "Are you in agreement?" he asked her.

Nijah's midnight gaze seared into her as though she wanted to turn her soul inside out. Bella stared back, unblinking. She'd just slit the throats of five demon bloods. She wasn't going to falter just because the leader of the Watchers was indulging in a show of power.

"I am." Nijah held out her hand, and Zane placed something on her palm. "Normally we would have a ceremony." Her voice was dry. "But this will have to do." She took Bella's right hand and slid a purple tourmaline ring onto her middle finger. "Welcome. The Forbidden Archives are now yours to peruse."

Bella glanced at the ring. It was a perfect fit. And it was her key to access all areas that until now had been prohibited. She wasn't concerned by Nijah's barb. Most members craved to know the hidden secrets of the Watchers, but only the Elite held that privilege.

"Thank you. With your leave, I'll retire." Given her newly elevated status she probably didn't need to formally request such a thing, but she didn't want to make an enemy of Nijah.

Nijah inclined her head in assent, and Bella left the platform and made her way to the elevator. As soon as she was back in her room, she gingerly pulled the headdress off. It weighed a ton and she placed it on her bed. Her headache was getting worse by the second and she massaged her scalp, as she tilted her hand in the glow of the bedside lamp. The oval, faceted, gemstone was so pretty.

Although she had many good friends within the Watchers, she had never been able to share everything with them because of her promise to Eblis. It had created a wedge between them, an insidious conviction that she didn't quite belong in the way everyone else did, even if that belief existed only in her mind.

It felt good, to finally be appreciated by her peers. And although they were still unaware of the full extent of her abilities, at least now she wouldn't be plagued by guilt that she was hiding so much from her friends. If not for Eblis and his insistence on secrecy, she would've received this honor years ago.

Why had he always been so insistent on that? She'd gone along with it because, in the purest sense of the word, he was her savior. And he'd alerted her to the existence of the Watchers. If he had reasons, they were sure to be good ones and even though she'd often wondered about it over the years, she'd always given him the benefit of the doubt.

But now, the questions wouldn't rest.

Seemed she was questioning everything lately.

Well, whatever Eblis' true motives one thing hadn't changed. He needed the immortal forged sword, and she'd pledged to discover whether the Watchers had it. Even though she suspected Nate had taken it, she didn't have any proof. But at least she could now access the Forbidden Archives, which was as good a starting place as any.

She glanced down at the glittery dress. She could change it, but that would cost her time, and right now she had more pressing concerns. Eblis might want her to find the sword, but she had another reason to go to the archives.

She wanted to find out more about Nate.

With a final glance at her ring, she picked up her phone and left the room. On the ground floor there was a public library, with enough history to satisfy new members for countless years. But the Forbidden Archives were subterranean, accessible from an antechamber open only to Elites.

The guard standing outside the antechamber opened the door as she approached. She went inside and walked across the thick rug on the floor, to the iron door set in the stone wall.

She took a deep breath, butterflies swirling through her, then pressed her ring against the lock.

The door swung open, revealing a spiral staircase that descended into darkness. How medieval.

How apt.

Before she'd mastered the art of teleportation, and long before she had discovered her true heritage, she'd spent years living on her wits, and always making sure she had an exit strategy. It had been a long time since she'd left that squalid existence, but the caution remained, hardwired into her reflexes.

She picked up a stone statue of an unfortunate-looking gargoyle, and wedged it against the doorframe, before once again peering into the dark.

Weren't there any lights? It was all very well keeping things mysterious, but she didn't want to trip on the hem of her dress and end up breaking her neck. Gingerly she patted the inside wall, but couldn't feel a switch, so used her phone light instead.

As she stepped on the second stair, the door behind her swung shut, catching on the gargoyle, leaving a comforting escape hatch. Shadows leaped from the walls and the black pit beneath her feet, and her heart hammered in her ears. It was a relief when she reached the final stair, especially when the light from her phone landed on a switch set into the wall.

She flipped it on, and dull electric light flooded the chamber.

It was a lot smaller than she'd imagined. An arch led to another, even smaller chamber, but it appeared empty.

Odd.

She glanced around. A lectern was in the center of the room and great leather-bound tomes filled the shelves that were set into the stone walls. There were no caskets on the floor that might conceal a sword. Maybe there was a hidden safe behind the books, but she wasn't counting on it. Despite Eblis' certainty, she'd never been convinced the Watchers were in possession of it.

Her glance came back to the adjoining room. Curious, she went over to the arch to get a closer look, in case she'd missed something. It really was tiny. If she stood in the center of the room and held out her arms, she'd almost be able to touch the walls.

A shiver skated along her arms and she stepped back. The room was empty, but there was something very *wrong* about it.

She went back into the other room and scrutinized the volumes. They were written in Sanskrit, Egyptian and Latin, and awe rippled through her as she traced a finger over their cracked spines. Were they copies of the originals, or really as ancient as they appeared?

None of those questions were important. She'd kept her promise to Eblis and risen in the ranks. Tomorrow, she'd join the Elite in their exclusive celebration of the Equinox and that was when she planned on raising the topic of an immortal forged sword. But right now, she needed to find any reference she could about Nate.

It took longer than she was comfortable with, but finally she found it. A volume from a Mayan scholar, dedicated to the Archangel Nathanael.

Guilt chewed through her as she pulled the book from the

shelf. She was an Elite. She had the right to read anything and everything within this library that she wished.

But that wasn't the source of her guilt, and she knew it. It was because this felt somehow as though she was betraying Nate.

She hesitated, unsure. The library upstairs had a great deal to say about him. How he'd been one of the foremost archangels in driving demons from Earth and had then made it his mission to hunt down any stragglers and their offspring.

What more could there be, that was so despicable that it needed to be hidden? More importantly, did she really want to know what greater sins he'd committed?

No.

Her fingers tightened around the book. Her personal feelings were irrelevant. Okay, that was a lie as they had *everything* to do with this. But just because she was getting cold feet was no excuse not to see this through.

She went over to the lectern, opened the book and began to read.

Nate

With barely repressed disgust, Nate replaced a book on the shelf. He'd lost count of how many he'd glanced through in this demon spawn library, but without fail the content had one aim in mind.

To distort the true history of archangels.

It might piss him off, but none of it was revelatory. He swung around and glared at the guard who had led him here.

"You wasted my time." His voice was low and throbbed with menace. "I can find this shit anywhere."

"You weren't specific."

Nate bared his teeth in a mirthless grin and his wings undulated. The guard swallowed, clearly rethinking his flippant attitude.

"I can take you to the Forbidden Archives. But I can't access it."

Nate didn't deign to answer, and the guard led the way through the empty temple before entering a passageway. Another guard stood at a door and appeared riveted by the sight of his wings.

"He needs access to the Forbidden Archives."

The other guard hastily opened the door and Nate strode into the circular room. Was this it?

"Nijah said nothing to me about this," the second guard said to the first.

Nate swung around. "Then contact her. I'm sure she won't mind the interruption."

His words meant the opposite, and they all knew it.

The guard stood his ground, but Nate was damn sure he wasn't sending a silent message to Nijah, not after his veiled threat. He stared them down until they retreated, shutting the door behind them.

He exhaled a long breath and strode across the room to where a door was ajar. He glanced at the gargoyle keeping it open. If this led to the Forbidden Archives, then the security was crap.

He pulled open the door. From far below, a glimmer of light glowed. Anticipation sizzled through his blood. Could it be Dagan? Doubtful, but he drew the sword in readiness, and the runes along its blade blazed with energy, before he stealthily descended the worn, stone steps.

The room came into view. Standing at the central lectern was the female who'd undertaken the initiations. She was in profile, her long blonde hair tumbling over her shoulders, giving him just a glimpse of her face. But that glimpse was all he needed.

Isabella.

Paralyzed, he saw her straighten and turn to him, and it was as though time had slowed and nothing existed but this subterranean hell. Blood thudded in his ears, a relentless tattoo that filled his head and blurred his vision.

Of everything but the woman who gazed at him in silent horror.

She didn't move and his gaze raked over her face. Her hypnotic eyes, delicate features, her tempting lips. His chest twisted, rebelled, and rejected the evidence standing before him.

"You." His voice was hoarse, accusing. His brain kickstarted, and ancient memories flooded through him. Of how demons had once enjoyed possessing feeble mortals and using them as puppets for their entertainment.

Isabella isn't feeble.

But it was the only context that made any kind of sense.

He leaped from the stair, extending his wings as far as possible within the confined space, and landed an arm's length from her. She didn't retreat, didn't even flinch. He bared his teeth and only then did she give a faint shudder.

"What have you done with her?" He spat the words at her. Isabella was strong, she could fight this. And when he discovered which demon had defiled her, he'd rip their heart from their chest and shove it down their throat.

Yet all the while a terrifying thread of denial whispered through him.

"Nate." Her voice was so soft he barely heard it above the cacophony playing out in his head. But he saw the truth in her eyes. Her beautiful, lying, *demonic* eyes. And his whole fucking chest cracked open.

He swung his arm and leveled the sword at her heart, the tip of its blade a hairsbreadth from drawing blood. And still she didn't retreat.

"Who are you?" He flung the question at her, quashing the irrational urge to grab her and teleport them both somewhere far from here. Some place where this nightmare could be explained and understood, and the toxic acid eating through his gut would miraculously vanish.

Her gaze flickered to his wings and for a fleeting second, wonder filled her expression. His chest cracked a little more and he gripped the hilt with both hands. He'd rip out his own fucking heart before he'd allow her to see his hands shake.

Self-preservation forced him to fold his wings, to force her to once again look in his eyes and dare to lie to his face.

"You know who I am." She licked her lips, and he drew a grim, despairing pleasure from the knowledge she wasn't as composed as she appeared. "I've never lied to you."

All demons lie.

Another truth splintered his stupefied reflexes.

She hadn't been surprised by his appearance. She hadn't *expected* to see him. But there'd been no questions, because she had damn well known who he really was.

Right from the start. She'd known.

And he'd fallen for it.

All the seemingly small inconsistences that he'd brushed aside, now flooded his brain in scorching derision. How difficult it had been to discover anything about her, either online or in public records. The mysterious family member who'd left her a fortune.

Her unexpected appearance in Romania, and how she'd just so happened to have packed a seductive dress and stash of condoms for their evening date. *Because she'd teleported.*

"Do you know what I do to my enemies?" He glared at her, waiting for the familiar wave of disgust that always accompanied any thought he had of demons and their spawn. But the only disgust that flooded through him was for himself.

"I know what I've read." Her gaze never left his. "But I don't know the truth."

"Your histories." He gave a bitter laugh. "I've read them, too. Who are you working for?"

Guilt flashed across her face, gone in a second, but it seared through him like a branding iron. Was she Dagan's creature? The possibility sickened him to his soul.

"I didn't know who you were, the night we met in my club."

Her club. The scent of demon he'd detected permeating the property. He'd been so convinced it was Dagan he hadn't considered any other possibility. Except she hung out with demon spawn. She might have held countless demonic rites at the place and that was why he'd picked up on it.

Or it could simply be her.

Rage licked through his blood. He'd checked her aura. There was *nothing* to indicate she possessed demon blood. She read as human. The faint strands of immortal heritage that had glinted hadn't triggered any alarms. Many humans possessed such traces. It didn't make them any less mortal.

"You shield your aura." He snarled the accusation at her. Couldn't help himself. Fuck, why didn't he just finish this? She'd betrayed him. There was no need for a trial.

Leave her or kill her. It wasn't that hard a decision to make.

"So do you," she shot back. "If I'd known you were an archangel I never would have got involved."

She'd read his aura? It shouldn't come as a shock, but it did. Wasn't this why he'd learned to distort it, so no other race could detect his true heritage unless he willed it?

Except it worked both ways. What fucking good was the ability to read auras, if the one time he'd needed the truth, it had failed?

"You expect me to believe that?" Worse, he *wanted* to believe she'd been ignorant of who he was. That it hadn't all been a lie. But it didn't add up.

"It's the truth."

"Demon spawn aren't known for telling the truth."

She flinched, as though he'd struck her, and anger flashed in her eyes. Instead of fury at her nerve, reluctant admiration licked through his blood. She knew he could destroy her in a heartbeat, yet she stood up to him.

"I'm demon blood. Don't refer to me as spawn."

It's what you are. The accusation remained locked in his throat, corroding him from the inside out. The evidence was before him, but he didn't—*couldn't*—accept it.

She still fucking dazzled him.

A strange, unnatural crackle filled the air, violet and white electricity sparking off the walls and floor. He tensed, his eyes narrowing, but she didn't appear to be the source. And then, in an unnatural flash, Dagan materialized behind Isabella, the tip of a dagger pressed against her throat. Nate bit out a curse and instinctively pulled back the sword, so it was no longer aimed at her heart. Was she working for him? A swift glance at her terrified face reassured him she wasn't.

Unless she was acting. It was possible. He wanted to believe it but couldn't.

Why didn't she teleport to safety, then?

"Hey, Nate." Dagan sounded as though they'd seen each other just the other day. He was wearing breastplate armor and a single vambrace on his right forearm. "I've missed you."

"Fuck you, Dagan," he growled. There was no satisfaction that he'd been right about Dagan being connected to the Watchers. Because this was the demon who had betrayed, not only him, but the entire archangelic race.

For millennia he'd searched for Dagan, obsessed by the need to face him once again and avenge the wrongs of the past. And now, when the demon was in his sights, when they could end this once and for all, he couldn't do a fucking thing about it because Isabella—a treacherous demon *spawn*—would be caught in the crossfire.

Collateral damage. That's all she'd be. But he couldn't risk her life for that.

For *this*. Something he'd wanted to finish for eleven thousand years.

"Astrid always made the best weapons."

"Why did you steal it?"

Dagan tilted his head. "Is that what she told you?"

Nate gritted his teeth. He wouldn't allow the demon to distract him. "Release Isabella. This has nothing to do with her. It's between you and me."

"On one condition. Give me the sword."

Fuck. He should've seen that one coming. He would have, if he wasn't so eaten up in trying to protect Isabella from harm. Even if she didn't deserve it.

The need for vengeance burned through him. But, damn it, he could *not* risk her safety. And he couldn't guarantee it once he and Dagan let loose.

There was only one thing for it. When he tossed the sword to the demon, he'd grab Isabella and teleport them both out of here. Dagan would have to wait for another day.

"Fine." He tightened his grip around the hilt of the sword and stepped back. The metal gleamed in the shadowy light and Nate tensed. Every fiber of him screamed to keep it. To not give it back to Dagan. To his enemy. But if he didn't—

He cut off the thought and threw the sword. It flew through the air in a glittering arc, landing to one side. Dagan swore and stepped away from Isabella to retrieve it. Nate wrapped his hand around her wrist and...

Nothing fucking happened.

What the hell...

"Sorry, didn't I explain?" Dagan said, as he sheathed his dagger without taking his gaze from Nate. Then he lifted the sword and gave a malicious smile. "Our powers are neutralized within Inanna's sacred mountain." He raised his hand and with a blast of unearthly power that belied his statement, catapulted Nate backwards into the adjoining chamber.

Nate swore. It had all been for nothing.

CHAPTER 18

BELLA

Slung against the lectern from the backlash of Dagan's power, Bella gasped as a shimmering barrier appeared in the archway. Nate threw himself against it and flames erupted, pushing him back into the small chamber.

It was a well-known fact among the Watchers that within the mountain, their powers only worked on Inanna's Eye and in the atrium, beneath the open sky. But this demon had managed to harvest enough raw material to counter its effects.

Who *was* he? Nijah's guest?

"I know you're many things, Dagan," Nate snarled. "But I never believed you were a coward."

Dagan shrugged, apparently unmoved by the insult. "I don't want you getting hurt. I'm guessing Inanna found a way to use her powers inside this mountain. Why else would she have a handy little dungeon here? It's been the perfect resting place for the sword for the last one thousand years. An archangelic artifact hidden in the heart of the Earth-bound demon bloods sanctuary. I've always found the irony amusing."

"Get me out of here."

"No. You can stay there while I sort some shit out. Your erstwhile friend Gabe fucked up my most promising cell and let me tell you. I'm pissed about it. Any idea where he is?"

"Remove this fucking forcefield."

"Not gonna happen. And before you fry your brains trying, there's nothing you can do about it."

Nate swore, violently, eloquently, the language one she'd never heard before. Yet the words flowed through her, touching something buried deep inside, and the savage beauty of his curse caused the breath to catch in her throat.

Dagan turned to her. He was as tall and well-built as Nate, with short, spiky, dark blond hair and midnight eyes. His laser gaze seared her, as though he sought to peel back every protective shield she possessed. "Interesting." He appeared fascinated by whatever he had managed to discover. "What powers have you inherited?"

Inside, terror curdled her blood, but she'd never let him know. She glared at him, and he responded with an amused smile.

"Keep your secrets. The Watchers have been a monumental disappointment to me." He threw Nate a glance. "As was Sakarbaal. That vampire lair needs eradication."

Another fear spiked through her chest at his unvarnished threat. Although Octavia hadn't belonged to Sakarbaal's order of vampires, she was at the castle. Bella doubted Dagan was the type to check IDs before administering his own brand of injustice. She needed to warn her friend that a demon had Nico and his Echelon within his sights.

Dagan returned his attention to her. "Take my advice. Don't let him out while I'm gone."

With that, and another spectacular display of lightning, he vanished.

She let out a shaky breath, as the static played through her hair. Slowly she turned to look at Nate. He glowered at her and unfurled his wings. Unwanted awe shivered through her and she couldn't drag her mesmerized gaze away. They were magnificent, silver-gray shot through with elusive glimpses of violet. How would it feel, to be enveloped in those beautiful, powerful feathers?

She'd never know. Whatever they'd had, was over. And even though she'd always known they had no future, this wasn't the way she wanted it to end.

I don't want it to end at all.

Like there was any choice.

"Congratulations." Venom dripped from the word. "You had me fooled. I should have driven the sword through your treacherous heart when I had the chance."

But he hadn't. And when Dagan had given him an ultimatum, he hadn't put her life on the line. He'd saved it.

The only reason she wasn't imprisoned with him now was because when Dagan had thrust him across the chamber, Nate had instantly released her wrist. Maybe it had been nothing more than an automatic reflex, but she wasn't convinced.

He'd saved her twice.

"I've never met him before."

"You expect me to believe that?" He thrust his fist against the barrier, and once again flames engulfed him. She tensed, but his flesh didn't blister, although it must have caused him pain as he backed off. "No wonder your club reeks of demon."

She'd wondered if he could sense the presence of Eblis in her club. But Nate was referring to her, and to Dagan, and he made it sound so obscene. Yet what was the difference between that, and the fact Eblis had detected archangelic essence in her office after just one visit by Nate?

Nothing.

Everything.

"You had the sword all along." It wasn't an accusation, although it sounded like it. Nate obviously thought so, since he slung her a withering glare.

"And now it's back in Dagan's possession," he shot back.

A dull ache twisted deep inside her chest. Would Nate ever look at her the same way he had before he'd become aware of her heritage?

Stop. She already knew the answer to that. And if she hadn't been such a bloody idiot as to almost fall for him, that question would never have crossed her mind. Because it didn't matter. This thing between them had always been nothing more than a fleeting dream.

Her defense echoed in her mind, a mocking refrain.

Almost? Who was she trying to fool?

"What does he want?' She knew Nate didn't have the answer. Even if he did, he wouldn't tell her. Any trust he'd once had in her had irrevocably died.

It shouldn't hurt. He was her enemy.

But he wasn't the enemy that the Watchers had made him out to be.

"If you want information, you can release me."

This was insane. The Archangel Nathanael needed her help. How often had she imagined having that faceless creature within her power?

Then she'd met him. He was no longer faceless. And he'd turned everything she'd ever believed inside out.

"I can't. I don't have the power." And if she did, would she use it to free him?

Yes. Because he'd saved her. She owed him.

His lip curled. It was obvious he didn't believe her. Slowly she raised her hand. Her ring glinted. Compared to whatever Dagan had, the power infused in the tourmalines that the Elite possessed was minuscule. The cosmic core of the mountain negated all demonic ability—all archangelic too—but a few decades ago their scientists had created a counterforce.

It was just enough to create locks that couldn't be broken by force, only by the primed gemstones, but was it enough to destroy whatever power held Nate imprisoned?

There was only one way to find out. The only way to pay her debt. She owed Nate that, at least, for not killing her the second he'd discovered she possessed demon blood.

She took a deep breath and clenched her fist.

"Stand back," she ordered. And thrust her hand into the shimmering barrier.

Her hand froze, as fiery agony exploded inside her head. A hoarse scream flayed her throat and crimson stars collided behind her eyes as the tourmaline battled the ancient force.

From a thousand miles away, she heard Nate shouting. Telling her to stop. But even if she could, she wouldn't. She owed him.

Her arm was shaking but her hand was trapped. The walls closed in on her, dark, menacing, and the shimmer faded. With a burst of orange flame, Nate shouldered his way to freedom, and she fell back, her lungs burning for elusive oxygen.

She never hit the ground. He caught her and pulled her upright, and she rested her forehead against his chest and sucked in raw, painful gasps of air.

"Fuck," Nate muttered. He grasped her hand, his fingers interlocking with hers, and she'd bet anything he tried to teleport again, but nothing happened. "Can you walk?" His voice was harsh.

"Yes," she said between her teeth. Even though she wasn't sure she'd ever be able to move again. Without releasing her, he edged her to the stairs, and she stumbled up them, tripping on her stupid dress. Relief washed through her as she finally stepped into the antechamber, but Nate still didn't let her go.

She tried to summon resentment at his attitude but failed. Because she had the despicable conviction that his grip was the only thing keeping her upright.

He strode out of the antechamber and one of the guards leaped in front of him, teeth bared.

"What the fuck?" he growled, but before he got any further Nate grasped him by the throat with one hand and catapulted him across the room. The guard smashed into the wall and slumped to the floor, unmoving.

She didn't even have the breath to protest. It took all her focus just to keep up with him, putting one foot in front of the other, and fighting the insidious blanket of fog that curled seductive tendrils through her mind.

Nate slammed open the main door and another two guards ended up unconscious on the ground before they even knew what hit them. The cool night air caused her to shiver but didn't help clear the dark wisps clouding her vision. Her right hand hung like a dead thing against her thigh, except for her ring finger, that throbbed like holy hell.

Abruptly he came to a halt, wrapped his arm around her shoulders, and teleported.

Disorientated, she staggered as he pulled back from her, although he still held onto her hand. And she was under no illusion it was because he enjoyed her touch. It was so she couldn't escape.

Lights flickered, and she blinked, as the room came into focus. It seemed to be an apartment, with timber floorboards and through the windows loomed dark shapes that could be warehouses.

Where were they? Was it London?

"Can you teleport?" His voice was grim. Her glance caught on their entwined fingers and a dull pain gripped her heart. Even though she knew there was no tenderness in the gesture, his touch still gave her a shred of comfort.

"Yes."

His grip tightened, as though he imagined she was going to vanish before his eyes.

"What else?"

This was pointless. "What does it matter? I'm half-demon. Isn't that enough?"

His lips flattened. "Half?"

She shrugged, as if it didn't matter. "Unknown father. My mother passed me off as her aristocratic lover's, but apparently I was a demon's offspring."

Anger sparked in the air. Surely he didn't still care how her relatives had treated her, now that he knew who she really was?

"You were born on Earth?" Distrust threaded through his words. She didn't blame him. To her knowledge, she was the only one in the Watchers who could claim such a strong bloodline. Even Nijah, powerful as she was, was three generations removed from her demon ancestor.

"My mother was mistress to an earl. She wasn't known for planet hopping." She tried to inject derision into her voice, but she was so damn tired she could hardly stand upright, never mind play word games.

His jaw tensed. He appeared to be having a hard time digesting her true history. She almost felt sorry for him, if her heart wasn't so full of wretched sorrow for what a mess this all was.

"How old are you?"

"*That's* your question? I could ask the same of you, but what does it matter?"

"It matters because you've always known who I am. But you..." His voice trailed off and he glared at her as though her very existence defeated him. "I don't know what you are."

She exhaled a ragged breath. She needed to check her injuries, but Nate deserved this answer, at least. "I was born in seventeen-eighty-two. My mother was barely eighteen and until I was five years old, she clung to the hope I was the daughter of her protector and not the result of one wild night with a demon."

And now he had it. Her sordid origins. She looked away. It was cowardice, pure and simple, but she couldn't bear to see the disgust in his eyes. Instead, she gritted her teeth and forced her right arm to move. Fire blazed through her muscles in protest, but she ignored it.

She stared at her hand and a hoarse gasp escaped before she could stop herself.

Her finger that was trapped within the charred remains of the ring was the color of ash, and gray threads were creeping beneath her skin to her wrist. It was horrific.

She could heal this. She sent out a tendril of power, but instead of seeping into the skin and bone it came to a halt. It hadn't worked. She tried again but couldn't breach the unyielding barrier. Panic bloomed in her chest, an untethered monster. Her hand. She couldn't heal it.

Pain ran through her like liquid fire, and lights flashed, distorting her vision.

She wasn't going to pass out. Not ever, but especially not now while in the presence of the Archangel Nathanael.

Shock kicked in, and the world turned black.

CHAPTER 19

NATE

Isabella keeled and he scooped her into his arms on sheer reflex. Her head dropped to his shoulder and her hair brushed his jaw in an ethereal caress. Heart thundering in his ears, he strode into the bedroom, but the sight of her damaged hand shook him to his core.

She'd risked her life to release him. Why hadn't he checked that she was okay before dragging her out of the mountain?

Carefully, he laid her on his bed. She looked so damn fragile. But she possessed the blood of demons. He dropped the last vestiges of his glamour. He didn't need to conceal his archangelic heritage from her anymore.

"I'm fine." She struggled to sit up, and he propped the pillows behind her head. "I'm just…" she glanced at her hand, and a sickly green tint washed over her face.

"Let me see." His voice was harsh. Self-disgust burned through him. He'd interrogated her while whatever power had held him captive had been eating her alive.

Gently, he held her hand. It was ice-cold. To fix it he needed to know what *it* was.

"Do you know why our powers are neutralized within Inanna's temple?" His words were clipped, in a vain attempt to hide his concern.

Rumors of such phenomena had been around for as long as he could remember. Of isolated pockets on far-flung, primitive rocks where life barely existed. He'd never investigated the truth of it. And now he was paying the price. Because if he knew what he was dealing with, it would help him heal her.

"They say a meteorite hit, millions of years ago, before the mountain range formed. Whatever properties it possessed permeated that area and renders our powers useless. But that's just the theory. I don't think anyone can know for sure."

Great. That was nothing he didn't already know. He glanced at her damaged hand and his gut clenched. He had to help her.

"I'm going to remove the ring. You okay?"

She gave a ghoulish smile that speared through his chest. "Go for it. I hope my finger doesn't come off with it."

"Not funny." He glowered at her hand and gripped the ring. If he messed this up—

Don't over think it.

He tightened his grip on the cold metal and eased the silver band over her swollen knuckle.

Isabella let out a strangled groan and he dropped the ring onto the bedside table before scrutinizing her injury. He could heal broken bones and ripped organs. But he wouldn't know what was happening with her hand until he psychically investigated.

"Tell me if I hurt you."

"Wait." She flexed her fingers and he glanced at her face. The sickly pallor had gone. "It's feeling better."

"You're healing yourself." It wasn't a question. He'd just forgotten, for a crazy moment, that she was capable of doing such a thing.

"No. I'm not doing anything. It was the ring, trapping the energy. I guess when it tried to escape, I got in the way."

She looked better already, and her hand was almost back to normal. Was the speed of her recovery because of her heritage?

Or had she faked her symptoms? Was this all part of an elaborate plan between her and Dagan? But for what purpose? To gain his trust?

He'd put nothing past the demon. But Isabella? The idea turned his guts but just because he didn't want to believe it, didn't mean it wasn't true. She'd said she hadn't known who he was when they first met. There had been a simple sincerity in her voice that made him believe her.

But she'd had a meeting that first night. And whoever she had met, had told her who he was.

Who else but Dagan could have shared that information with her?

Never trust a demon.

He folded his arms, so he wasn't tempted to pull her close. Just to make sure she was okay. Except it was more than detached concern for her wellbeing that churned through his chest and scrambled his brains, and he damn well knew it.

When she'd fallen in that subterranean cave, he could have abandoned her to her fate. She'd concealed her true identity from him, even though she'd been aware of his. Whatever way he looked at it, her reasons didn't augur well for him. But leaving her behind had never been an option. Whether she'd been working for Dagan or not.

Maybe she'd genuinely helped him and escaping from the mountain had nothing to do with an ulterior plan from Dagan's warped imagination.

It still didn't mean he could trust her. He threw up a psychic blockade around her. Until she told him why he'd been targeted, she wasn't going anywhere.

It was nothing less than she deserved. The prospect filled him with bleak resignation.

She gave a delicate shudder and then frowned. "What... did you just do something?"

"I can't have you disappearing on me." He braced himself for her outrage. It wouldn't change his resolve.

"I'm not going to disappear on you. I need your—" She bit off her words as comprehension, and unwarranted shock, swept across her face. "You've disabled me."

Her accusation stung which made no fucking sense, since it was the truth, and what the hell else did she expect?

"Yes."

"Am I your *prisoner*?"

"No. But if it makes you feel better, you can tell yourself that."

She sucked in a ragged breath. He refused to allow her evident distress to touch him. She'd played him once. Never again. "That doesn't even make any sense. I *saved* you. Dagan would have left you there to rot."

Did she want him to thank her? "Tell me when you first met Dagan."

"I've already told you. I'd never seen him before tonight."

If he chose to believe her, that meant someone else had been at her club. Someone as powerful as Dagan. Another player. "Who did you see the night we met?"

The same guilt he'd witnessed before flashed over her face, and the knot in his chest tightened. She was hiding something. He needed to discover what it was. And he couldn't afford to let the memories they'd made over the last few days distract him.

Consume him.

The memories were false. He needed to remember that.

"I can't tell you." She sounded reluctant to admit it. "I promised him a long time ago I'd never reveal his name to anyone."

Acid tore through him, blazing through his chest. Ugly. Unprecedented. He didn't know where it came from. Didn't want to know. *Stay focused on the goal.*

"Your lover?" He bit out the words as though they defiled his tongue. To hell with his goal.

"Absolutely not." Ice speared through each word and her blue eyes dared him to challenge her. He glared right back because what else could she mean? "You've got no idea what it's like. How can you? You've always known your heritage. Always known you were immortal. You never had to watch people you cared about grow old and die, while you just *kept on living.*"

Shit. This was the last direction he'd expected the conversation to go. There was a wild gleam in her eyes and although she wouldn't believe him, he did understand where she was coming from.

In a way.

But she was right. He'd always known of his immortality. It had given him a shield, foreknowledge that if he became close to any mortal, he'd suffer the consequences.

It had served him well.

"Isabella." He wasn't sure what to say, only that he had to say something. But she didn't give him the chance.

"I was fourteen when my mother threw me onto the streets. But I didn't stay in the gutter for long. I could do tricks, you see. Tricks that didn't involve me having to service men the way so many of the girls did. Because my tricks were magic and they earned me coins so I didn't starve."

He unfolded his arms, shifted his weight from one foot to the other, and his wings undulated. "Isabella," he said again, but the words died in his throat when she looked at him. No filters. Pain glowed in her eyes, and the agony of centuries slammed into his chest, paralyzing the oxygen in his lungs.

How long had she survived, not knowing who she truly was?

"My mother's protector always believed I was his daughter and ensured I had a good education. Once I crawled out of the slums, I made good use of it."

"You don't have to relive all this." He could imagine her life.

Hell, he already had. Except he'd been wrong. She hadn't been a vulnerable mortal.

That didn't make what had happened to her any better.

"Yes, I do." A thread of scorn tainted her words. "It's the only way to make you see. I didn't understand, Nate. I got to a certain point and I didn't *age*. And I didn't *die*. I couldn't even kill myself because I kept on *healing*. That was in eighteen-twenty-five."

Shaken, he gazed at her in silence. It had never occurred to him how abandoned demon spawn—*demon bloods*—had coped with their immortality if they'd been isolated from others of their race.

In Ama-gi, whenever a precious Nephilim had been born, they'd been beloved, protected. Educated in their heritage, and their immortality—when compared to humans—had always been understood and accepted.

"I know what you're thinking." Her voice was bitter. "I'm aware if I'd cut out my heart or put a bullet through my brain I'd die. Just never quite screwed up the courage to do that."

"That's not what I'm thinking." He clenched his fists, fighting the need to pull her into his arms, because how the fuck would that help? "I've never encountered those with demon blood who were unaware of their lineage. It's rare, Isabella."

"Not on Earth, it isn't."

She was probably right. Now he considered it, the ones he hunted on Earth could all trace their roots back to the Fornax Galaxy, where demons had fled after their goddess had exiled them from this planet.

And while he'd always known descendants of demons were spread across the face of the Earth, unless they caused trouble, he ignored them. But the Earth-born ones never caused that kind of trouble, and now he understood why.

Because they were unaware of who they really were.

The Watchers knew, though. Where did they fit in? Yet he

couldn't ask her. Not now, when he'd inadvertently forced her to return to the nightmare of her past.

"I'm sorry." He choked on the words. They didn't come easily, not when he'd rarely uttered them before. What was he even apologizing for? He wasn't responsible for what she'd been through.

But there was nothing else he could say.

The savage gleam in her eyes faded and she released a long breath as she sank back against the pillows. She pushed a shaky hand through her hair before giving him a wary look.

"I know."

He hadn't expected her to accept his words at face value and the fact she did caused a strange pain to twist through his chest. He sat at the end of the bed, his forearms on his thighs, and leaned forward, his gaze fixed on the floorboards.

"I gave up trying to make friends." She said it so matter-of-factly, and the pain twisted deeper. From the moment of his creation, he'd been surrounded by other archangels. He hadn't been alone, or lonely, and many of them he had counted as close friends.

Some of them he still did.

"I was…" Her voice trailed off and from the corner of his eye he saw her grip her fingers together. "I was in a bad place when my mentor found me. Turned out he'd been watching me for years. Gauging my powers. Anyway, he finally decided I was worth saving."

Who was she talking about? A demon, for sure. And not Dagan.

"I owe him my sanity. But I'm not blinded by gratitude to the truth. He needed me, and I've always been a willing partner."

Slowly, he turned to look at her, and caught her steady gaze. Questions seared his mind, and he clenched his teeth. He would not allow them to escape. He had to accept that he might never know who her savior was. But the *not knowing* was eating him alive.

Uncertainty flickered over her face as though his silence was unexpected. "My mother and relatives used to call me the devil's daughter. That I was filled with nothing but sin. But he—my mentor—told me I possessed the blood of demons, a noble race, and I should be proud of my heritage. It was…" again she hesitated as though she struggled to find the right words. "It was a revelation, Nate."

A noble race. He'd never found them so. But he'd tear out his tongue before saying that to her.

"You're not saying anything." She sounded unnerved.

"I'm listening." And deep inside, in a place he barely knew existed and sure as hell didn't want to examine, a piece of him was dying.

"He told me there were others like me. Said there was an organization especially for the forgotten ones if I was interested in joining. Of course I said I was."

The forgotten ones? He'd not heard that term used before when referring to the offspring of demons. But it was apt. Demons had always bred with impunity with the mortals on countless worlds, and rarely cared about the resulting child.

Unless that child was exceptional.

Another question burned. And this time he couldn't remain silent. "Is this mentor your father?"

He hadn't expected her to smile, even if it was a sad one.

"Apparently not. I believe him, though. If I were his daughter, there's no reason why he'd deny it."

Maybe not. It was strange, though. Demons had little enough time for their own spawn—*children*. Why had this demon taken Isabella under his wing if, as she asserted, it hadn't been for sex?

He needed me. But why? And then an answer came to him.

"He needed you to join the Watchers."

"Yes." She didn't appear surprised that he'd guessed. "Sometimes I liked to pretend his motives were purely altruistic, so I could meet others of my race. But you're right. His overriding motivation for helping me was so I could find out what the Watchers are doing."

"A spy." How did that make sense? "Why didn't he just join himself? They'd love a full blood demon in their ranks." Unsure, he frowned. "Wouldn't they?"

"You'd think." She sighed and looked so weary it physically, fucking, hurt. "Yes, probably. That's not the point. He didn't want to reveal himself. He wanted to know what they were doing, as an organization. I wasn't doing anything underhand. Just sharing with him what went on."

He bet the Watchers wouldn't feel that way if they ever discovered what she'd been doing. But even so. She'd only been reporting to a demon.

Something just didn't add up.

"But," she hesitated and the vulnerability in her voice twisted his pain into something unbearable. "I don't think I would've survived without them. Finally, after one hundred and fifty years, I could make friends without that fear that had been eating me alive for so long. I found my family."

Silence weaved between them, and guilt ate through him. Merely a decade or so before Isabella had discovered her people, he'd tried to enter the Watchers' headquarters. While he hadn't gone with the sole intention of destroying every demon blood inside, it had certainly crossed his mind. If he'd believed them dangerous, he would have found a way to wipe them out without a second thought.

He would have been responsible for the annihilation of her family. That she hadn't yet found them was irrelevant.

"I know this wasn't the first time you've breached the Watchers security." Her voice was soft but there was a thread of condemnation there, too. He guessed he deserved it.

"Only once before," he said, as if that would absolve him. It wasn't a great feeling, knowing she'd learned things about him from the perspective of his enemies. "One hundred years ago, when I tried to find out what they were doing. But I never got inside the mountain."

Uncertainty flickered across her face. "You didn't slaughter a dozen demon bloods who tried to stop you from destroying the temple?"

Had she truly believed that, all the time they'd been together? A dull ache settled deep in his chest. Because the lies the Watchers had told her could so easily have been the truth.

"No." It was all he could say. He had no other defense.

She was silent. He had no idea if she accepted his word or not. It shouldn't matter to him. Nothing between them had been real.

He'd destroyed other demon bloods in battle, across the universe. She could condemn him for that. But he didn't want her despising him for something he hadn't done.

I don't want her despising me for anything.

He sucked in a harsh breath. He couldn't change the past. It was the future he had to focus on, and something else she'd said gnawed at the edges of his mind. Her mentor had told her who Nate was, but it didn't answer a deeper question. Had the demon been following him? Was *he* working in tandem with Dagan?

His gaze roved over Isabella's face. Dark smudges pooled beneath her eyes and her lashes flickered in exhaustion. She needed to rest. But he needed this one last answer.

"How did he know you were seeing me?"

"Oh." She gave a tired smile. "It must be some demon/archangel witchy sense you share. He knew an archangel had been in my office the second he arrived. And then I spoke to you on the phone—and called you Nate."

The demon hadn't stalked him, then. And if he hadn't called Isabella that night, just so he could hear her voice again, her mentor would never have known which archangel she'd been with.

Yet another damn coincidence.

The unearthly power that infused the walls of Isabella's club had nothing to do with demons collating their forces. Nothing to do with Dagan. All he'd sensed was her mentor's demonic presence.

And hers.

Brooding, he couldn't tear his eyes from her as she gave up the struggle and slid into sleep. The knowledge she'd kept her true identity from him after discovering his own, thudded through his head, a constant reminder of how she'd betrayed his trust.

He wasn't used to not being in control of the situation. Even among other immortal races archangels had the advantage. Because thanks to their megalomaniac goddess and her experimentation with DNA, there was only one degree of separation between archangels—and demons—and the original Alpha Immortals of antiquity.

The numerous minor gods and goddesses had been worshipped across the universe on untold worlds by countless mortals. They were powerful, arrogant, and sometimes entertaining. In the past, he'd taken many as lovers and enjoyed the distraction. He'd never come close to losing his ability to compartmentalize. There was business. There was pleasure. And there were friends.

But somehow Isabella had slipped through his defenses and he didn't have a fucking clue how to categorize her. She should be his enemy. Yet he couldn't think of her as such.

He stood and draped a blanket over her. Paralyzing her abilities had been the right thing to do. He couldn't afford for her to escape and cause more chaos.

Is that the reason why I'm keeping her captive, though?

What chaos had she caused? He couldn't prove anything against her, except for her heritage. The brutal truth was he hadn't bound her to his side to save the planet.

He'd done it because he didn't want to lose her.

Jaw clenched, he went into the sitting area and took a chair back to the bedroom. Derision burned through hm. Did he intend to watch her the entire night, now?

He sat down, folded his arms, and couldn't shift his gaze from her. He couldn't trust her. But he couldn't keep her prisoner. Grim resignation settled like a rock in his chest and he released the binding that tethered her abilities.

In the morning, she'd be gone.

CHAPTER 20

BELLA

Sunlight pierced the gloom and Bella stretched her aching muscles before slowly opening her eyes. Nate was sprawled on a chair beside the bed, head back, sound asleep. His wings cushioned his back and trailed to the floor, in magnificent, breathtaking glory.

She exhaled a silent sigh. How many times over the last few days had she wondered how he'd look, without his protective glamour? Even her wildest fantasies had fallen short of the reality.

But she couldn't afford to waste time, drinking in his unearthly beauty. Dagan's careless threat thudded in her mind and she pushed herself to her feet. It wasn't just her life that might be in danger.

She had to warn Octavia.

Where was her phone? If Nate hadn't immobilized her, she'd teleport to Romania right now.

Awareness slithered along her spine and she sent out her senses, testing the boundaries of her power. The tingling sensation that had sunk into her bones last night, when he'd disabled her, had gone.

She teleported to the bedroom door. He'd released her. While she slept. *Why?*

He stirred, his feathers rippling and muscles flexing, and she couldn't drag her mesmerized gaze away. Within seconds he'd be fully awake, and her chance of freedom would vanish.

Would it?

He hadn't loosened the bonds in error. He was giving her the choice. To stay or flee.

She held her breath as he shifted in the chair. Although she couldn't see his face, he was staring at the bed. Motionless. As though waiting for... something.

Her breath thickened and chest grew tight. The distant hum of traffic from the outside world faded, and the silence within the room was almost tangible. Despite how she'd tried to avoid the truth, she'd fallen for him. Hard. Maybe from the first moment she'd seen him among the sea of mortals in her club.

The only one she didn't have to fear outliving.

She could go home right now. He wouldn't stop her. And what then? How did she think she could protect her friend against the wrath of a demon?

Far better to have an archangel by her side.

She took a step closer to him and he swung around as though she'd cracked a whip. Shock etched his face, instantly smothered, but it was enough.

He thought she'd left him.

It meant something. But he'd never admit it. So what did it matter?

More than it should.

"Good morning," she said, sounding like a complete idiot. Not that he seemed to notice. It was insane that she didn't know what else to say to him. What a shame she hadn't suffered from that last night when she'd spilled her guts.

Too late for regrets now. Maybe he'd released her because he felt sorry for her. Inside, a raw sliver of her heart shriveled. The last thing she wanted from Nate was his pity. Why wouldn't he say something?

He rose from the chair, his wings unfurling, and her mouth dried. Eblis' wings were impressive, but they'd never affected her in the way Nate's did. But then, she'd never been ensnared in Eblis' demonic glory.

For too many years she'd despised Nate's race, based on the teachings of the Watchers, and how humankind had elevated archangels, at the expense of demons.

The ancient truths had been twisted. Even as a child, she'd known of the myths surrounding demons. But those myths had been perpetrated by archangels. And of them all, the archangel Nathanael blazed through the histories in his quest to eradicate her kind.

It was reason enough to hate him. But more than that she had despised him for trying to destroy the one refuge on Earth where she'd found others like herself.

Then she'd met him and started to question it all. He'd told her he had never entered the sacred mountain one hundred years ago. That he hadn't slaughtered a dozen demon bloods.

And she believed him.

"Going somewhere?" His voice was rough from sleep and ignited an unholy hunger deep inside her heart.

"I need to warn Octavia and the others about Dagan," she said, hating how desperate she sounded. But Octavia was like a sister to her. She had to ask him. Even if it meant swallowing what was left of her pride. "I could use your help."

"I can defeat him by myself."

She didn't doubt it. "He threatened Octavia. And Nico. The entire Echelon could be in danger."

"And?" The faintest trace of belligerence tainted the word. It was clear he wasn't used to a mere half-blood demon questioning his word.

"I won't let you leave me behind," she said, but his face was unflinching. She would have to play her ace. And hope she wasn't wrong. "I'm on Dagan's radar too, now."

His dark eyes smoldered. It was hard to concentrate when all she wanted to do was throw her arms around his neck and hold him close. Feel his heart. Know that maybe, somehow, there was a light at the end of this bottomless abyss.

"If he wanted you dead, you would be."

That was true. And not the answer from Nate she'd been hoping for.

"There's nothing to stop him from changing his mind."

"I need someone by my side who I can trust."

And there it was. The mountain between them. She didn't even blame him but that didn't make his barely concealed allegation any easier to accept. But she couldn't give up. He hadn't killed her when he could have. He'd released her when he hadn't needed to. Some part of him, no matter how deeply buried, believed in her.

"You can trust me on this."

"You'll betray your own kind to help me?"

His question was unwarranted. She gave him the haughtiest look she could manage. "I won't let a demon harm my friends. I'm half human, and so is Octavia. I pledge my loyalty to those who deserve it. Blood only goes so deep."

"Does it?" He took a step toward her, his wingspan obliterating the rest of the world. "You pledged your loyalty to a demon long ago. How do I know he's not the one orchestrating this whole thing with Dagan?"

"What?" Ice pierced her chest. It had never even occurred to her that Eblis and the demon who had so casually held a knife to her throat might be working together. "No. I don't believe it. There can't be a connection between them. He isn't like that."

"But it would make a difference, wouldn't it?" His gaze was relentless, peeling back the layers of everything she'd believed in for so many years. "If it came to a showdown between your mentor and me, then blood would out."

No, it wouldn't. The denial screamed in her mind, a devastating revelation that despite what Eblis had done for her and despite the fact he'd saved her, she wouldn't let him touch Nate. She'd defy anything—*anyone*—to keep him safe.

She clamped her teeth together, keeping the damning confession inside her head, where it belonged. Even if she did lose every shred of self-preservation and blurt out those words, he'd never believe such an outrageous declaration. Hell, she wouldn't believe it either, if he said such a thing to her.

Even though she'd want to.

"I gave him my word I'd never betray who he was. And I've told you how much I owe him. But my integrity remains my own."

"Spying on the Watchers." It wasn't even a question, and his accusation stung.

But even though it wasn't the word she'd choose, he wasn't wrong. "I made that choice, yes. Will you help me?"

Silence filled the room before he gave a curt jerk of his head. "Yes."

"Thank you." She let out a breath, relieved she had his word.

He folded his wings. His hot gaze never left hers. "At least if you're by my side I know you're not plotting behind my back."

She flinched. Did he have to keep telling her how little he trusted her? "If I wanted to *plot* against you, there's nothing you could do to stop me. I'm telepathic, too."

Probably not the wisest thing to say under the circumstances, but at least he couldn't accuse her of holding anything back.

The ghost of a smile softened his features for less than a heartbeat, but it was enough. She'd been right to tell him.

"If you betray me, I'll take you to an uninhabited planet in the Sextans Galaxy and disable all your powers."

She snorted. "Bit dramatic. Even for an archangel."

"Beats slitting throats in archaic rituals."

He'd watched her do that? But he'd been confounded when he'd seen her in the forbidden library. Hadn't he recognized her in the atrium?

He shrugged, even though she hadn't said anything. "I'm not judging. Archangels have had some weird fucking rituals done in their name in the past."

"Just so you know, that was my first time. It was a test."

"They randomly decided to test you?"

She didn't need to tell him anything more. But he had spared her when he could've destroyed her, and he'd released her, giving her the choice to escape his clutches—or stay by his side.

She'd made her choice.

"It was more complicated than that. Until yesterday, they didn't know I could teleport. That's one of the abilities that allows a member to ascend into the Elite."

Nate's gaze became laser sharp. "Why did you keep that hidden?"

She wanted to tell him. But it was tied back to Eblis and she'd never betray him. Nate's accusation that Eblis and Dagan might be working together gnawed through her mind. She'd never believe it. And yet...

Why had Eblis wanted her to reveal herself now, of all times? How much had he been keeping from her?

Sharing a little more with Nate wouldn't expose Eblis. "My mentor thought it prudent."

"Interesting."

She couldn't tell if he was being sarcastic. "Yes. Very, considering what happened."

"Have you been in contact with him since last night?"

It was a reasonable question. As soon as she'd discovered Nate had released the binding on her powers, she should have done two things. Got out of here, and contacted Eblis.

Yet the demon hadn't even crossed her mind.

"No."

"Why not?"

Another good question. She wasn't sure she knew the answer.

"I'll contact him when I'm ready to. First, we need to warn Octavia about Dagan. Unless you've changed your mind."

Nate contemplated her, his eyes narrowed. "I haven't."

"Okay." She tore her gaze from him and glanced down at her dress. "I need to get changed first. Can you give me ten minutes?"

"I'll give you five."

For the first time in what felt like forever, she smiled. She hadn't been sure that he'd agree she could go home unless he came with her. It was a small step, but significant. "Fair enough. Meet you back here?"

"I'll come to you."

"Fine." She hesitated, unsure how to end the conversation. She could hardly kiss him but teleporting without a farewell seemed wrong. "See you shortly."

He didn't respond, but his dark eyes assured her that yes, she certainly would.

She arrived in her bedroom a moment later, a half-smile on her face. And instantly froze.

A smoky cloud snaked up the stairs, and as if to punctuate the wrongness, something smashed from a room below, the sound reverberating up the walls and shattering the windows.

Had Dagan found her?

From the corner of her eye she caught a distortion in the air and swung around, as Zane materialized at the far end of the landing. Murder glowed in his eyes.

"Traitor." His cold voice sent ice into her veins, and as blue-white power launched from his hand she teleported into the bathroom from sheer instinct. Beside her, the dilapidated bath exploded into a million pieces, and she instantly teleported to the drawing room before the flying shards ripped her to shreds.

Nijah was there, but despite the danger all she saw was her

beautiful, elegant, room that she'd spent so long creating, was now nothing more than a ruin of scorched fabric and shattered memories.

"My instincts were right," Nijah said, as Zane appeared by her side. "I've never trusted you. To betray us to an archangel."

Lightning fast, both Nijah and Zane hurled daggers her way. She threw up a protective shield, and the daggers hovered in mid-air, suspended inches from her face. In the split second as shock dulled the Elites' senses, Bella activated her rarely used telekinetic power and flung the sad remnants of her once-gorgeous grandmother clock into the back of their heads. They crashed to the ground, and even though she knew they were only temporarily stunned, and she had to get out, she couldn't move.

Zane had been one of the Elite for years, but she'd always considered him a friend.

And he had just tried to kill her.

CHAPTER 21

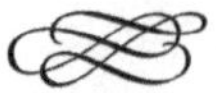

NATE

Nate exhaled a long breath after Isabella teleported. She'd never know how much it cost him not to have gone with her. But if he couldn't trust her in this one small thing, there was no way in hell she'd accompany him to see Gabe.

Because Nic and his Echelon weren't the only ones Dagan had threatened.

He pulled out his phone and called the vampire. Unlike the creatures of myth, Nic didn't limit his working hours to those of darkness.

"Nate," Nic said.

Briefly, he recounted what he'd discovered about the strange, liquid smoke that had been found at the castle.

"I'll let Octavia know. Anything else?"

"Sakarbaal received the sword from a demon. He fucked up and now Dagan is pissed. He might be coming after you."

"Inconvenient."

"Tell me about it. Take everything you need from the castle. I wouldn't put it past Dagan to raze it to the ground just for the hell of it."

"Understood. Did you locate the whereabouts of the sword?"

Should he tell Nic he was the one who'd taken it from the castle? Not much point, now. "Dagan has it."

There was a heartbeat of silence. Did Nic suspect the truth?

"Good hunting," Nic said at last, a dry note in his voice, and hung up.

Frowning, Nate shoved his phone into his pocket. He guessed he owed his friend the truth but first he needed to find out what Gabe had done to Dagan.

He teleported to Isabella's house. The stench of burning timber and demonic power hung heavy in the air. *Fuck.* Adrenaline punched him in the chest, propelling from the hallway into the drawing room.

The room was unrecognizable, but relief streaked through him when he saw her by the window. She was breathing and there was no blood on her clothing. Electricity crackled and sparks flashed and from the corner of his eye he saw two figures trapped beneath a shattered grandmother clock vanish.

He was across the room in an instant and roughly pulled Isabella into his arms. She was rigid, unmoving, and the relief twisted into a black, unformed fear.

"Are you all right?" His voice was rough, and he inched her back so he could see her face. Glazed eyes gazed up at him and the unnatural fear magnified. "Isabella. Speak to me."

"It's all gone," she whispered. "There's nothing left."

The air stunk of demons and the scorch marks on the walls were similar to ones he'd encountered over the years. The Watchers had come after her.

And they'd tried to kill her.

Rage flooded through his blood and he sucked in a harsh breath. There was a time for vengeance, and it wasn't right now when Isabella needed him.

"You're safe now." And by all the cursed gods, he'd ensure she remained so. He shouldn't have allowed her to go home alone. He should have been with her. Should have damn well protected her. "I won't allow them to harm you again."

"My home." Her voice broke on the words and she slumped against his chest, as though all the strength had been sucked out of her.

Unease twisted through him. What was he missing? She couldn't be this upset over the wreckage of her house.

"What did they take?" He tried to keep the urgency from his tone in case it made her worse but failed. Seeing Isabella shattering before his eyes was freaking the shit out of him. But if he knew what the problem was, he could fix it. "Whatever it is, I'll get it back for you."

"All those years," she whispered, as though she hadn't even heard his question. "I never had a real home. Just places to stay. Until I found this house. It was my sanctuary from the outside world." She hitched in a ragged breath and her body shuddered. "All my beautiful pieces. Gone."

He glanced around the room. When he'd been here before, he'd noticed the antiques and authentic period style. She had great taste and he appreciated the aesthetics.

But they were just things. Apart from his collection of weapons that he'd amassed over the centuries and kept secured in an underground cave system on an uninhabited planet in Andromeda, he wasn't attached to any of his shit. Hell, even if he lost all his weapons he'd be more pissed off at the inconvenience, and gall of the perpetrator than anything else.

He tightened his grip around her but had no idea what to say. Isabella was strong, for fuck's sake. She'd defied Dagan to release him and thrust her hand into an alien forcefield without a second's thought to her own safety. And she'd managed to fight off at least two attackers before he'd arrived.

But the loss of her home was breaking her.

He had to get her out of here. As far away from the Watchers as possible.

He wrapped his arm around her and teleported, to a place he hadn't been in decades.

A lush planet that although teemed with life, was on the primitive side of the Andromeda Galaxy, which meant the chances of anyone finding them were zero. The timber dwelling was constructed high in the trees, offering a hundred-and-eighty-degree view of the island and although there wasn't much in the way of luxury here, at least she'd be safe while he crushed the Watchers and hunted Dagan.

She sucked in a sharp breath and stiffened in his arms as she took in their surroundings.

"It's okay." His voice was rough. "No one's going to find you here. If you need anything, let me know. You're telepathic. I'll open a link for us."

She grasped his shirt. "Octavia." Fear threaded through the word, but at least that terrifying blankness had left her eyes. "You said you'd go with me. You promised."

"She's safe. I contacted Nic."

"She can't die because of me."

"She won't. And the connection between you is irrelevant. Sakarbaal is the linking factor, not you."

"We saved each other's life," she said, still gripping his shirt as though it was her lifeline. "Well, we thought we did. Neither of us knew the other was immortal back then."

"Okay." He attempted to inject a soothing note in his voice but wasn't sure he succeeded.

"We met on a train going across Europe. Oh, so long ago—the middle of last century."

Was it a good sign she was telling him this? Or was she sliding into shock, and not even aware of what she was saying? He'd wondered how she and Octavia had met. But if this was the price, it was way too high.

"There was a terrible accident. Fire raged through the carriages, trapping everyone. Octavia and I managed to force open one of the doors, but we were hanging over a ravine. People were jumping, but a human didn't stand much chance of survival. I knew I would, and I knew I could shield Octavia from the worst of the fall. Funny thing is, she was thinking the exact same thing about me. So we jumped, and that's how we discovered we had more in common than a love of ancient European architecture."

"Still must have hurt."

"Gods, yes. We broke so many bones between us. But at least we managed to walk out of there before the rescue teams arrived. Her regenerative powers are almost as fast as mine. It would've been hard to explain how we barely had a scratch on us just hours after the accident."

"There's always mind manipulation." This wasn't the conversation he'd imagined having with Isabella right now, but she was sounding more like her usual self by the second. And there was no way he was going to leave her until he was certain she was okay. Gabe wasn't in imminent danger since Dagan had no idea where he was.

"Sometimes walking away is the easier option." She relaxed her death grip on his shirt and curled her fingers over his shoulders. "And sometimes you just have to fight."

She wasn't talking about the train wreck or its possible aftermath anymore. It made no difference that she wasn't a vulnerable human who needed his protection. There was no way he was going to let her get anywhere near Dagan again. "Leave the fighting to me."

The ghost of a smile touched her face and pain speared through his chest. He didn't try to analyze it. No point. Somehow, Isabella had carved through his armor and the damage was done.

She didn't remind him she was half-demon, or she possessed powers that would, at least, give her a fleeting chance. They both knew that, and it wouldn't change his mind. Instead, she slid her hands around the back of his neck and linked her fingers together.

He drew in a deep breath, savoring the elusive hint of her perfume in the air, and attempted to pull back. But his good intentions dissolved before they even took form, and he remained locked in place, her delectable curves a tantalizing promise of eternity against his body.

Her lips parted, so close to his. This wasn't the time, it wasn't the place, and now he knew of her heritage, how could he even think of taking her again?

She rolled onto her toes and captured his mouth. His groan of defeat echoed in his ears and throbbed through his mind, as he cupped her ass and tugged her closer. Her kiss was desperate, savage, an affirmation of life and even as the knowledge pounded through him, he discarded it.

He didn't care why she wanted this. Only that she did. And if this was the last time they'd ever be together, he was going to take every last damn thing she offered.

As she feverishly tugged his shirt from his pants and shoved them down his thighs, he unzipped her dress and trailed his fingertips over her naked back. She sighed, the sound reverberating inside his mouth, before she pushed the sparkling material to the floor and kicked it aside.

Her exploring fingers found his wings, and her touch was exquisite fire. She wasn't the first to caress his wings, but it had never been like this before. Protectively, he wrapped them around her, and she broke their kiss to lean back, cushioning her head against his feathers.

A dark, damning wave of possessiveness gripped him. Her tangled blonde hair spread against his silver-gray wings and the guileless blue of her eyes gave her such a vulnerable air. He knew it was an illusion. But it didn't change the truth.

He'd protect her with his life.

"Stop thinking." Her husky whisper stoked the lust in his

blood but a question he couldn't ignore gnawed through his brain. And not for the first time. No matter how impossible it should be.

"Are you reading my mind?" Did he care if she could? His wings shifted, tightening around her, inexorably pulling her closer until their breath mingled.

"I don't need to. I can see it in your eyes. We don't need anything else, Nate. Just this."

She cradled his jaw, her deceptively fragile fingers branding his flesh. But even as he hoisted her in his arms, and she wrapped her legs around his hips, discordance prickled along the edges of his mind.

I want more than this.

The revelation flared through his brain, a supernova brightness, and for an eternal moment paralysis held him in a punishing grip. When it came to sex, he never wanted *more* than this moment in time. Never looked ahead or thought about the woman in question when they weren't together.

What the fuck am I doing?

Isabella dug her nails into his jaw. "Stop," she whispered, her lips brushing his and their kiss was hungry and wild.

He backed up to the bed and sat on the edge, Isabella straddling him. Her curves pressed against his chest, exquisite torture, and his groan echoed in his ears as she tore his shirt from him before pushing him onto his back.

Her hair was a silken caress against his burning flesh as her mouth and teeth engulfed his senses with primal fire. His fingers explored the warm satin of her skin, and the sound of harsh breaths and beating hearts filled the heated air. There was nothing beyond this primitive room, nothing except Isabella and the promise of forever glowing in her eyes. It was an illusion. He didn't care. All he wanted was here, now, and he'd take it, savor it, damn well inhale it, without analyzing the *why*.

She gripped his shoulders, bracing her weight, and slowly

glided her wet slit across the length of his cock. His thumbs played with her nipples and her sigh touched a hidden sliver of his soul that he had never known existed before today. Infinity beckoned as finally she sank onto him, and her addictive heat embraced him with mind shattering passion.

Her nails scored his skin and he reared off the bed, gripping her hips. She arched her back, and her gorgeous breasts were a visual feast, a temptation he couldn't resist. He cupped her breast, relishing how she filled his palm, and sucked her luscious nipple into his mouth.

"Harder," she breathed. A command he was powerless to resist.

She rode him, pounding him into the bed, and the scent of sex and need swirled with reckless abandon. He stroked the tips of his feathers along her back and she shuddered, her eyelashes flickering in ecstasy. Her tight sheath convulsed around him, a glorious cocoon of pure sensation and wordless content, and he fell. *Ama-gi.*

Home.

CHAPTER 22

BELLA

*E*nveloped within Nate's wing, Bella didn't want to move. His feathers were soft, silken, warm with life and so breathtakingly powerful she could barely imagine it.

The steady beat of his heart beneath her hand was hypnotic. So was the sound of his breathing, and the way his fingers idly traced patterns across her shoulder.

She could stay here forever, her body entwined with his. If only it could be this easy.

Reluctantly, she forced open her eyes and drank in the magnificent vision of his naked chest. The fragile world she had built for herself had been destroyed in one vindictive swoop. But she hadn't fallen into his arms through shock. She'd wanted him. Needed him. And had used the only way she knew how to have him one last time.

She wasn't proud of it. But she didn't regret it. Unable to stop herself she pressed her body against him, a final, lingering touch before this moment out of time shattered.

His arm tightened around her, and his wing flexed, drawing her closer in his feathered embrace. He wasn't making this easy. But nothing with Nate was easy.

Except for how I fell for him.

A ragged sigh hitched through her as she finally faced the truth. A truth she'd known almost from the moment she'd met him. She'd sworn off love so long ago. Never wanting to go through the heartrending agony of watching the man she loved grow old and die.

The irony was great. If anything, she was the one who would grow old and die, long before Nate.

Obviously, this was the bitch of the universe letting her know there was more than one way to break a heart.

"You okay?" His deep voice vibrated through his chest, tingling her fingers, and it took every shred of willpower she possessed not to simply crawl on top of him and lose herself once again.

She'd indulged enough. But real life still waited out there, and she had to face it.

"Yes." Her lips brushed his skin. It would be so easy to press a kiss on his beautiful flesh, but it felt too intimate. As though by doing such a simple thing she'd give herself away.

Stupid thing to think, after the way she'd practically devoured him just now. But that was different. Because that was just sex.

She squeezed her eyes shut. There was no distinction, except inside her messed-up head. And that was where it was going to stay.

Her interlude was over. And so was her self-indulgent grief. There would be plenty of time to mourn her broken home when Dagan was dealt with.

And not just my home...

Gently, she eased out of Nate's embrace. He didn't try and stop her. Had she expected him to? She refused to think about it, and instead reached across the bed and picked up his discarded shirt. He sat up and leaned against the timber wall but didn't take his steady gaze from her as she pulled his shirt on. It was miles too big for her, and his scent clung to the cotton, like an ethereal caress.

She concentrated on doing up the buttons, so she didn't have to look at him. Just in case he saw more in her eyes than she wanted. After everything they'd been through together it was ridiculous that she didn't know what to say to him and she glanced around the place for inspiration.

It was certainly impressive. Some sort of treehouse, by the way the view through the many windows gave a fabulous view of exotic treetops. As inspiration went, it worked.

"This is amazing." She waved her hand in the general direction of the view, but still couldn't bring herself to look at him. "Did you build this yourself?"

"A long time ago. Although I freely admit I cheated with the glass. I imported that from off-planet."

Her suspicion had been right. They were no longer on Earth and despite the circumstances, excitement flared through her. "Where are we?"

"The far side of Andromeda."

She sucked in a sharp breath. For some reason, that now she thought about it didn't even make sense, she'd assumed they were still within the Milky Way. "Wow. Okay, then. I didn't expect *that.*"

"I found this planet soon after the exodus from Earth. It's in the backwaters of the Galaxy. I'd be surprised if anyone else even knows it exists."

The exodus from Earth? She knew the historical story, of course. How archangels had abandoned their own half-blood descendants in the chaos of floods and earthquakes that had hit the planet when Earth reset her celestial clock. But over the last couple of days she'd questioned the truth of it.

It didn't fit what she knew of Nate. He'd never leave the vulnerable behind, no matter what other archangels might have done. And she'd found proof in the archives that the Watchers taught one version of history while they concealed another.

Yet he'd just confirmed that he had, indeed, been part of the exodus.

"Really?" She turned to him, but her questions dried in her throat. His hair hung over his shoulder in thick ropes of gorgeousness, and his dark eyes were fixed on her, a smoky gaze that caused sharp ripples of need deep inside.

"When I say it's primitive, I'm not joking." He gave a faint smile, which didn't help settle the plague of butterflies currently invading her stomach. "But it suited me at the time."

Stop gawping at him. She wasn't a starstruck mortal, and she wasn't going to behave like one. Frantically, she clawed through her mind because there was something she needed to ask him. And it had nothing to do with how advanced or otherwise the indigenous people of this planet were.

"Why did you leave Earth?" She couldn't—*wouldn't*—believe he'd left the vulnerable to perish.

"There wasn't much left of the Earth we'd known once we escaped." His voice turned grim. "Also, it was the one thing our damn goddess didn't want us to do."

Enthralled, she gazed at him. Questions tumbled through her mind, demanding answers that only he could give.

"What do you mean, after you escaped? What happened?" There had never been a whisper of such things in the histories. Were they another secret buried in the Forbidden Archives?

"Don't you know? I'd have thought the Watchers reveled in our downfall."

"*Archangels'* downfall? I don't know anything about that. It was the demons who were banished. Are you telling me that's not true?"

"The demons were banished before archangels were created."

She wrapped her arms around her knees as shreds of information she'd picked up over the years twisted through her mind.

Humans had their own fables of archangels and demons, but the informed had assumed that they were nothing more than fairy stories.

But just how informed were the Earth-born descendants of demons? It seemed truth was an elusive concept when it came to the immortals of antiquity.

The knowledge she and her kind had been lied to burned through her chest like acid. But after all that had happened over the last day or so, she wasn't surprised.

Just disappointed. And in the distant shadows of her mind, a familiar sensation of once again being adrift in an alien world crawled from its tenuous slumber.

"I didn't know that." By rights, she should hate admitting that to Nate, the enemy of her people. But she didn't. Because right now, she didn't have any people. No allegiances, no loyalty. The eerie sense of disconnectedness snaked like corrosive lava through her brain and she forcibly shut it down. She'd deal with it later. When she was alone. Nate had seen her fall apart once. She'd never let him witness such weakness again. "Our histories tell us that archangels were instrumental in having demons sent into exile."

"That's creative. But untrue."

"So you didn't poison the great goddess' mind against demons?" She already knew the answer. But wanted to hear him confirm it.

"Her mind was poisoned long before she started her damn experiments." Bitterness threaded through the words. "Demons were her first experiment. When they didn't turn out the way she wanted, she started over. With archangels."

How easily truth could be manipulated. In her version, demons had been created from divine love. But she guessed *experiment* worked just as well. There was every possibility that Nate was lying but, in her heart, she knew he wasn't.

"You said you escaped. I still don't know what you mean."

"Do you know of Ama-gi?"

She'd only heard the word once before, when Nate had spoken it in the guesthouse in Romania, yet it whispered through her, evocative and oddly comforting, as though it called her to a long-forgotten home.

"A place you knew long ago." She gave him a sad smile as she repeated his words from Romania back to him.

"It's been given many names throughout history." There was a brooding, faraway look in his eyes that inexplicably made her heart ache. "Somehow, its essence survived in the genetic memory of humanity. It was the true cradle of civilization on Earth and the place we lived for almost a thousand years."

The glorious paradise, before the demonic fall from grace. Which, despite the propaganda, hadn't been due to an almighty battle between the great goddess' two opposing creations.

"Why are we even enemies, then?" If there had been no epic battle, and if the archangels hadn't persuaded their great goddess to disown her first beloved children, what the hell was the problem?

"Archangels and demons aren't the same, Isabella."

"It seems we've more in common than not."

"Only superficially."

He was deliberately searching for reasons why their two races were incompatible. It shouldn't hurt. But it did. It was almost as though he was trying to tell her why they could never have anything more than this fleeting moment together.

But she already knew that. He didn't have to shove it down her throat.

"I don't agree," she said. He obviously believed in the superiority of his race, but she wasn't going to agree with him. Especially when she now doubted demons were the ones who deserved that distinction, either. "I think there's nothing to choose between us."

His beautiful wing curled around her, the tips of his feathers dusting her cheek in a tender caress.

"I'm not talking about you. You're different. But demons are fundamentally flawed. They can't be trusted. They've wanted nothing more than our destruction from the moment of our creation."

How could his touch be so gentle, when his words were weapons, ripping her apart?

"I'm not different, Nate. I'm not just some human with a trace of immortal blood. I'm half-demon and I don't believe we're all flawed, or that all archangels are so damn perfect."

"I never said we're perfect." His feathers trailed over her arm and across her back. She willed herself not to react, but treacherous need shimmered through her body regardless. "And you're not flawed."

She let out a ragged sigh. They were going in circles. He'd never acknowledge his prejudice. Did she really want to spend this time debating the finer points with him? There was no point. In her heart she wanted him to remember her as *someone different.*

Not flawed.

Pathetic. But she wasn't going to analyze it. Because she didn't want her own memories of Nate tarnished by a useless argument based only on her gut feelings, and no hard facts, when the outcome wouldn't even change anything.

Real life couldn't be ignored forever. At least Octavia had been warned, and she had every faith Nico would do all in his power to protect his Echelon.

But now she needed to get to Eblis and find out the truth. Why had he wanted her to reveal her powers to the Elite? *Did* he know about Dagan? It was time to find out what, exactly, Eblis' agenda was.

She reached out and touched Nate's hand. It was meant to be nothing but a brief stroke across his knuckles, but he caught her fingers and for endless seconds she remained a willing captive within his smoldering gaze.

"I need clothes," she said at last, breaking the spell, and regret squeezed her heart as he reluctantly released her. She left the bed and glanced at the windows. They needed to find Dagan, but right now she was on an alien planet. How could she leave without taking a quick look outside?

He reached her side, magnificently naked, and opened the door that led directly onto a deck that wrapped around the outside of the treehouse. *Remember which view I'm supposed to be admiring.* It was hard to tear her bewitched gaze from his spectacular pecs.

She gripped the wooden handrail, so she wasn't tempted to grip him instead, and focused on the view. Birdsong filled the air, and flashes of metallic blue and bright red-orange wings flashed through the leaves. They were on an island in the middle of an archipelago, surrounded by sunlit-glinting aquamarine water. The mainland wasn't far away and looked like it was mostly forest with a wide sandy beach.

Movement rustled the trees on the mainland, and she stared, transfixed, as a massive creature emerged from the forest. Its long neck was thick and tinged with green while its elongated jaw snapped at the branches.

"Oh, my gods." She couldn't tear her gaze away. "It's a *dinosaur.*" Not like any she'd seen in museums, but there was no mistaking the genus.

"Yeah. Told you this planet was primitive." There was a hint of amusement in his voice. "Luckily, this island is too small to accommodate the main inhabitants of this world."

"This is amazing. A front row seat in prehistory."

"Any time you want to come back here, let me know."

"I'll do that." She never would, and they both knew it. *Move on, Bella.* She'd wasted enough time as it was. "Can you take me home so I can get changed?" For real, this time.

"Tell me what you need, and I'll collect your stuff."

She turned to face him. "I'm going with you."

"It's not safe."

"I don't think abandoning me on a world full of dinosaurs is exactly safe, either."

He frowned as though her accusation was unwarranted. "Dagan will never find you here. And I'm not abandoning you," he added, as though that was an afterthought.

"Okay. Worst case scenario. You disable my abilities and then something happens, so you lose your powers. Wait." She raised her hand at him, and whatever he'd been about to say clearly stuck in his throat at her nerve. "Right. So there you are, incapacitated on Earth, with no way to rescue me. I could die of starvation, or be poisoned by eating something, or even end up as some creature's supper."

"And you said archangels are dramatic."

"I'm being realistic. You can't leave me here, Nate."

"You're—" He bit off his words and glared at her. "Frustrating."

"Why? Because I'm right?"

He growled something in the language he'd used once before. It was obviously a curse, and the poetic cadence was enchanting.

Maybe Dagan wanted to harm her, although she wasn't convinced. But one thing she did know for certain.

Both Nijah and Zane were out for her blood.

CHAPTER 23

NATE

Nate prowled through the wrecked kitchen of Isabella's home. There was no sign the Watchers had been searching for anything. They'd been out for nothing more than vindictive destruction.

And Isabella's head.

Teeth clenched, he marched into the drawing room, where he'd found her just a couple of hours ago. Currently, she was upstairs in her bedroom, the only room that hadn't been destroyed, changing her clothes, and he still couldn't wrap his brain around the way she'd managed to manipulate him.

The problem was, she was right. When he'd seen her looking so vulnerable surrounded by her ruined possessions, his overriding impulse had been to protect her, but he hadn't thought it through. Like everything when it was connected to her, his good sense was fucking scrambled.

He'd have to revert to his original plan and keep her by his side when he spoke to Gabe about the demon.

Hey, Az.

Azrael answered at once. *What?*

You still with Gabe?

It was a pain in the ass that Gabe no longer possessed the archangelic telepathic link. He should've got his phone number, but it hadn't occurred to him.

Yes.

I need to speak with him. I won't be alone.

Okay. There was a thread of curiosity in the word, but Az didn't push it. Nate disconnected their link, as Isabella walked into the room. She'd pulled her hair back into its usual ponytail and was wearing black jeans with a sweater that matched the color of her eyes. He stifled a sigh. When had he ever noticed such a thing about a woman?

She glanced around the room and swallowed before returning her attention to him. "Are we still going to Romania? You said you'd warned Nico."

"We're visiting Gabe."

"The one Dagan's pissed off with? Who is he? A human?"

Nate wasn't sure what Gabe was anymore. "He's the Archangel Gabriel."

Her eyes widened. "Oh."

There was no reason to tell her anything else, yet that didn't stop him. "He's lost his immortality. If Dagan finds him, it won't be an even fight."

"I didn't know archangels could lose their immortality. Is that a *thing*?"

"Yeah, seems that falling in love is dangerous for archangels' health." He wasn't just thinking of Gabe, either. An image of Azrael's severed wing flashed through his mind. And before he could stop himself, the vision of Isabella, with her hair tumbling over her naked shoulders as she wrapped her arms around him, filled his head.

Fuck. He wasn't going there. He sucked in a sharp breath and didn't miss the questioning glance Isabella gave him.

Questioning? Or knowing?

Enough.

"Ready?"

"Sure." Once again, she glanced around her ruined room, and pressed her lips together. He was going to hunt down those bastard Watchers and fucking enjoy feeding them their entrails. But first, he had to discover what Gabe had done to Dagan.

He held out his hand, and Isabella threaded her fingers through his. His thumb stroked her knuckles. Her bones were so fragile. So easily broken.

She's more than she appears. He had to remember that.

A moment later they arrived outside Gabe's house. The weather was dull and drizzling and instinctively he wrapped his wing around Isabella, protecting her from the rain. As the door opened, he reluctantly released her hand. There'd be enough questions regarding her presence without adding more speculation to the fire.

Gabe gave him a quizzical glance, before stepping back so they could enter the hallway. He closed the door before focusing on Isabella.

"I'm Gabe," he said. "Welcome."

"Bella. Thank you."

Huh. Did she usually introduce herself as Bella?

Gabe folded his arms and transferred his gaze to Nate. "Az said you need to speak to me. But before we get into that, there's something you should know. I no longer have the advantage of being able to read auras."

His unspoken question was obvious. *Who the hell is Bella?*

Then again, even if Gabe hadn't lost that ability, he wouldn't have gained much by trying to read Isabella's. She shielded her true nature, just like he did.

"Isabella and I are working together. She's aware of what happened to Az." He wouldn't reveal her heritage. It wasn't his secret to share.

Gabe scrutinized her. It wasn't threatening or even unfriendly, but Nate's feathers bristled, regardless.

"I'm half-demon," Isabella said, as though she wasn't dropping a fucking great revelation. "I was searching for the immortal forged sword before I teamed up with Nate."

"Why were you searching for it?" Azrael walked across the hall to them, and Isabella sucked in a sharp breath as she turned to him. He sympathized. His gut still knotted every time he saw Azrael's wing.

She licked her lips as indecision flashed across her face. Then it was gone. "To discover its origins," she said in a cool voice.

Shit. He still needed to tell Az who had forged the sword. And that it wasn't a fucking demon.

Az contemplated Isabella in silence, before turning to Nate. "You're working with a half-demon?"

That's all he said. But Nate got the subtext. It wasn't only because Az knew of his aversion to demons. It was because, only weeks ago, Nate had raged at his friend for falling for a dhampir, when Az had spent a thousand years loathing their very existence.

"Yes." He failed to keep the belligerence from his voice, which as good as told Az that Isabella was more than merely his working partner. But he wasn't prepared to discuss Isabella with anyone. "That isn't why I needed to speak with Gabe."

Gabe and Az exchanged a glance that grated along his nerves. As though they shared a secret communication. But since Gabe was no longer telepathic, he was clearly paranoid when it came to anything even loosely connected to Isabella.

"My office, then." Gabe led the way to the back of the house and parked his ass on the end of one of the desks. "Is this about Mephisto? Have you seen him?"

Fresh irritation swept through Nate at the mention of Mephisto. "It isn't. And yes, I have."

"He didn't have any insights on that atmosphere shit?" Az flexed his damaged wing, and grimaced.

"He's dealing with it." Disgust dripped from each word. "But decided not to share."

"Typical Mephisto." Gabe exhaled an impatient breath. "What's this about, then?"

Nate glanced at Isabella and she gave him a faint smile. It was a struggle not to take her hand. He folded his arms instead, to ward against the temptation.

"What did you do to Dagan?"

Gabe stared at him. "What?"

Fuck, had Gabe's memory been affected by his mortality?

"The demon, Dagan. He—"

"Yeah, I remember Dagan. Wait. A demon? Thought he was a demigod."

"He was a demon?' Az cut in. He sounded fascinated. "I always thought there was something about him."

"What was he doing in Ama-gi?" Gabe said. "Spying on us?"

Nate had no doubt that was exactly what the bastard had been doing. Except it was irrelevant to the current problem. Because it was obvious Gabe hadn't confronted the demon since the destruction of Ama-gi.

He might as well get straight to the point. "He's after you, Gabe."

Gabe frowned. "Why?"

"I was hoping you could tell us that."

Gabe glanced at Isabella. "Are you connected to Dagan?"

"No," she said. "But the last time we saw him he was pretty mad about something. Said you fucked up his most promising cell."

Comprehension glowed in Gabe's eyes. "What the fuck." He sounded shaken. "Dagan was behind that?"

"Behind what?" Nate demanded.

"There was a pirate cult on Anzu. They were hunting down forgotten descendants of archangels for their blood."

"What's Anzu?" Isabella asked.

He sucked in a harsh breath. "It's the largest planet in the Seventh System of the Fornax Galaxy." Did she even know the truth of where demons had fled when they'd been banished from Earth? "Fornax is demon domain."

"The Primus of Anzu crushed the cult in her Sector, but only because Aurora and I discovered what they were doing. Fuck." Gabe pushed himself from the desk and strode to the French doors that led out into the garden. "If he comes anywhere near Aurora—"

"He won't. I'm going to find him, Gabe."

Gabe swung around. "I know someone who might help. If I could just fucking contact him."

"I don't need any help."

Gabe ignored him and turned to Az. "Eblis has contacts throughout the universe. I need a way to speak to him."

"Don't look at me. I still can't teleport." Frustration burned through Az's words. "And I've never had a telepathic link with him."

"Eblis?" There was an oddly strained note in Isabella's question and he only just stopped himself from taking her hand. *Again.*

"He's a powerful demon." They'd crossed paths several times in the distant past, but Gabe's comment thundered through his head, making it hard to focus on anything else. He glanced at Gabe. "Why would Eblis help you?"

"Long story."

"I'm sorry," Isabella said, looking at Gabe. "May I use your loo?"

"Sure." He went to the door and opened it. "It's just down the hall, on the right."

There was a silence after Isabella left the room. Nate only dragged his gaze from her when she disappeared into the bathroom and turned to find the other two staring at him.

"What?" He knew he sounded belligerent and couldn't help it.

"Can you trust her?" Gabe said.

It was a fair question, but he didn't have to like it. He trusted her in this. He had to. "She wouldn't be here if I didn't."

"How do you know she's not in league with Dagan?" Az demanded.

He'd asked himself the same thing more than once. It was possible. Anything was fucking possible. But he didn't believe she was.

"She risked her life for me." It was true. She might have died when she thrust her hand into that forcefield. But she'd done it anyway.

"Demons are masters of deception," Az said, as though Nate wasn't fully aware of that fact. "Look how Dagan fooled us all back in Ama-gi."

It was my fault he was in Ama-gi. Guilt corroded any defense he might have constructed against his own gullibility, but he wouldn't allow Az to slight Isabella.

"I believe in her."

Neither Az nor Gabe said anything. But they didn't have to. The expression on their faces was more than enough to let him know they'd read way too much into his statement.

Curse the gods. Just because he cared more for Isabella than he should, didn't mean he was in any danger of *falling* for her.

Deep in the darkest recesses of his psyche, his words mocked him, ruthlessly.

He wasn't in any danger of falling for her.

Because I already have.

CHAPTER 24

BELLA

Bella closed the door and let out a ragged breath. The downstairs cloakroom Gabe had directed her to comprised of an original Victorian high tank toilet with a pull chain and any other time she would've admired the tasteful renovations which appeared to be only half-complete.

But right now, she had other burning issues on her mind. Mainly, what the hell was Eblis up to?

He'd told her Earth would become a battleground for ancient immortals if they didn't find out who had given Sakarbaal the sword. She'd assumed he was talking about demons and archangels.

Was he, though?

She'd gone to Romania to track it down for him. Put her life on the line with the Elite. Because she believed Eblis had told her the truth.

Had he?

Anger bubbled. It wasn't because Eblis had used her for his own ends. She'd always known he had his own reasons for every-thing that he hadn't shared with her. It was because it hadn't crossed her mind that the damn sword might not have been as important to him as he'd made out.

Something else was going on, and Eblis appeared to be involved. She needed to have it out with him, but now wasn't the right time to accuse him of anything. Not when Gabe wanted his help and she was the only one who could contact him. She gritted her teeth.

Eblis.

She wrapped his name in urgency, something she'd never done before. Seconds passed. What was he doing?

Hey, Bella. He sounded annoyingly unconcerned. *What's the problem?*

She had so many questions for him. But they would have to wait.

What's your relationship with the Archangel Gabriel?

Gabe? His shock was palpable. If she weren't so churned up inside about everything, it would almost be funny. *Where are you, Bella?*

And she wasn't falling for that one. *Would you help him if his life was in danger?*

Gabe's in danger? The sharp concern that spiked his response told her everything she needed to know.

How were Eblis and Gabe such good friends when demons and archangels were supposed to be such deadly enemies?

Then again, look at her and Nate.

Things got complicated. I'm the only one who can contact you. Can you meet with us if I arrange it?

Why can't Gabe contact me? Obviously, he had no idea Gabe was no longer an immortal. She'd bet anything he was attempting to connect with Gabe right now.

I don't have time to discuss it. She didn't even try to hide her impatience. This was important, and she was willing to put her own issues with Eblis aside for now. But that didn't mean she wasn't going to grill him on what, exactly, his agenda was with having her go undercover in the Watchers.

Very well. It was a dismissal, but she cut their connection before he could—another first. She was done deferring to him anymore.

When she returned to the others, only Nate met her eyes. It was blatantly obvious they'd been talking about her. Not that she could blame them. Azrael's damaged wing snagged her attention for a second but this time she managed not to react. Maybe he deserved such retribution for the way he'd hunted dhampirs in the past.

She pushed the archangel's fate to the back of her mind and focused on Nate. Because he was the only one who mattered. "I know a way to help. But you're not going to like it."

"What is it?"

"My mentor… it's Eblis."

"Your *mentor?*" Gabe repeated. "Are you telling us Eblis visits Earth?"

She didn't know why he found it so unbelievable. Archangels had allegedly abandoned Earth millennia ago, and yet here they were.

"He's agreed to meet. I just need to let him know where," Bella said as two women entered the room. From sheer force of habit, Bella scanned their auras. One was human, although her aura was unlike any other human she'd met before. The other was…

Awe trickled along her spine at the unique structure of her aura. She had no idea what the other woman was.

"Hi." The human smiled at her. "I'm Aurora, Gabe's other half. This is Rowan." She introduced the dark-haired female, who also smiled at her before going over to Azrael.

Rowan? The dhampir Octavia had told her about? What had *happened* to her? There was no trace of dhampir in her aura. She tried not to stare but couldn't help it as Azrael wrapped his undamaged wing around Rowan in a protective gesture, while Gabe threaded his fingers through Aurora's.

When Nate had said falling was dangerous for an archangel's health, she'd guessed he was talking about Gabe. But Azrael, too? And the price was his wing?

"Gabe tells me you're in contact with Eblis," Aurora said. Clearly, Gabe *hadn't* lost all his telepathic ability when he'd turned mortal, if he'd already explained things to Aurora.

"Yes. But I didn't let him know where I was if that's what you're thinking. I told him I'd get back to him once we'd decided on a safe place to meet."

The tips of Nate's feathers caressed her arm, a silent show of support. It took all her willpower not to glance at him. Because if she did, she wasn't sure she'd be able to hide just how much that simple gesture meant to her.

"If Aurora agrees, he's welcome to come here."

"Eblis?" Azrael frowned. "He's a warped bastard. We should find somewhere neutral."

"We go way back," Gabe said. "I trust him. But it's up to Aurora."

"I've no objections." Aurora gave Gabe a faint smile. "He'd never betray you."

She'd always got the impression from Eblis that he held archangels in contempt. Not that he'd ever ranted about them, unlike some members of the Watchers, but he'd never had anything positive to say about them on the few occasions the subject had come up. And he sure as hell had never mentioned his friendship with the Archangel Gabriel. But why would he?

She really didn't know him at all.

"What about the baby?" Azrael said to Rowan, concern threading through the words.

"She's fine. She's sleeping. Do you want to leave?"

They had a *baby*?

Azrael threw a dark glare at them all. "It's different when you've a family to consider."

This was the archangel who had mercilessly slaughtered a thousand dhampirs in the past? She'd find it hard to believe, if Octavia hadn't confirmed it. Without quite meaning to, she inched a little closer to Nate.

I hope no one noticed.

"I'll take you wherever you want to go," Nate said. Then he leveled his gaze at Gabe. "How do we know Eblis and Dagan aren't working together?"

He'd asked her the same thing, and although in her heart she didn't want to believe it, the seed of doubt he'd planted had been one reason why she hadn't shared any more information with Eblis.

So much had happened in less than a week. Who would have thought she'd put the word of an archangel above that of the demon who had saved her sanity?

"We don't," Gabe said. "But I guarantee he won't put any of us in danger."

Azrael cursed in that beautiful, ancient language. Frustration radiated from him. "Nate, if things turn to shit, promise me you'll get Rowan and the baby to safety."

"You have my word." As he spoke, his feathers caressed the small of her back. An unspoken promise; made between the two of them. Even though she didn't need it. *I'll save you, too.*

"Tell Eblis where we are," Gabe said to her, and she relayed the message.

Within seconds, Eblis materialized by her side. He spared her only a fleeting glance before zeroing in on Gabe. "What the fuck happened to you?"

"I'll tell you later," Gabe said. "You'll love it."

"Spare me," Eblis growled. "Hey, Aurora." He turned to Azrael and distaste flickered over his features. "Fuck." Without missing a beat his laser glare zapped to Nate. "Find what you were looking for?"

"Tell me about Dagan," Nate shot back.

Confusion flashed in Eblis' eyes. He recovered instantly, but it was enough. He wasn't in league with the other demon, and relief rushed through her. Eblis might have kept secrets from her, but at least he hadn't knowingly sent her on a potential death mission this week.

"Dagan tried to kill me," she said. Which wasn't exactly the truth. If he'd wanted her dead, she would be, but she wasn't inclined to reveal that to Eblis right now. "And so did two of the Watchers."

"What?" Finally, Eblis returned his attention to her. "Why didn't you alert me of this earlier?"

"This is the first chance I've had." Now wasn't really the time to question Eblis' motives, but she needed to know. "Why did you want me to reveal my powers to the Watchers?"

It only made any sense if he'd known Dagan was going to be there. Except what had Eblis hoped to achieve?

"It was the only way to ensure the Elite would allow you unfettered access to their confidential gatherings." Eblis' eyes turned flinty and he swung back to face Gabe. "Dagan's threatened your life?"

"Turns out he was behind the pirates I tracked to Anzu who were working for the Guardians."

"Demons from Anzu are working with the *Guardians*?" Nate sounded outraged, and his wing curved around her in blatant possession.

This was moving too fast. And it appeared she was the only one out of her depth. "Who are the Guardians?"

"Misbegotten creatures from the dawn of time." Disgust dripped from each word. "They should've become extinct millennia ago."

"The pirates were part of an underground cult," Gabe said. "As far as I know, the pureblood demons weren't involved. Eblis, are you in contact with Kala, the Primus of Anzu? She's the only one who might have more information that Nate can use."

Eblis gave Gabe an assessing look. "I didn't know you were on speaking terms with Kala."

"I didn't know you mentored demon spawn on Earth," Gabe shot back.

"Demon bloods," Nate said, a dangerous edge to his voice. "Not spawn."

Silence thundered around the room as though Nate had just tipped the known world off its axis. Probably because, in the current company, he just had.

"No one should be judged purely on their bloodline," Rowan said. "Because in the end, blood *isn't* everything."

"Unless you're a demon." Eblis gave Bella a sardonic grin. "Kala's agreed to meet. In the meantime, we need to talk in private. Your office."

CHAPTER 25

NATE

Nate arrived in Isabella's office, and drew in a harsh breath. The antique furniture had been destroyed and the walls slashed. The Watchers had been here, too. Beside him, Isabella shuddered, but didn't say anything. She didn't have to. The stricken look on her face as she took in the malicious damage was more eloquent than any words.

He threaded his fingers through hers. To hell with whatever Eblis might think when he arrived. "We'll fix it, okay? We'll fix everything."

Even if he had to search to the ends of the Earth, he'd find replacements for every last antique she'd lost.

She squeezed his fingers. A tiny gesture. Strange how it meant so much. Before she could answer, the fucking demon appeared.

Eblis' lip curled in distaste when he caught sight of their entwined hands, but he appeared unmoved by the destruction. "I received word an immortal of renown was due at the Equinox ceremony. That's why you needed to ascend into the Elite, so you were in a position to find out more. I didn't anticipate Nate fucking things up."

Rage flared through him. "You knew Dagan was going to be there, and you still sent Isabella in without backup?"

Eblis unfurled his wings. "I didn't have a name. Could have been an archangel masquerading as a demon. Wouldn't be the first time."

"You received *word*? Who from?" Isabella demanded.

"I don't share the names of my operatives." He glanced around the wrecked room, as Isabella sucked in a sharp breath. Nate knew she'd never seen herself as a spy, but Eblis, the bastard, had just casually informed her that's all she was to him. "I'm going to make an exception in this case."

A male materialized beside Eblis.

"Zane?" Ice dripped from her voice, and the male's jaw tightened as he transferred his steely glare from Isabella to him. "Who else do you have undercover in the Watchers, Eblis?"

Eblis ignored her question. "The only reason I called you here, Zane, is so you don't attempt to eliminate Bella again. I'm assuming you and Nijah are responsible for the attack. As for who else I may or may not have in the Watchers, is none of your concern."

Zane. Now he knew why the male seemed vaguely familiar. He'd been trapped under the grandmother clock in Isabella's house.

Nate battened down his temper. Much as he wanted to smash his fist into Eblis' smug face, they still needed the demon's help. "Your ill-conceived machinations put Isabella's life in danger."

"Only because you gatecrashed the party, Archangel."

"Dagan told Nijah that you'd betrayed us to an archangel," Zane said to Isabella. "That you were the one who gave him safe passage into the temple. She won't rest until she has your blood."

"For the record, I didn't betray the Watchers to Nate."

"And I had no idea she was a member until I saw her there," Nate said. What a farce. Except it had been devastating for Isabella. "The real question is what the fuck are you doing, Eblis?"

"You hunt rogue demons. I hunt rogue archangels. What's your problem?"

Rogue *archangels*? "What are you talking about?"

"Really?" Derision dripped from the word. "You're that shocked by the notion? Typical."

Irritation sizzled through him. Eblis was deliberately goading him but he wasn't about to take the bait. Not when Isabella herself was half-demon.

Not all demons were the same.

"Even if I believe you," which he didn't, "infiltrating a cult of demon bloods is a bizarre place to search for rogue archangels."

"I don't give a shit what you believe," Eblis said. "My reasons are my own."

"Have you both finished?" There was a caustic edge in Isabella's voice. "Is that the reason we're here, so you can take swipes at each other?"

"I want to know why he thought it was okay to put you in danger." He knew he sounded belligerent but couldn't help it. She could have fucking *died*. "You weren't even safe from members of the Watchers."

"How the mighty are fallen," Eblis said, apropos of nothing. Nate glared at him, and the demon responded with a mocking grin. "You forget—or don't you know? Bella is a powerful demon blood. She doesn't need the cursed benevolence of an archangel to survive."

He did know that. It didn't make any difference. *I'm losing my fucking mind.*

"What now?" There was a thread of hostility in Zane's voice as he tossed Nate a glance of contempt. "Do I terminate Nijah?"

"Not yet," Eblis said. "She could still prove useful. Just keep her away from Bella."

It was a dismissal, and without another word, Zane vanished.

"Eblis," Isabella said.

The demon raised a finger. "Much as I'd love to chat," insincerity oozed from each word, "Kala is ready to see you. Do you know Eta Hyperium, Archangel?"

"I thought that hellhole had been swallowed up by its sun eons ago."

"No. I have an establishment on the last remaining habitable sector of land. Kala doesn't want to tarnish her reputation on her own planet by welcoming a random archangel into her domain." Eblis flashed his teeth in a mirthless smile. "Do you need help with the coordinates?"

"No."

Eblis shrugged and vanished.

"Eta Hyperium?" Isabella raised her eyebrows. "Another alien planet?"

"It's in the Sextans Galaxy. The mortals are technologically advanced but morally bankrupt. Remind me to take you somewhere civilized in Andromeda when all this is over." Inspiration struck. "I'll introduce you to Inanna. It's the least I can do."

He wasn't joking, either. But when all this was over, would they even see each other again?

"I'll hold you to that." She smiled, but there was a hint of sadness in her eyes. Disquiet gnawed the edges of his mind. As though he should say something profound, something that mattered.

Something that could change everything.

They needed to leave. He didn't know Kala personally, but she wouldn't appreciate being kept waiting, especially when she was bestowing a favor by seeing him.

"Ready?" His voice was gruff with all the things he didn't know how to say.

She hesitated. Despicable anticipation flared. Could she put into words what he couldn't?

"As I'll ever be," she said. What else was there? He crushed the hollow ache deep in his chest and offered her a careless grin.

How could an action he'd done a billion times in the past now be so damn hard?

"Hold tight."

He teleported to the only habitable sector on Eta Hyperium. The air was clogged from centuries of pollution and an ominous red glow from the lowering sky spread across the withered landscape.

"Not as impressive as your dinosaur planet." Isabella glanced around and shivered. "What kind of establishment would Eblis have *here*?"

He could take a good guess. Eta Hyperium had never been known for legitimate activities.

"Nothing good." He scrutinized the few buildings scattered across the dying land. He had no idea which one belonged to Eblis. It was galling, but maybe he should've got more information from the demon before they'd left Earth.

"That one." Isabella nodded to one of the buildings that was some distance from the closest sprawling spaceport. When he tossed her a frown she shrugged and gave him a half-smile. "I just asked him. Thought it would save some time searching."

As they approached the deceptively dilapidated-looking building, their hands untangled. He wasn't sure how. He flexed his fingers and ignored the loss that drilled through him. It was fucking crazy. He had to focus. Dagan had to be hunted down.

Eblis met them at the door and waved them through the sophisticated security system into a dark, incense-filled club. "Kala's pissed that you've kept her waiting." He sounded obnoxiously gleeful by the fact. "Way to impress, Archangel."

Nate didn't deign to answer as they reached a semi-secluded booth where a female demon lounged, her wings partially unfurled, hostility radiating from her.

"Primus Kala," Eblis said. "The Archangel Nathanael and Isabella Beauchamp."

"Primus," he said, but she ignored him, her gaze fixed on

Isabella. It was blatantly obvious she was scanning Isabella's aura. A glimmer of grim satisfaction spiked through him at the knowledge the demon wouldn't learn much, given Isabella's shields.

"You're from Earth?" Kala said, in one of the demon languages.

"Yes." Isabella didn't pause for a heartbeat, and her ability to understand Kala clearly impressed the demon.

"Don't you find it horrendous?"

"What, living on Earth?" Isabella sounded unsure as to what the demon meant. He kept his mouth shut only by pure force of will. Kala was ignoring him deliberately, expecting him to object to the breach of protocol. But she wasn't the only one who could play games.

"I meant living among humans." Her feathers shimmered. "I've heard how primitive they are. When Eblis told me of his pet, I didn't expect you to possess such power."

What the *fuck*? He was done with keeping silent.

"Isabella is not Eblis' pet."

Finally, Kala acknowledged his presence. But the malicious gleam in her eyes told him that he'd just fallen right into her trap.

"No," she said. "The human hybrid isn't, is she?"

Her implication was clear. He managed not to unfurl his own wings in response. This wasn't a fucking pissing contest. "Isabella," he said, enunciating each syllable, "is no one's pet."

"The Archangel Gabriel said you might be able to assist us." Isabella shot him a warning glance. If he weren't so pissed by Kala's comment, it would have been funny. A half-demon daring to silently reprove an archangel in public.

"What's happened to Gabriel? He's vanished off the radar."

"I don't know," Isabella said. "And even if I did, that's for him to share with you."

Eblis sat, a satisfied expression on his face. Isabella sat next to him.

"Park your ass, Archangel," Eblis said, daring him to refuse.

He'd much rather stand. Not least because he'd be smashed right up against Isabella and it would mess with his focus.

Curse the gods. If he didn't need information, there was no way he'd take Eblis' taunts in silence. He gritted his teeth and slid in beside her. The warmth of her body pressed against him, even though she shuffled along the seat to give him more room, and her scent was a tantalizing whisper in the air. He folded his arms and glowered at the demons. It appeared both Eblis and Kala were highly amused by the whole thing.

The sooner they got down to business, the faster he and Isabella could get out of here.

"I'm hunting a rogue demon. I've reason to believe he's the one behind the pirate cult Gabe uncovered on Anzu. Do you have any more information on them?"

Kala's knowing smile faded and her eyes flashed with annoyance. "I obliterated their cult on Anzu. And destroyed every last member throughout my entire Sector. Any pathetic remains are currently awaiting mortal justice, but that's out of my jurisdiction." She leaned across the table, her eyes never leaving his. "The pirates are filth, but I have some sympathy with their desire to see the rightful fall of archangels. However, no pureblood demon would support anything connected with the Guardians. You're looking in the wrong place, Nathanael."

The rightful fall of archangels. He clenched his fists. "I don't agree. I knew Dagan long ago, and this is exactly the kind of shit he'd do."

Her eyes narrowed. "Dagan?"

"Before your time. He's an original." Created by their mutual goddess. Kala, on the other hand, was demon born. If he had to hazard a guess, he'd say she was a pureblood second or third generation.

Kala shrugged. "You've given me no reason to assist you in your hunt. Where's your proof that Dagan is behind this cult?"

"He's been involved in a demon blood underground movement on Earth. When we confronted him, he admitted Gabe fucked up his most promising cell. Gabe and Dagan have never met since we left Ama-gi, which points to one thing. The cell he spoke of is the one Gabe uncovered on Anzu."

"Really." Derision dripped from the word. "You expect me to take your word on that?"

"It's the truth." He ground between his teeth. Why had he imagined that, because Gabe knew her, the demon would be reasonable? "I've no reason to lie."

"You're an archangel. Lying is embedded into your DNA."

Why the fuck had Kala agreed to meet with him if she'd no intention of helping?

"I was there," Isabella said. "I heard Dagan say it."

Kala leaned back and contemplated Isabella. He didn't like the speculative gleam in her eyes at all.

"You intrigue me," the demon said. "Here's my deal. I'll grant the archangel permission to go through the ruins of the pirates' nest, if you accompany me back to the capitol of Anzu."

He surged to his feet, looming over the table at Kala as his wings unfurled with outrage. "No fucking way. Keep your claws out of Isabella. She's not a pawn to be used in your negotiations."

"You speak for her, do you?" Kala stood, malevolence pulsing from her. "Are you her keeper, Nathanael?"

"I'm impressed," Eblis said to Isabella. "You've brought an archangel to his knees."

Nate gritted his teeth. Was it so fucking obvious he'd do anything to keep her out of danger? He should have left her someplace safe, far from the venomous machinations of demons. Except where the hell was safe anymore?

"That's enough." Isabella slammed her hand on the table. Eblis raised his eyebrows but didn't appear enraged that she was glaring at him. "Is this all the enmity between demons and archangels comes down to? Petty squabbling?"

Despite the danger crackling all around, he admired her

courage. Full blood demons weren't known to tolerate differences of opinion from those they considered beneath them. It was a well-known fact they possessed little respect for mixed bloodlines.

The pirates were proof of that. Their ancestors had been pureblood demons, but their heritage was now so diluted they were shunned by the upper echelons of their own race.

"What do you *do* on Earth?" Kala sounded fascinated. "Is it difficult to blend in with the rabble?"

"No. I'm half human."

"Fortunately, your demon blood is dominant."

With difficulty, Nate folded his wings and hauled his temper into line. It didn't sit well with him, but there was another direction he could take with the demon. "Primus Kala, Dagan has threatened Isabella. I need to find him."

He sent a silent appeal to Isabella. *Don't disagree with me.* Why hadn't he initiated telepathic contact between them before they'd come here?

"Isabella would remain safe within *my* domain."

Caution vanished. "What's your real interest in her? And don't give me any bullshit about keeping her safe. Why would you care about that?"

"Here's my deal." Isabella didn't stand or raise her voice, but she commanded all their attention anyway. "I've pledged to stay by Nate's side until we've found Dagan. If you grant us the help we've requested, when Dagan is dealt with, I'll come with you to the capitol of Anzu."

"The hell you will." There was no fucking way he'd allow her to go to Kala's planet alone. "You don't need to make any kind of deal with the demon."

Isabella's smile was oddly sad. "The truth is, I'd like to see how that half of my heritage lives, Nate. It's not a permanent arrangement. I have a life on Earth." She glanced at Kala, who shrugged.

"Sure. The choice is yours. But you might not want to go back there when you see what you're missing."

He kept his mouth shut. There was nothing more to say and it wasn't his business. But a dull ache gripped him deep inside. The mission they'd set themselves had not yet finished.

But Isabella had already moved on.

He exhaled a long breath. It didn't matter if she stayed on Earth or Anzu. When this was over, when he knew she was safe, they'd never see each other again. He was an archangel. She was half-demon. There was no getting away from the truth. She'd never had a family until she had found the Watchers.

Millennia ago, he'd almost destroyed his family. And because of her involvement with him, when the Watchers had seen them together in the temple, Isabella had all but lost hers.

She was safer without him.

"Do we have a deal?" Isabella asked.

"Very well." Kala cast a critical glance his way. "You have my permission to visit the pirates' nest. Not that you'll find anything of use." She gave him the location. "You'll be safe from my guards as long as you're with Isabella."

Her mocking taunt echoed in his ears as he took Isabella's hand and got them out of there.

CHAPTER 26

BELLA

The nest was underground, the air was bad, and a massive hole gaped in the ceiling, revealing a deep turquoise sky. She glanced at Nate, and his gaze captured hers. If it wasn't for the fact hers and Gabe's lives were on the line, she almost wished they'd never find Dagan, just so they could continue to search for him, together.

"Guess Kala forgot to tell us she'd nuked the place." His voice was sardonic. "We'll be lucky to find a trace of DNA in this wreckage, never mind anything else."

"I don't understand why Gabe thought she'd help. How do they know each other?"

He shrugged. "No idea."

It was hardly the time to ask, but she might not get another chance. "Do you know Eblis well?"

"I barely know him at all. We met a few times, millennia ago. He didn't get in my way, I didn't get in his."

What had she expected? That Nate could provide her with an in-depth analysis of Eblis, so she could somehow piece together his real motives in recruiting her, all those years ago?

"This is," she hesitated. Would Nate think she was being

ridiculous? Yet who else could she talk to of such things? "It's a lot to wrap my head around. Demons and archangels are fabled enemies. And when I joined the Watchers, the histories they shared just confirmed those tales. But you all work together."

"I wouldn't go that far." His voice was dry. "There's no love lost between us."

"But Gabe trusted Eblis enough to let him come to his home. I didn't expect that."

Nate's fingers tightened around hers. "I don't have an answer. All I know is demons *can't* be trusted."

He was so adamant. Yet he'd trusted her enough to take her to Gabe, who had mysteriously lost his immortality, and Azrael, whose powers were as disabled as his wing. Could he even see the contradiction?

"But I'm half-demon, Nate."

What did she want from him? A passionate declaration that he didn't care about her heritage, that he wanted them to at least try and forge a future together?

It was crazy. For so many reasons. But mainly because she wanted him to accept the immortal side of her heritage. Not discount it.

"You're half-human." There was an edge in his voice and his wings unfurled in all their glory, but he didn't let go of her hand. "You have integrity."

She couldn't work out if she was touched or exasperated by his comment. It was a backhanded compliment whichever way she looked at it. "Not all humans are trustworthy. And why shouldn't demons have integrity?"

Why were they even having this conversation? Did she hope to change his mind?

Demons and archangels were enemies. It was hardwired into their very existence. This was the history she'd learned from the Watchers. It was even woven through the hidden texts she'd read of the Archangel Nathanael. The buried history, which showed he never had indiscriminately hunted every demon blood he discovered.

Except that fundamental tenet of the legendary enmity between their races wasn't true. Eblis and Gabe had a bond she didn't understand but couldn't deny. And Kala, a powerful demon who appeared to control an entire sector of a galaxy, had seen them on the strength of her relationship with Gabe.

Maybe Gabe was the anomaly here. But she wasn't convinced. Her view of archangels had been warped for years, until she'd met Nate. And discovered what he was really like. He wasn't an arrogant hunter of innocents, and he wasn't blinded by prejudice.

Except when it came to demons.

He exhaled an impatient breath and swept a condemning glance around the debris. "There's nothing here that will lead us to Dagan."

And there it was. Gently she tugged on his hand until he faced her, a frown slashing his brow.

"Why are you hunting Dagan?"

He didn't look at her. "You know why. He threatened you."

"No." She wouldn't be deflected. Not this time. "You were searching for him before you even met me. Why are you really after him, Nate?"

His jaw tightened. "I knew him once. Long ago."

She already knew that, but the conversation at Gabe's flickered through her mind, presenting a possible answer. "When he masqueraded as a demigod in Ama-gi?"

"Yeah." He ground the word between his teeth. Leashed rage thudded between them. What wasn't he telling her? There had to be more than the fact Dagan had lied about his heritage. Nate wasn't that shallow.

"What did he do that was so bad?"

Tension spiked from him, fed the rage, a lethal cocktail that caused a shiver to race over her skin. Instinctively, she took his other hand, facing him, willing him to share. She didn't even know why it was so important. Only that it was.

"He betrayed us all." The confession sounded as though it had been torn from the bowels of hell itself. "And everyone archangels loved in Ama-gi were destroyed."

That was bad. Worse than she'd imagined. "How did you find out who he really was?"

Silence grew heavy in the air, a suffocating presence that closed in on her like a physical entity. He wasn't going to confide. It shouldn't hurt. But it rammed home to her that despite his determination to protect her, when it came to anything deeper, the connection just didn't exist.

And then he spoke, the words grinding from him as though they were dredged from the bottom of his soul.

"I always knew what he was."

It was the last thing she'd expected him to say and confusion spiked through her mind. What had she missed?

"You knew he was a demon in Ama-gi? But how? Did you see through his masquerade?"

His grip on her hands tightened. She doubted he was even aware of it.

"I knew he wasn't a demigod," he said through clenched teeth, "because I was the one who suggested he conceal his true nature."

Nate

Nate glared into Isabella's beautiful blue eyes, bracing for her contempt. It was nothing less than he deserved. Why the fuck had he said anything at all?

It was something he'd never spoken of. His deception, which had seemed so minor at the time, had led to the destruction of the precious Nephilim.

Except no one had ever asked him such a thing before. Why would they? Only he had known who Dagan was. Or what he had done. But her questioning gaze had burned into his soul. Although he'd never lied to her, he'd been economical with the truth, but that ended right now. Even if it ripped him apart.

"I don't understand." There was no condemnation in her voice. But then, she didn't know the full extent of his guilt. *And she never will.* He could barely live with the knowledge himself. There was no way he wanted the magnitude of his sin reflected in her eyes every time he looked at her. And now, it wasn't only that he was responsible for the deaths of the Nephilim. A century ago, he'd also come close to destroying Isabella's chosen family. "Why would you do that?"

Because he sucked me into his deception.

But that wasn't true. Dagan had had no need to weave a web of lies, because Nate had been only too willing to subvert the status quo. He just hadn't wanted to admit it, even to himself. Even after all these eons.

There's no need to respond.

Release her hands. Turn away.

He remained rooted to the spot. Ensnared by her gaze. Bewitched by her beauty.

Deluding himself once again. Her eyes or her face or the sound of her voice weren't the reasons why he couldn't get her out of his mind.

He was an archangel, answerable to no one. Least of all a half demon. He owed her nothing. Yet her very existence captivated the essence of his soul, and to deny her the truth would corrode whatever was left of his honor.

"He was injured and stranded on Earth." Nate had believed his tale of being hunted by radicals from the Demonic High Council and it had fed into his own streak of rebellion against the dictates of his goddess. But for all he knew, Dagan had been a spy from the Council itself. The way he'd been so easily used sickened him. "I healed him."

She didn't answer right away, but her gaze never wavered

from his. He should have kept his mouth shut. There was no way to change the past. It was done. But in one misguided comment he'd risked changing Isabella's belief in him.

If it weren't so fucked up, he'd appreciate the irony. He wanted her good opinion. Yet here he was, spilling his guts about the most despicable thing he'd ever done.

Giving his trust to a demon.

Something he'd vowed never to do again. And the universe, the screwed-up bitch that she was, had led him to Isabella. His unlikely confessor. *End this now.* It wasn't too late. She need never know the part he had played in the devastation that had ravaged Earth.

"You took him to Ama-gi." It wasn't a question and there was no condemnation in her words but the consequences of that one action had condemned him long ago. "Where he betrayed you. And that's why you can't trust those with demon blood."

He let out a bitter laugh, then silently cursed when Isabella flinched as though he'd struck her. She was right, but there was so much more to it.

Dagan wasn't the only demon he'd trusted. Because it didn't matter how hard he'd fought against it, she—a powerful demon blood— had managed to secure his trust.

And so much more. Even if he could never find the words to tell her.

"If all he'd done was betrayed the friendship I thought we had, I'd have forgotten him long ago. My ego's not that fragile." He attempted to give her a mocking grin, anything to lighten the darkness that had descended around her but failed. Did he really think by voicing his deadly error of judgment he could cleanse his tarnished soul?

All he'd do was prove how despicable demons could be. Truth was, he didn't want to be the one to shatter any illusions she had about her race. It wasn't her fault. He wouldn't be the one to burden her with the truth of what had really happened eleven thousand years ago.

Or confess his part in it. Even if the need to unburden his guilt was eating him alive.

It was nothing less than he deserved.

"What did he do, Nate?"

"It doesn't matter." He tore his gaze from her and glared around the chamber. But he didn't see the ruins. He saw the scorched Earth, the floods, and the deaths of the beloved Nephilim.

"Yes, it does. It's the reason you're hunting him. It's why you can't let go of the past."

"You don't need to know the reasons."

She pulled her hand free and pressed her palm over his heart. Did she know she was destroying him, piece by piece, from the inside out?

"Tell me." Her voice was gentle, and it was his undoing.

She'd risked her life for him. Almost killed herself trying to free him. He owed her the truth.

"My only excuse is I was young." No. Why was he still lying to himself? Worse, why was he trying to deceive Isabella? His sin had nothing to do with his youth. He covered her hand, but the pressure against his heart didn't ease the pain. It reinforced the memories of everything archangels had lost.

Because of him.

His sigh raked through his chest. "I liked him. Demons had been banished from Earth and I enjoyed the subterfuge of going against the word of our goddess."

Her smile was so sad it clawed a wretched talon through his heart. But she didn't say anything.

"No one questioned his heritage. For decades, we hung out together. Unsurprisingly, he harbored a hatred for our goddess I hadn't encountered before, but I found it intriguing. The things he told me, from when demons had lived in Ama-gi and been the favored ones, didn't align to the history she had shared with us."

He sucked in a harsh breath. It had been a revelation, to discover how easily their goddess had turned on her first children. And while he had no doubt Dagan had lied and embellished the truth to suit his own purposes, their goddess' betrayal of the demon race had been savage.

At the time he'd been so certain that archangels were above her wrath. How wrong he had been.

"History's always written by the victors," Isabella whispered, no censure in her voice. "I just never realized it had been written by the goddess."

The goddess had played her part. But if not for him, she would never have discovered the truth of the archangels.

"I told him things." The confession burned his throat, corroded his tongue. "Things that should never have been shared, least of all with a demon. I confided our plan in him, and by so doing, condemned our precious Nephilim."

CHAPTER 27

BELLA

The agony of ages threaded through each word, and Nate's eyes were filled with bleak despair. There was nothing Bella could do, nothing she could say, to ease his pain. A pain she had once imagined a cursed archangel could never feel.

But Nate was nothing like the hunter of demons she'd despised for so many years. The tome in the Forbidden Archives on the Archangel Nathanael began with a great betrayal between him and the last, unnamed, demon in their lost paradise. She hadn't managed to read much of the ancient volume, but she'd read enough.

That great battle had been the catalyst for the devastation that had befallen Earth, and the beginning of Nathanael's quest.

He was a demon hunter, yes. But not the cruel slayer of every demon blood descendant he encountered, as all new recruits were taught. The truth hadn't been lost. It had always been known by the Elite.

And she had known it too, deep in her heart, from the moment she'd discovered who he really was.

"Nate." She tugged his hand to her lips and kissed his knuckles. He was on the precipice of sharing what had really happened

253

so many millennia ago. Not merely an eyewitness to events or an unreliable chronicler of history. But the leading player.

And now, when she was so close to discovering the truth, she wasn't sure she could bear to hear it.

"I've never spoken of this before." His voice was raw, as though each word had been mercilessly hacked from the fabric of his existence. "Tell me to stop, Isabella."

His dark eyes consumed her, torment and despair a suffocating cloak around him. Why hadn't she noticed the ache behind his smile before? Was it because, even after she got to know him, she'd still been so prejudiced against his race that she couldn't fathom such a thing?

He'd given her an out. She could take it.

But she'd never been a coward. There was a reason they were here, now. A reason why he needed to share what had happened during Ama-gi's twilight hours.

"What did you tell him?' she whispered.

He drew in a jagged breath, and a shudder wracked his big body. It was clear a battle raged within, and she pressed his fist against her cheek.

I'm here. A foolish gesture. But it was all she could offer him.

Finally, he spoke. "Ama-gi was a civilization built on mathematics and science. In many ways they were more advanced than humans are now, in the twenty-first century. They knew when the celestial body they'd been tracking for centuries passed through our solar system, it would devastate life on Earth."

She knew the stories. Of how archangels had fled when Earth reset her clock. Over the last few days, when everything she'd believed had been twisted beyond recognition, she'd doubted the truth of it all.

But Nate had been there.

It had happened.

A sick sensation gripped her stomach. He'd mentioned the Nephilim. The offspring of archangels and mortals, who had all perished during the so-called Cleansing. Until now, she hadn't given much thought to them, except to despise the archangels for having left them behind.

The raw pain in his eyes told her that wasn't true.

What had Dagan done?

Nate remained silent. Was he waiting for her to ask him the question?

"What did you tell him?"

He ground his jaw, a deadly emotion flickering across his features. "We never had any intention of allowing nature to take her course. Not when it came to the lives of our beloved Nephilim. When the time came, we planned to save them, and our lovers. I made the mistake of thinking Dagan was on our side. That his thirst for vengeance was directed solely at our goddess. I shared our plans with him. And he betrayed us to her."

She wasn't to blame, but acidic guilt ate through her. This was why he despised the demon race. The archangels hadn't abandoned their half mortal children. Somehow, Dagan had prevented them from saving the Nephilim.

"I'm sorry." How inadequate, but she needed him to know that at last she understood his personal animosity against her race. "His actions were despicable."

"His actions?" Nate gazed at her as though he didn't understand what she meant. "Yes. They were. But the fault is mine for taking him to Ama-gi and perpetrating the lie of his origins."

"You weren't to know Dagan would double-cross you, Nate. You were just trying to help him."

"A demon. The one race we'd been forbidden to interact with. If I'd turned my back on him as soon as I discovered what he was, no one would have found out about our plans."

"Listen to me." She pulled her hands free and cradled his jaw. This tough, warrior, archangel who carried a guilt that wasn't his to bear. "You're not responsible for the actions of anyone else. Do you hear me? Dagan deceived you for his own purposes."

"I vowed to hunt him down and exact retribution, no matter how long it took." There was a fanatical gleam in his eyes. Had he even heard her? "But he disappeared without trace. Not one of the rogues I encountered knew where he was, and as the centuries passed, they didn't even know his name."

A terrible, wondrous, realization dawned. "You could have fought him in the mountains. But you let him go. Because of me."

His gaze sharpened, boring into her like a laser. "The outcome was too unpredictable. I wouldn't put you in danger."

"I'm the reason you lost your chance for retribution."

"He's surfaced again. I'll find him."

Even if it took another eleven thousand years? Yet he wasn't directing any justifiable frustration her way, even though they both knew that, but for her, Nate and Dagan would have fought to a bloodied end in the sacred library.

Except that wasn't true. Dagan had possessed an unfair advantage. He could have destroyed Nate in the blink of an eye.

An icy shiver crawled over her arms. She could so easily have lost him.

"We will." She dropped her hands to his broad shoulders and warmth unfurled deep inside when he encircled her waist, linking his fingers together against the small of her back. She'd hunt Dagan into the depths of hell, if it helped Nate to achieve the vengeance he needed. She just hoped it would assuage his misplaced guilt.

There was still something she couldn't work out, though. The enigmatic comment he'd made on the beautiful dinosaur planet haunted her.

There wasn't much left of the Earth we'd known once we escaped

Had Dagan somehow disabled all the archangels? She couldn't imagine such a thing could be possible, but what else could Nate have meant?

"How did he imprison you all?"

"Dagan didn't imprison us." Nate's beautiful, aristocratic

features hardened. "He whispered into the humans' ears. Spread discontent and anger that we—the archangels—had chosen who would live and who would die. His final act before leaving Earth was to confront our goddess and tell her of our unforgiveable sin. He knew it was the one thing she would never tolerate."

"Your unforgiveable sin?" The Watchers indoctrination espoused a multitude of sins that archangels were guilty of. But she no longer believed in their propaganda.

"She created archangels to worship her, to love only her. She had no idea how many had fallen for mortals on Earth. How they waited for their beloved to be reborn, life after life. But even if she'd decided to turn a blind eye to that, she'd never forgive the reality of the Nephilim."

"The goddess imprisoned you?" Horror at what he was telling her shivered across her skin. She should have guessed. Only an immortal from the Alpha Pantheon, the ancestors of every minor god and goddess who now existed across the entire universe, could possibly have possessed the power to do such a thing. "And abandoned the Nephilim on Earth?"

"I was one of the last to answer her call. I saw the start of the uprisings but even then, I didn't realize her true motives." He clenched his jaw, as though he'd been about to say more but had changed his mind.

What more could there be? He'd shattered any remaining thread of illusion she'd held about the corrupted morality of archangels.

"And when you managed to escape her prison, it was too late."

"We destroyed her prison." Bitter satisfaction painted each word. "The planet Nibiru where we'd been created. Her laboratory. By then, Earth was unrecognizable, the Nephilim killed, and the mortal population decimated."

The legacy of the catastrophic events had lived on, embedded in myths and legends, an unheeded warning to future generations. But the truth had still been perverted.

Not only by humanity. Even Nate couldn't separate his own distorted convictions from the unvarnished facts.

"Dagan betrayed you," she clarified, not just for herself but to make him see it, too. "And the goddess prevented you from saving the children. You aren't the guilty one here, Nate."

Self-loathing distorted his features. "I was the one who told him of the plan. If I hadn't, we would have taken them all to Nibiru."

"And she would've be fine with that?"

"It would have been too late for her to do anything about it."

"Do you really believe that?" She took his hands and squeezed his fingers. "You might have saved them from the natural disaster. But what about afterwards? Even if Dagan hadn't told her about the Nephilim, she would have found out about them, when they went to Nibiru. If she hated their existence so much, do you think she would have really allowed them to survive?"

For the first time, uncertainty flashed over his face. "We could have protected them."

"Maybe. But you're talking about one of the Alpha Goddesses and she managed to incarcerate all the archangels. That's some incredible power, Nate. If she went to all that trouble to keep you from saving the Nephilim, I can't see how she would have behaved any differently toward them, no matter when she found out about them."

Silence echoed between them. Obviously, he had once known the goddess and she never had. But her logic was sound.

Slowly he exhaled a long breath. Was it her imagination or did some of the tension ease from his body? "You could be right." He sounded reluctant to admit it. "But we'll never know, will we?"

She was convinced she was right, but he had a point. "Nate." She gave his hands a little shake. "Humanity survived. And so did the Nephilim. Archangels were wrong when they thought they all perished. But Dagan knew. And the question is—why was he using the pirates on Anzu to hunt them down for their blood?"

CHAPTER 28

NATE

Isabella's question drilled through his mind, wrenching him from ancient memories and into a present nightmare. He'd been so caught up in hunting Dagan because of the past, he'd overlooked what had been right in front of his nose. Disgust curdled his gut. "No. The real question is why is he working with the Guardians?"

"I don't know. Are they very powerful?"

Were they? He knew next to nothing about them, except for the fact their race had been ancient even before the Alpha Pantheon had come into existence. "They live in the shadows of the universe. And hate any living thing that is different from themselves. Which is basically the entirety of creation."

"There's no mention of them in the Watchers history."

Frustration gnawed through him and he slung a glance around the ruined pirates' nest. "We should sift through this rubble. There might be something we can use."

"Since we're here." She gave him a faint smile. It was obvious she held out as much hope as he did of finding anything useful.

They split up and he prowled the underground chamber. The

demons had done a good job of destroying every trace of the pirates' existence. Charred remains of their technology were scattered across the floor and when he flattened his hand on the wall, there was no lingering sense of who had once inhabited the place.

He crouched and picked up a mangled piece of hardware. Had Kala downloaded the information before destroying all the evidence?

"Nate."

He stood and swung around. Isabella was across the room, looking at whatever had caught her attention. "What have you found?"

"I don't know. It's—unnatural." She backed away, her focus still on something he couldn't see.

He was by her side in an instant. And then had to forcibly stop himself from recoiling.

A ribbon of the Guardians dark atmosphere floated in midair.

"It's like it's trying to escape something." She sounded unnerved. "But there's nothing there."

Gingerly, he circled the phenomenon. Her description was apt. As though an invisible door had slammed shut, trapping a fragment of atmosphere in this underground chamber.

"It's from the Guardians' domain, within the Dark Matter. But it's not trying to escape. It's trying to return there."

She shuddered. "There's something not right about it."

He knew exactly what she meant. "It's poison to archangels. Maybe even to demons."

"What does it mean?" She turned to look at him. "Is there a gateway to their world from here?"

If there was, he sure as hell didn't want to open it.

"It's proof the Guardians have been here." But had Dagan?

"We should capture it."

He eyed the malevolent darkness, that continued to ripple in a nonexistent breeze. They already had samples that were being examined. There was no need for any more.

Except it was the only damn thing they'd found here.

"Agreed. I don't suppose you have anything we can collect it in?"

"Sorry. I left all my hazardous chemical containers at home."

He grinned, before he recalled how the Watchers had destroyed her home. Nijah had yet to pay for that. And so would Zane, even if he was working for Eblis.

"I'll find something. Will you be okay here for a few seconds?"

He knew she would be. But he had to ask. Just because.

"I'll be fine." She smiled and pushed her hands into the pockets of her jeans. How could two such simple gestures be so mesmerizing?

"Before I go." He went up to her and cradled her face. "May I initiate a telepathic connection?"

She sighed. "That's the most romantic thing anyone's ever asked me."

Despite where they were, he laughed. "Yeah, I have my moments."

"No, seriously. I didn't know it was a thing. Eblis never asked and I've always hidden my telepathic abilities from other demon bloods."

"What can I say? You need to get out more," he said, before creating a telepathic connection with the delicate threads of her mind.

Sure you'll be okay? He didn't need to double-check. He just wanted to hear her voice in his mind.

Don't worry. I'll scream your name if I need any help.

He was still smiling seconds later when he rematerialized next to her. She hadn't moved.

"This should hold it." He'd acquired a high-grade medical phial from one of the premiere hospitals in Andromeda. As

Isabella nodded in approval, he pulled on his leather gloves. At least they'd give him some protection against the alien substance.

Isabella attempted to take the phial from him. When he held it out of her reach, she gave an exasperated sigh. "I'm only half-demon, remember? This stuff won't affect me as badly as it might affect you."

That might be true, but he still wasn't going to risk it. "Let's just get this done. I've more questions I want to ask Kala."

"That's assuming she'd even see you again. I could ask her when I go to the capitol."

He clamped his jaw shut before he told her there was no fucking way she was going to the capitol. At least, not without him. Instead, he concentrated on easing the alien atmosphere into the phial. It shouldn't be this hard. But despite fierce concentration, his hand shook and sweat prickled his skin.

Isabella wrapped her hand around his, steadying his grip, until the last wisp had been captured. He sealed the phial and let out a harsh breath. "That was fun."

She took it from him before he could stop her, and held it up, scrutinizing the contents.

"I can still feel its affect, even through the glass."

"Here, give it to me."

She turned and then stiffened. "Zane just contacted me. Dagan's back at the mountain with Nijah."

Fire pumped through his veins. "I'll take you to Gabe's. You'll be safe there."

She shoved the phial into her pocket and grabbed his hand. "We're going to the mountain. Your powers will work in the atrium. It's only when you go inside that they'll be suppressed."

He hesitated for only a fraction of a second. It was long enough for him to imagine every possible, horrifying outcome that involved her. But in the end, the choice had already been made.

"Stay out of his way," he warned. And teleported them both to the entrance of the atrium in Inanna's former temple.

Dark anticipation throbbed through his blood. This was it. After millennia of searching, he was finally about to confront the demon who'd betrayed his people.

Dusk had fallen and swathes of red and deep purple painted the sky. On the raised platform where he'd witnessed Isabella conducting the initiation ritual, stood Dagan and Nijah.

Zane emerged from the shadows that led into the heart of the mountain, his focus on Isabella. "Eblis should be informed."

"No." He released Isabella's hand and stepped forward. "Dagan is mine."

He strode along the aisle to the platform, where Dagan faced Nijah. Deep in discussion, neither of them appeared to realize they were no longer alone.

Suited him.

Without warning, Nijah shot into the air, clutching her throat, her eyes bulging in terror. With a casual flick of his hand Dagan catapulted Nijah across the atrium and she smashed into the wall behind Nate.

Even when the demon didn't know he had an audience, he was fucking dramatic.

As Dagan followed the progress of his victim, he caught sight of Nate, and a mocking grin spread across his face. "Hey, Nate. I knew you'd be back."

Nate drew his sword. It wasn't immortal forged, but in the two thousand years since he'd acquired it from a renown warrior race in the heart of the Andromeda Galaxy, it had served him well.

"Then you know why I'm here."

Dagan leaped from the platform, his wings outspread, and landed two sword lengths from Nate. "Unfinished business." With a flourish, Dagan drew his own sword. "Very well, if it will help appease your conscience."

"Fuck my conscience. This is vengeance for the Nephilim."

Bella

Keeping her back to the wall, and eyes on Nate, Bella followed Zane to where the broken body of Nijah slumped. Blood matted her hair and streaked her face, and her arm was a mess. Bella swallowed at the sight of Nijah's snapped humerus that poked through the shredded flesh.

"I didn't betray our demon lord." Nijah's hoarse whisper sent shivers along her arms. Zane crouched by Nijah's side, his face impassive. "I've served him faithfully for more than two hundred years, since the day he revealed that my destiny was to lead the Watchers. I should have entrusted you with the truth, Zane." Her glazed eyes caught sight of Bella and her body convulsed. "This is all your doing, traitor."

Zane placed his hand on Nijah's forehead. "Be still."

She exhaled a ragged breath. "Yes. Heal me so I can avenge this treachery."

Shit. Bella backed up a couple of steps, her skin prickling. Eblis might have told Zane she wasn't to be harmed, but that didn't mean he'd obey.

Before she got the chance to strike, Nijah stiffened. The whites of her eyes glowed crimson and her lips peeled back revealing her teeth before her head tipped to the side. Zane stood and their gazes clashed over the lifeless body of their former leader. He had picked his side.

"I take it you're staying." His voice was grim. "Do we even know who we're fighting for anymore?"

She glanced at Nate. There were no fireballs or lightning bolts illuminating the scene, but silver sparks showered him and Dagan as their swords clashed. The echoes rasped around the atrium and the air hissed with unfettered menace.

Her heart clenched. Dagan wielded the sword she'd been

searching for. The one that could mortally injure an archangel and most likely destroy one, too.

For so long she had wanted the Archangel Nathanael to pay for the wrongs he'd inflicted on her hybrid race. But she was the one who'd been wrong about him.

Terror that her wish might be granted lodged in her throat. *Stop.* She refused to think of it.

Nate was a feared warrior. He wouldn't succumb.

But Dagan was a formidable match for him.

The clash of forged steel rang in the air as Nate countered the deadly blow that Dagan had struck. The demon's face twisted in a maniacal grin as he was forced to step back to avoid the sweep of Nate's counterattack.

Two immortals, fighting a remorseless battle reminiscent of Dark Age knights. Something that, since meeting Nate, she'd never wanted to witness. Except in place of medieval armor, their wings were unfurled, giving flight to their leaps across the stone floor and walls.

It was magnificent. Breathtaking.

Terrifying.

Armor. Realization struck.

"He's wearing his armor." And was slowly, but surely, maneuvering them both to the mountain entrance. And once inside, while Nate wouldn't be able to use his powers, Dagan would. She grabbed Zane's arm. "Dagan's armor neutralizes the effect of the mountain."

Forcing herself to remain calm, she opened her mind to Nate.

Watch your back. Dagan's pushing you into the mountain.

Don't worry about me. I know what he's doing. Keep out of danger.

Of course he'd been aware. She dragged her gaze away as Zane stepped away from her, hugging the shadows of the wall. His face was set in a hardened mask as he moved with agile ease. She opened a telepathic link with him.

Zane. What are you doing?

Closing the gate.

It could only be closed manually and would prevent Nate from being backed into the mountain. Except Nate would never allow such a thing to happen.

But Zane didn't know that.

It's okay. You don't—

Her words froze as Dagan tossed a dagger in Zane's direction. It glinted silver as it sped through the air. She sucked in sharp breath. Zane didn't stand a chance.

She flung every particle of telekinetic energy she possessed at the dagger. Pain spiked through her head as she focused on forcing it from its trajectory. But it was powered by a full blood demon, and instead of smashing into the wall as she'd intended, the dagger barely swerved.

It embedded in Zane's shoulder, catapulting him to the floor. At least it had missed his brain. Dagan smirked and reached for a second dagger before Nate shoulder charged him, sending the demon sprawling. Panic caught in her throat as Dagan rolled on the ground and sprang to his feet several yards from where he'd fallen. Nate charged a second time, sword in front of him.

Zane let out a soft groan and Bella ran toward him and crouched by his side. "You need to stay out of sight."

Zane gritted his teeth before inhaling a ragged breath. "I assume I owe you my life. Dagan wouldn't have missed."

"Do you want me to pull it out?"

"Leave it. I'll do it." He cast a stony glance at the battling immortals. "What the fuck are they doing? They can't kill each other unless one of them lets down their guard. No chance of that."

But it could happen. Panic flared and Bella shook her head. She couldn't let Nate get hurt.

"There must be something I can do to distract Dagan's attention."

"Sure. If you want him to melt your brain."

"He won't if he doesn't know I'm doing anything." She scanned the area, drew in a deep breath, and ran to the nearest column. Heart banging, she flattened her back against the cool marble before risking a quick glance at the oblivious immortals. She couldn't afford for Dagan to see her. She dropped into a crouch and inched forward, every strike of the swords causing an eerie glow to illuminate the enemies.

Dagan's armor glinted in the light and an idea glimmered. If she loosened the buckled straps around his vambrace, and then ripped it off at the right moment, it might be just enough to work.

She focused all her energy on the buckles. Her head throbbed and mouth dried, and her entire body shook with the effort.

But it was working. In her mind's eye, they loosened.

Don't let go.

Seconds stretched into eternity. Sweat dripped from her temples.

So close. Almost there.

It was done. She released the pressure that was keeping the vambrace molded to his forearm, and the armor hurtled across the atrium. For a split-second Dagan stumbled, his attention fractured, and Nate attacked, whipping his sword beneath the guard, and twisting it from the demon's grasp. The immortal forged sword flew from Dagan's hand and Nate caught it, aiming the tip of both blades at the demon's throat.

Instantly, an invisible fist closed around her own throat. She gasped and her hands flew to her neck, trying to release the pressure. Nothing. She tried to scream but her voice was frozen as she was unceremoniously dragged across the floor to Dagan's side where he suspended her on her toes.

"Release Isabella." Nate's voice was low and deadly. In her mind he spoke.

Can you breathe?

She hitched in a fractured shred of oxygen.

Yes.

"The hybrid interfered. That's against the rules."

"We have rules?" Scorn dripped from Nate's voice. "Isabella has nothing to do with us. Let her go."

"Ever feel like history's repeating itself?" He flashed her a grin. "I knew you'd allow him to escape the dungeon. Thank you for being so predictable."

She tried to respond, but all she could manage was a strangled gurgle.

"You had no way of knowing that. Is this why you returned here tonight? To see if I was still imprisoned?"

"The bond between you is so amusing. It's the only reason I allowed her to live."

"You're a perverted bastard."

"I know. And you're the only one who ever had the balls to tell me to my face. Frequently."

Why was Dagan reminiscing about the past? He sounded as though he was enjoying this exchange.

"I should have left Maahes' knife in your neck."

"No. You should have come with me, Nate. You know it."

Nate bared his teeth. "You stabbed me in the back."

Dagan shrugged, and his grip on her relaxed a fraction. Hastily, she sucked in more oxygen and the fog in her mind faded. She tried to teleport out of his grip and failed. Dagan had bound her power.

"It wasn't personal. I was handed the key to avenge my race. What would you have done?"

"It was the sole reason you came to Earth."

"I didn't lie to you that day. I was being hunted by the Council. Earth just so happened to be the planet I ended up on. It was dumb luck when I met you and found passage back to Ama-gi. The birthright of demons."

"It was our goddess who cast you out. Not archangels."

"And my actions ensured she lost her precious archangels for all time." A trace of bitterness seeped into each word. "There was no way archangels would forgive her for her final, ultimate betrayal."

The destruction of the beloved Nephilim. But Dagan had lived in Ama-gi. He must have known the archangels' half-human children. Yet he'd still gone ahead with his egotistic plans for vengeance. It was reckless, but she couldn't stay silent any longer.

"Didn't you care at all about the loss of the Nephilim?" she said, her throat ragged from where he held her.

"The abominations of nature?" His teeth flashed in a mirthless smile. "Hybrids. Like you. I cared nothing for them. Their demise was merely a means to an end, and the humans were collateral damage. And the best part? It was all down to a natural disaster."

"If that's true, why are you helping the Guardians to hunt down forgotten descendants of archangels for their blood?"

"Feisty little thing, isn't she?" Dagan returned his attention to Nate.

"The question stands," Nate said through his teeth.

Dagan gave a dramatic sigh. "Everyone needs a hobby, right? I like being worshipped on countless worlds. The one who will lead the mindless rabble back to their rightful place in paradise. My underground network is spectacular. Kala might have cut off one head, but there are a dozen more in her Sector that she doesn't have a clue about. The Guardians approached me, by the way. I'd no idea any Nephilim had survived. But since archangels had abandoned them, hunting them down gave the believers another avenue where they could prove their devotion to me."

"But what about the Watchers? We've never worshipped you and we sure as hell don't hunt Nephilim for you."

"Nijah had been working on her most trusted of Elites for decades. Sounding them out. Evaluating their loyalty to her before she moved forward to the next stage of initiating them into my cult." He rolled his eyes, clearly unimpressed by Nijah's methods. "Talk about pandering to the ignorant. In the end, she was less than fucking useless."

"And what of the vampire, Sakarbaal?" Nate demanded.

"That bloodsucker was a twisted fucker." Was that a thread of admiration in his voice? "He was obsessed with destroying Az. Did you know Sakarbaal had a side hustle going on with the Guardians? Something to do with transcending dimensions. Fascinating. In exchange for information on what those perverted little shits were up to, I offered him custodianship of the sword."

"So he could destroy Az?"

Dagan shrugged. "To be fair, I didn't think he stood a chance against an archangel. Az must have really slacked off over millennia. But it was entertaining, nevertheless."

"It's all been a game to you?" Nate's words throbbed in the air.

"There was a time when life was nothing but a game to you, too," Dagan shot back.

"That was before you showed your true colors. I only regret that I didn't kill you the day we met."

"You're going to regret that more in a minute." Dagan's smile was chilling as he released his ironclad hold around her neck. Bella sucked in precious oxygen. The welcome air burned against her damaged throat and it wasn't until her second gasp of air that she realized his intention. His psychic grip hoisted her above his head and slung her high into the night sky.

She flung her arms up, desperately trying to steady herself as air rushed past her, but it was useless, and wind whipped her hair across her cheeks as gravity sucked her back to the earth.

"No." Nate roared from somewhere below, his wild voice whipping through the sky like an arrow. Bella gasped as the cool air turned warm and the wild rushing descent slowed. Unseen energy cocooned her. She was no longer falling. Instead she was feather light, hanging in the air. Safe in the protective bubble he'd made her. His gaze locked on her and she let out a choked gasp.

"Watch out," she tried to scream, but her damaged throat was hoarse, and she was forced to watch as Dagan charged at Nate.

Nate staggered and fell to his knees, the swords clattering to the ground as he grasped his head. No longer cushioned within his power, Bella crashed into the wall before falling onto the floor. Panting, on her hands and knees, everything was blurred. Everything except for the way Dagan towered over Nate, ruthlessly pulverizing the essence of his being.

Get up.

She willed Nate to stand as primal fear clawed through her. It couldn't end this way. If she hadn't been so stubborn and insisted on accompanying Nate, Dagan would never have discovered a chink in Nate's shields. But the raw agony ripping open her chest wasn't the only thing tearing her apart. Ice burned her flesh, and as waves of nausea rolled through her, she pulled the glass phial from her pocket.

It was cracked, and the noxious substance oozed through the fissures, turning her fingers numb. The essence that had the power to destabilize archangels and demons alike.

"We need to get out of here." Zane grasped her arm and hauled her to her feet. "They're pulling the mountain apart."

Rocks tumbled down the walls and fractures raced across the floor as the two immortals battled on the psychic plane. Storm clouds rumbled in the lowering sky and a desert wind whipped through the atrium, scorching her skin.

"No. I won't leave him."

"There's nothing you can do."

She raised her hand, and Zane recoiled at the sight of the phial.

"Yes, there is." It was a shit plan, but she was out of options. And it was her fault that Dagan had been given an advantage over Nate. "You should go, Zane. If this doesn't work, you don't want to be here."

He opened his mouth, but she ignored him, and she ran at the demon.

Dagan had his back to her, and golden sparks shattered in the air around him, as he held Nate in his psychic grip. Fury and terror of what he was doing to Nate burned through her. She leaped, her momentum carrying her forward, the same second as Zane's body rammed into her, giving her the extra impetus to smash against Dagan's shoulders.

She slammed the phial into his neck, shattering the glass.

Blood splattered where the glass tore into his skin and she pushed the phial in as deep as she could. Dagan roared, and it echoed around the crumbling mountains.

He rolled his shoulders and unfurled his wings as he stretched out his arms. His fist connected with her cheek and pain flared through her as she fell back onto the floor, Zane following her. She groaned and tried to sit up as Dagan staggered.

Black threads appeared under his skin, spreading across his neck and face, and turning the whites of his eyes ebony.

Nate pushed himself to his feet, his chest heaving, and without taking his gaze from Dagan, moved between her and the demon. *Protecting me.*

But she could still see Dagan. His wings drooped, dragging on the ground, the color fading to ash. As he took a couple of unsteady steps toward them, a handful of charred feathers floated to the ground.

She had done this to him. A powerful demon, a member of her noble race, to save the archangel who hunted rogue demon bloods.

Nate. The archangel she loved.

And I'd do it again to save him.

Dagan grasped Nate's shoulder, and leaned in close. For an endless moment his gaze caught hers, but instead of the crazed gleam she expected, there was a strange flicker of regret in his eyes.

Then he pressed his mouth against Nate's ear. "Forgive me, brother. I already knew. And tell her I'm sorry."

Her?

"Tell who?" Nate demanded, but there was no reply and a different kind of fear gripped her.

I just killed a demon.

CHAPTER 29

NATE

Nate grasped Dagan's arm, the demon who had been both his friend and his enemy, his dark blood coating his fingers.

Pain erupted through his hand as Dagan's blackened skin turned red. Nate snatched his arm away as the demon's skin began to smoke. Searing heat blasted out and in a fiery shimmer, he vanished, leaving behind a thousand ruined feathers that floated to the ground like spectral condemnations.

He spun around and pulled Isabella into his arms. She held him close, the warmth of her body slowly seeping into his frozen blood.

"Are you hurt?" He'd seen her plummet from the sky and had been unable to do anything to save her. For that alone, Dagan had deserved his fate.

But is he truly dead?

"No." Her voice was hoarse, and she pulled back, so she could trace her fingers over his face. Briefly, he closed his eyes, and her gentle touch sank into his soul, healing the jagged wounds even if he didn't deserve it. "Are you?"

"I'll survive." He glanced at Zane. The demon blood had

proved his worth and was no longer in his sights. "You need some help?"

Zane gritted his teeth and pulled the knife from his shoulder.

"No." He dropped the knife to the floor, swept his gaze over them, and then teleported.

"Is Dagan…" she hesitated, her beautiful eyes filled with concern. "I had to do it, Nate. I thought he was destroying you."

"He was." It was a brutal confession. Dagan had found a crack in his defenses and used it mercilessly. Yet even then, as they had fought each other's psychic powers, Dagan's offer had remained, a deadly beacon in the darkness.

Pledge me your loyalty. Come with me.

Except this time, unlike eleven thousand years ago, Nate hadn't been tempted. And Dagan had known it.

He pressed his forehead against hers. He'd told her so much. But he hadn't confessed all his sins. Not the one he kept buried so deeply that sometimes he even managed to fool himself that he had forgotten it. "When our goddess called her archangels home, Dagan asked me to go with him, instead. The two of us, against the universe."

She shivered but didn't say anything. What was there to say? He should shut the hell up. But the dam had burst, and the words poured from him as though after millennia they craved an escape, no matter how destructive the aftermath would be.

"I should have struck him down. But I hesitated. Because he offered me something I craved. Freedom from the shackles of our goddess. The chance to find a home far from her shadow."

Self-disgust burned through him, corroding what was left of his pride. He hadn't appreciated how much he'd loved Ama-gi until it was gone. And while its destruction wasn't his fault, the mystical city had haunted him for millennia.

His only true home.

Vengeance should have been his, here, tonight, in this ancient temple of Inanna's. Just before Isabella had struck, he'd found a weakness in Dagan's shields. He should have been the one to end this. By doing so, it might have finally eased the guilt that had been a part of him for years without number.

He'd tear out his tongue before he gave her even the slightest glimpse of his conflicted soul. She could never come close to guessing how the roar of thwarted retribution reverberated through his psyche. It was his burden to bear.

"You guessed he'd betrayed you to your goddess. There was no way of knowing what she was going to do with that knowledge. She was the one who prevented archangels from saving their children. It wouldn't have made any difference to the outcome if you'd obeyed her call instantly or not."

Once again, Isabella saw what he couldn't. Dagan was no more. If he wanted a future with her, it was time to let go of the past.

He cast a glance around the atrium. It was wrecked, but salvageable. But only if that was what Isabella wanted.

"I can destroy the temple. Just say the word."

"Inanna's temple?" There was a wistful note in her voice.

"It hasn't been hers for more than a thousand years."

"With Nijah gone, the mantle passes to Zane. The decision should be his. But I don't want it destroyed. It's still a place for demon bloods to find others like us and learn of our heritage. The true histories of our races, not the propaganda."

Maybe. But an archangel had been involved in the destruction of a powerful demon and part of the temple. Tonight's events would live on in the archives of the Watchers and he doubted his part in it would help heal the rifts between their races.

"Want to get out of here?" He'd promised to show her the wonders of Andromeda. Right now, all he wanted was to get as far away from Earth as possible. He didn't even care where.

As long as Isabella was there.

"Yes." She gave a wan smile. "I need to tackle the mess at home."

Not what he'd had in mind. "That can wait. You need to unwind."

"What I *need* is to get my life back on track. And I'm not wound up."

Fine. He was the one who was wound up and attempting, with little success, to harness the restless energy that pumped through his blood like a marauding virus. "Then I'll help."

"Okay." She didn't sound especially happy by his offer. What *did* she want from him? The question lodged in his throat. Because once spoken, it could never be taken back, and the grim truth was—he wasn't sure he wanted to hear her answer.

He was well aware she could make her own way to her house, but he held her hand anyway, and a moment later they arrived in her drawing room. Over the centuries he'd been responsible for the destruction of a great many things. It was the first time he'd had to face the reality of the aftermath.

Even if he hadn't been the one to smash her beloved possessions, he was still responsible. Indirectly. And Isabella knew it.

She let out a long breath and their fingers untangled. "I don't even know where to start."

Her things hadn't simply been broken. They'd been tainted by demon vengeance, which meant any restoration would involve the painstaking extraction of demonic essence. Something no one on Earth had the ability to do.

"I know people who might be able to fix this." They weren't exactly people. They were immortals who had evolved on the far side of the Andromeda Galaxy and the price they'd demand for such a favor would be brutal.

But she didn't need to know that.

"I don't know." She toed a shard of wood from the shattered grandmother clock. "It could never be the same. All I'd see is Nijah and Zane trying to kill me." She offered him a mocking smile, but it wasn't hard to hear the pain beneath her words. "It'll be best just to start over again."

He folded his arms and tried to ignore the hollow burning sensation that twisted through his chest. She'd spent decades collecting her antiques and creating her home, but to forget all the shit she'd gone through during the last few days, she saw no alternative but to throw it all away.

It didn't take much of a leap to figure out she was including him. Did she see only death and destruction every time she looked at him? Since they'd met, her life had been in constant danger. Not just from Dagan. But from those she'd known for years. Truth was, he couldn't even blame her for wanting to get as far away from him as she could.

Yet when he looked at her, he saw a woman who had captured his mind and stolen his willing heart. And she didn't even know it.

Tell her.

But the words were locked so deep inside he didn't even know how to rip them into the light, let alone tell her what she meant to him. It was too big. Too terrifying. To split open the raw remnants of his soul and risk her walking away forever.

For millennia, he'd been alone. His friendships were solid, and pleasure was a transient pastime. It was only now, as he faced the reality of not having her in his life, that he understood how empty his existence had been.

He'd do anything to keep her. Even if it meant concealing the truth from her.

"Sounds like a plan." It almost fucking killed him to sound as though he was unaware of how much she was hurting inside. But if she wanted to keep him at arm's length, he'd take it. It was preferable to the alternative. "Do you want me to get rid of this stuff for you?"

She pushed her hands into the pockets of her jeans. "It's okay. I'll do it the mortal way. I feel like I need to, you know? It'll seem more final that way."

Final wasn't a word he wanted to hear from her. He had to get out of here, before he said something that shattered this strange, unnatural accord between them.

"Sure. There's something I need to sort out. I'll swing by later with some food. Sound good?"

"Uh, yes." Not that she sounded thrilled by his suggestion.

Was this how it would always be for them, now?

Intimate strangers.

The prospect twisted his gut. But there was nothing he could do about it. Not when he planned on maintaining the status quo even if it damn well nearly destroyed him.

Bella

Nate gave her a careless grin, and it was so achingly familiar yet strangely detached that her heart squeezed in sorrow. He was willing to continue the farce that nothing had changed between them when everything manifestly had.

He disappeared, and she exhaled a long breath. Despite everything that Dagan had done, it was clear Nate had still been hurt by the betrayal.

She'd seen it in his eyes when he'd told her how he had ignored the call of their goddess. And when she'd plunged the Guardians' deadly atmosphere into Dagan's neck.

She sat on her sofa and stared at the ripped fabric and stuffing that had been strewn across the floor. Once, her beautifully restored furniture had given her such joy. The perfect buffer between her gnawing need deep inside to love and be loved, and her fear that anyone she grew close to would inevitably die.

Her ruined possessions meant nothing to her now, except for an ethereal sadness that yet another era of her long life had faded. She'd told Nate she could replace her property.

But she couldn't replace her heart.

She slumped, clasping her fingers together between her

knees, her forearms resting on her thighs. A dread suspicion prowled the darkest recesses of her mind.

Had she made a terrible mistake by destroying Dagan?

She could live with the knowledge she'd broken a demon. It had been the only way to save Nate and she'd never regret that. But what if the price she paid for turning on one of her own kind was to irrevocably lose the fragile bond between her and Nate?

I would have still done it. At least this way Nate was alive, even if he could never look at her in the same way again.

She sucked in a ragged breath. Whether or not she had a future with Nate, things would never be the same. She had the chance to find out more about the demon side of her heritage, and she had every intention of taking Kala up on her offer.

She had questions for Eblis, too. He owed her some answers, at least.

But first, she needed to get her life here on Earth back on track.

A shiver danced over her skin and the hair rose on the back of her neck. She leaped to her feet, unaware of what the danger was, only knowing it was here, in her home.

The breath stalled in her lungs and paralysis gripped her heart. Standing by the door was a tall blonde creature, her long hair twisted into an intricate tapestry of plaits, her vivid green eyes like poisoned emeralds drilling into Bella's brain. Her aged leather tunic and leggings clung to her figure, a dagger sheathed at her hip, and a sword strapped to her back.

The beautiful immortal spread her wings, and ripples of venom sucked the oxygen from the room.

"Isabella." Her voice was strangely devoid of emotion but that didn't stop the icy dread from slithering through Bella's blood. Or prevent her mind from making the obvious connection.

Her actions had destroyed Dagan. And this demon was here for vengeance.

Belatedly, she attempted to read the demon's aura, for all the good that would do, but her powers were bound, rendering her useless. Gods, she could barely even breathe. The atmosphere was oppressive, bearing down on her as though trying to force her to her knees.

She braced her muscles, fighting against the relentless imperative. The demon would have to strike her down before she'd give into the subliminal demand.

"Dagan said you were strong." A hint of scorn iced the words. "He spared you because of his love for Nate." Her eyes flashed with malevolence. "I harbor no such sentiments for a misbegotten hybrid. I don't care if you're protected by an archaic covenant. You'll pay for what you did."

Archaic covenant? What was she talking about?

"Dagan was killing Nate. I couldn't let that happen."

"No, he wasn't. He would never harm Nate."

She managed to take a staggering step forward. "How do you know? You weren't there. And if you had been, you would've destroyed Nate."

A tortured expression flashed over her face, as though Bella's words had hit a nerve. "Don't presume to tell me what I would or wouldn't do."

Burning pain slashed into her side and she doubled over, gasping, her hand pressed against her sweater. Warmth seeped over her fingers, and blood dripped onto the carpet. She forced herself upright and glared at the demon. "What is this? Death by a thousand cuts?"

"No. That would be too merciful a death, compared to the one you inflicted upon Dagan. I have a far better idea."

The woman held out her gloved hand, and a phial containing a swirling, dark material, materialized on the palm of her hand.

The Guardians' atmosphere. Had Dagan taken the last sample from the castle?

"Where did you get that?" Her voice was hoarse with dread. Had Octavia escaped in time?

For the first time, the demon smiled. It was beautiful and terrifying and radiated lethal despair. "From my beloved friend, Nate."

Bella panted, but the air was too thin, and the dizziness filling her mind made it hard to think straight. She'd simply assumed the only demon friend Nate ever had was Dagan.

She'd been wrong. And was about to pay with her life.

It wouldn't help. But she had to know. "Who are you?"

The demon removed the lid of the phial, and tendrils of the atmosphere floated up, as if seeking escape. "I'm the Archangel Astrid."

An archangel? She should have guessed. For decades, archangels had been the true monsters lurking in the shadows without mercy or a moral compass. Except since meeting Nate, her perception of archangels as despicable creatures had crumbled. The only reason she'd imagined Astrid was a demon was because she had loved Dagan.

Nothing in the histories of the Watchers even hinted such a union could be possible. But the histories didn't know everything.

Astrid approached. Her psychic grip on Bella was absolute, rendering her powers useless. But that wasn't all. She was also physically paralyzed. Frozen in place, her gaze fixed on the phial as the archangel slowly raised it, only for her to pause over the wound she'd slashed in Bella's side.

"No." She choked on the word but couldn't help it as the image of Dagan flashed through her mind. She was only half-demon, but that wouldn't be enough to save her.

"Beg." Astrid breathed the word against her ear, before dropping a thread of the poison into her body.

Fire scorched her flesh, scalded her blood, and distorted her vision. She couldn't move, but her body was falling through the void beyond the universe and her soul splintered into a million shards of rainbow bright light.

Was this how it ended? Before she even had the chance to tell Nate how much she loved him? Death, from the hand of an avenging archangel.

Her powers were bound. She couldn't reach him with their telepathic bond. But he was all she could think of, all she could see, and with every shred of energy she possessed, his name filled her mind.

"Nate."

CHAPTER 30

NATE

Nate caught up with Inanna in *Zega*, and they were on a rooftop garden that gave a spectacular view of the lush valley. The last time he'd been here with Mephisto, he'd vowed to let her know of the possible danger from the Guardians' atmosphere. Whether archangels liked it or not, they were created from the same DNA as that of the gods. And while he didn't give a fuck about most of them, he and Inanna went back a long way together.

She stood beside him and contemplated the view. "Is Dagan dead?" There was mild curiosity in her voice. "If he teleported, there's no way of knowing for sure."

"I didn't behead him." That was one sure method of killing any immortal. "But I've never seen anything like that stuff before. It destroyed him from the inside out."

He exhaled a long breath. He'd kept Isabella's name out of it. There was no need for Inanna to know everything.

Gods, he should never have allowed Isabella to accompany him to the temple. She was strong, and she was a survivor, but until she'd met him, she hadn't been a killer.

She'd chosen to save him, at the cost of one of her own. But the true price was far greater. When they'd arrived back at her home, he'd seen the despair in her eyes, even though she'd tried to hide it. And it had nothing to do with her shattered possessions.

"He must have thought it a great joke to desecrate my temple in such a way." Now Inanna sounded pissed. "I've a good mind to cleanse the entire mountain in fire."

The Watchers' archives would be destroyed. Did he care about that?

"It's the only place demon bloods on Earth have to learn of their history." Yeah, he guessed he did care, after all. Because the Watchers had saved Isabella when she'd needed them the most and with Nijah gone, she could have her surrogate family back.

"And since when has *that* ever concerned you?" Inanna turned to face him, and he saw comprehension gleam in her eyes. *Fuck…* "Are you involved with a demon blood, Nate?"

"It's irrelevant."

"You *are*." Inanna sounded inordinately delighted. He couldn't think why. "Although I shouldn't be surprised. You were always one of the rebel archangels."

Every word was like the slash of a dagger against his feathers. If everything had been great between him and Isabella, he wouldn't care what Inanna said. Hell, he'd probably tell her how he'd finally fallen, and laugh with her when she mercilessly mocked him.

But things weren't right. No matter how much he tried to convince himself they were. And tangled up with the mess he'd made of everything with Isabella was the gnawing unease that he was missing something vital, that there was unfinished business just beyond his comprehension, and he couldn't escape its relentless grip.

He was grasping at straws. There was nothing else. The only reason he was feeling like shit was because of the chasm that was tearing him and Isabella apart. And he had no idea how to heal the rift.

There was no miraculous act that could reset the clock.

"What really happened between you and Dagan?" Inanna gave him an assessing look. "Why did you turn your back on him? I confess I've occasionally pondered on it, over the years."

Of all the immortals he'd known in Ama-gi and had remained in contact with, Inanna was the only one who had always known he'd been aware of who Dagan truly was. Archangels had scattered across the universe, oblivious that a demon had shared their paradise on Earth with them. Only Inanna would have considered it noteworthy that he'd severed ties with Dagan after the destruction of Nibiru.

"He betrayed me." It was all she needed to know. He'd shared his deepest secrets with Isabella, and that was how it would remain until the end of time. His guilt was deep, but she'd been right. Their goddess would never have allowed the Nephilim to flourish once she'd learned of their existence.

"That's no big revelation." Inanna sounded disappointed. "He was a demon. What did you expect? Demons and archangels can never be trusted." She tossed him a mocking smile. "Present company excepted."

He glared across the landscape, but all he saw in his mind's eye was Dagan as he'd clutched his arm in those final moments in the atrium. The demon's last words echoed through his brain.

Forgive me, brother. I already knew.

A shudder crawled over his arms as a thousand possibilities collided in his mind. At the time he'd barely acknowledged what Dagan was saying but there was only one thing the demon would have spoken of in the end. Only one thing his whispered confession could have meant.

Another archangel had told Dagan of their rescue mission. He'd already known the details, before Nate had shared them with him.

Why hadn't he seen it before? When he and Dagan had spoken of the immortal forged sword, the demon's reply had been enigmatic.

Is that what she told you?

He'd shrugged it off as unimportant. Not worth his time attempting to analyze. Yet Dagan had offered him a fucking great clue on a platter.

Tell her I'm sorry.

Another archangel had told him, and there was only one other archangel it could've been. His lover.

Astrid.

"Nate, what's going on?" Inanna's voice was sharp.

He turned to her, but he didn't see the goddess. He saw his own blind prejudice when it came to his own immortal race. So eaten up by the sins of his past, he'd not even contemplated another archangel might have shared the confidential plans with Dagan.

He should have known that no one, not even an immortal, could have gained access to Astrid's prized weapons unless she herself had allowed it. Images from Ama-gi flashed across his mind, of the times when Astrid and Dagan had indulged in biting exchanges. He'd assumed they couldn't stand each other.

How wrong he'd been. They had been playing a dangerous game of their own.

She had given the sword to her demon lover before their goddess had called them from Ama-gi. And millennia later Nate had returned it to her.

Ice clutched his heart. He needed to speak with her. Fast.

Astrid.

I'm busy. Her response was instant. And dismissive.

Cold certainty gripped him. She knew what had happened to Dagan. Which meant she most likely also knew who had been responsible.

"What's going on?" Inanna's imperious demand rang through

the evening air as a horrifying possibility hit him. Did Astrid also know about Isabella?

"I'll get back to you," he told the goddess. And in the nanosecond before he teleported, Isabella's petrified voice filled his entire being.

Nate.

He arrived in her drawing room and his heart damn near froze. Isabella stood at an awkward angle, slumped to one side, blood spreading across her sweater. Her gaze caught his, but she didn't seem to hear his frantic telepathic message. Or maybe she did but could no longer respond.

And Astrid was by her side, holding the phial of atmosphere that he had given her to analyze just days ago.

"It's right that you witness this," she said, speaking in the language of Ama-gi. "Yours for mine. Vengeance will be served."

She intended using the toxic substance on Isabella. His stomach clenched at the thought of her suffering the same fate as Dagan. He responded in English, so Isabella could understand. "Astrid, we need to talk about this."

"No, we don't. There's nothing more to be said." As she spoke, once again in the language of the ancients, her hand shifted a hairsbreadth away from Isabella. If he could keep her talking, keep her distracted, he'd be able to grab the phial.

"I didn't know you and Dagan were together. Even back in Ama-gi?"

The ghost of a smile shadowed her lips. "It's thrilling, isn't it, Nate? Keeping a forbidden secret that no one else would possibly guess."

And look where his secret had led them all.

"You were working together with the Guardians?"

"Dagan had his projects. I had mine."

Didn't she know everything Dagan had been doing?

"He didn't tell you, did he?" Isabella said, her voice raw with pain—but she was speaking the same language as Astrid. The one she'd told him she couldn't understand. "You loved him, but he didn't love you back."

"Be silent." Astrid's voice was like ice. "You know nothing."

"Maybe he did love you," Isabella persisted. Why did she keep drawing attention to herself? He couldn't even warn her. Their link was still blocked. But with Astrid momentarily diverted, he stealthily took a couple of steps closer to her. "But not enough."

"We can work this out, Astrid," he said. "There doesn't need to be more bloodshed over this."

She rounded on him. "The hybrid bitch destroyed Dagan. It's divine justice that I destroy her. Only then will the universe be in balance once again. You know this is true."

"I destroyed Dagan. Not Isabella. I deserve your vengeance, not her."

"Stop. I won't kill you, Nate. We're of the same blood."

Rowan's words from when they'd been at Gabe's thundered through his head. *Blood isn't everything.* But for too long after the destruction of Ama-gi, he'd thought it was.

Blood meant nothing compared to his love for Isabella. He'd die for her, if it would save her. But there was only one way out of this. There always had been.

For a split second, Astrid's gaze wavered as she steadied the phial over Isabella's wound. Faster than lightning, he whipped her sword from its sheath at his hip. The runes danced along the blade and then burst with light as he plunged it through her heart.

The phial tumbled from her hand onto the carpet as she turned to him. Shock glazed her eyes. But he hadn't finished yet. There was, after all, only one sure way to kill an immortal and he wouldn't—couldn't—allow Astrid to go free when she'd set her sights on Isabella.

Astrid reeled, her gaze never leaving his, as she reached for him, her fingers clawing through the air. She pushed images of

Ama-gi into his mind, but it was too late. Ama-gi was his past. And he didn't want to go back.

Ruthlessly, he pulled the sword from her, gripping it with both hands as he swung it into a killing arc. Her blood dripped from the blade and she let out a gasp of pain before holding up her hands. Then she grinned, and without warning the blade disintegrated into glittering, ethereal specks of electrons, spiraling up to the hilt and vanishing beneath his fist. Astrid emitted a low, hoarse laugh, as her body mirrored the sword, fragmenting into subatomic particles that radiated from her wound, before being sucked into it, like a whirlpool from hell.

Was she dead? She'd always claimed her weapons had souls. Was it because she had bound her own soul to them? Had her sword preserved her life?

The moment she vanished Isabella staggered from her paralysis into his arms. She clutched at his coat, her breath rasping. "The poison's inside me."

Relief transmuted into raw terror. *I arrived too late.*

He shouldn't have left her. He should have been here for her, to protect her from Astrid's vengeance. But instead, he'd fucked off to Inanna, because he'd been unable to find the words to tell Isabella how much she meant to him.

Because he hadn't wanted to risk discovering she didn't feel the same for him.

His arrogant pride might yet cost Isabella her life.

He swung her into his arms and gently placed her on the sofa. There were no black threads shifting beneath her skin but what other damage was happening inside her body, that he couldn't see?

He pressed his palm against her wound. There was no precedent for anything like this. But that was irrelevant. If he didn't try, she could die.

"I'm going to drain the poison. If it's too agonizing let me know. I'll put you under."

She gritted her teeth in the semblance of a smile. "Like hell you will. I'll help. I can feel it sliding through my veins, like a separate entity. Should be easy enough to isolate."

Once again, the last moments of Dagan flashed through his mind. Was Isabella's mortal blood helping her survive?

How ironic, when for countless ages both archangels and demons had considered the blood of humans to be inferior to their own.

"Okay."

He slowly inhaled, forcing his mind to calm and heartrate to slow. He couldn't afford to let any negative energy escape when he accessed his regenerative abilities.

It wasn't usually this hard. Brutally, he focused on the only thing that mattered.

Healing Isabella.

His mind brushed hers, an ethereal touch that echoed through his blood and sank deep into his heart. The damaged cells radiated with alien darkness. He focused his regenerative forces, intertwining with Isabella's lighter energy, and together they fought the enemy, driving back the poison's insidious invasion.

Something cold and alien scorched his hand.

"That's all of it," Isabella panted. He looked at his palm. One small drop slithered, like black quicksilver. Within a second, the phial was in his other hand, and he tipped the altered element into it, where it merged into the swirling mass. He slammed on the lid and placed the cursed thing beside him before turning back to Isabella.

Her skin was unblemished, without even a trace of a fading scar. She had already healed her wound.

A strange buzzing filled his head and the room tilted. His hands were clammy, and it had nothing to do with the dull throb of his palm where he'd caught the poison. The relief and fear intermingled, soul deep, pervading every atom of his existence, and for endless seconds he couldn't move and could barely think beyond the one thundering reality in his head.

She's alive.

She brushed her fingers over his arm. "I'm sorry," she whispered.

The words made no sense, but it didn't matter. Nothing mattered except she was safe. He exhaled a ragged breath. If anyone other than Isabella was witnessing his inability to function right now, he'd never live it down. But there was no one else in the universe who could ever witness such a thing. Because she was the only one who had captured his soul and held his life in her heart. She was his reason for being.

"Nate, I'm so sorry," she repeated, and he still couldn't fathom what she was talking about. A shudder wracked his body. *Move, damn it.* But he appeared incapable of doing anything but drinking in the fact she hadn't succumbed to the Guardians' toxic atmosphere.

Her hand dropped to her lap. "I won't pretend to know how you feel. I wish I'd been able to stop her, so you hadn't needed to make that terrible choice between us."

The meaning behind her words penetrated his fog. She blamed herself? That was insane. He grasped her hands, pulling them to his chest, and pressed her palms over his heart.

"No." His voice was harsh, couldn't help it. "You or her, Isabella? There was never any choice. Don't you get it yet? You're all I want. I'd destroy anyone who tried to harm you, archangel or demon, there's no difference to me. Astrid made her choice when she came after you."

"I thought I'd lost you when I destroyed Dagan. But I'd do it again, to save you."

There was a strange blockage in his throat. Something he'd never experienced before. Then again, he'd experienced a whole lot of things he never had before since meeting Isabella.

"If you hadn't, I would have. I just hate knowing it's my fault you were faced with that. A member of your own race."

She let out a little *huh* and shook her head. "That's why you went all distant when we came back here? Because you felt *guilty?*"

"Hey, come on." He gave her a half-grin, attempting to lighten the mood. The way he always did because that was so much easier than digging deep and facing stark reality. "I do it so well."

"You've nothing to feel guilty about." There was a fierce note in her voice that slayed him. "Even if Eblis himself had been the one threatening your life, I wouldn't have hesitated. The bond of blood only goes so far, Nate."

She was right. More than she could ever know. He'd spent so long avoiding the hard questions and ignoring the truth beneath his flippant words. But he didn't need to hide those buried slivers of his soul anymore. Not from Isabella.

He rested his forehead against hers and breathed in deep. Beneath the blood and fear that had so recently saturated the air, he caught the elusive hint of her smoky, woodsy scent that conjured up mythical groves in ancient forests.

He'd known her for so short a time, but her scent was so familiar, as though he'd been aware of her forever, and wherever she was, he was home.

But that alone didn't absolve him.

"I've persecuted demon bloods for millennia, Isabella. Because of their heritage."

"All demon bloods? Or rogues?"

He acknowledged the distinction. "Point is, would I have been as vigilant if not for what happened in Ama-gi? There are plenty of other races out there doing unspeakable things in the name of their beliefs."

She stroked the tips of her fingers over his knuckles. "You did what you had to do."

He threaded his fingers through hers. He wasn't proud of

everything he'd done since the destruction of Nibiru, but one thing was certain. "I'd do it all again, if it led me to you."

Her smile was sunlight, bathing his world after the storm. "You're such a charmer."

"I aim to please." And then it struck him. They'd been speaking in the language of the ancients. "Isabella, you understand Ama-gi. What happened?"

A frown flickered over her face. "When Astrid poisoned me, it felt like my consciousness fell over the edge of the universe. But..." she hesitated as though searching for the right words to explain. "I think it got into my brain. I remember flashes of dark places that I've never been to, constellations I've never seen. It's all fading away, but the knowledge of your language is a part of me now. Maybe it was buried inside my head all along and I just couldn't access it before."

"Maybe." He glanced at the phial. Much as he wanted to destroy its contents, he didn't even know how. But since both archangels and vampires had a sample, it was only fair the gods did, too. He'd give it to Inanna. "Hell of a way to discover hidden knowledge."

"I wouldn't recommend it." Her smile faded. "Astrid said something strange. That Dagan wouldn't touch me because I'm protected by an archaic covenant. I don't even know what that means."

"Don't you?" It was wrong that Dagan had seen the truth before he'd faced it himself. Before he'd had the chance to tell Isabella. But they'd been given a second chance and he wasn't going to screw it up. "I'm guessing in the mountain the shielding to your aura was neutralized. That's when Dagan saw the truth. That you're the beloved of an archangel."

Her bottom lip wobbled. Just once. It damn near broke him.

"The beloved?" Her voice was husky.

"Yeah." He aimed for nonchalance. Failed with honors. Hell,

just tell her already. "I love you, Isabella. I want to spend the rest of eternity with you by my side. You're my everything."

My only chance of salvation.

"Nate." Her whisper was a caress against his skin and her blue eyes captivated him, the way they had the first night they'd met. "I spent so many years thinking I could live without love. That all I needed to be happy was to surround myself with beautiful things. And then I met you." She traced her fingers along his jaw, his incomparable, demon blood beloved. "You're all I need in this world. Or any other. I'll love you until the end of time and beyond."

For too many years he'd mourned the loss of Ama-gi, his only true home. But he didn't need the magnificent city of his youth anymore. His home was with Isabella, wherever in the universe that might be.

Her lips met his and their kiss ensnared his soul, filled with an unbreakable promise of an endless tomorrow.

ACKNOWLEDGMENTS

As always, a huge thanks to my fabulous writing buddies, Amanda and Sally. Your support and friendships are everything!

Massive thanks to Amanda Ashby, for always making me dig deeper, and for asking the hard questions and not letting me off the hook! Your insights and ability to find the heart of the story are amazing.

And thank you to Mark, who never complains when I have a meltdown and ask you to fix my laptop problems (had a few of them this year!) and basically for putting up with my writerly weirdness! I couldn't do this without you!

ABOUT THE AUTHOR

Christina Phillips is an ex-pat Brit who now lives in sunny Western Australia with her high school sweetheart and their family. She enjoys writing paranormal, historical fantasy romance and contemporary romance where the stories sizzle and the heroine brings her hero to his knees.

She is addicted to good coffee, expensive chocolate and bad boy heroes. She is also owned by three gorgeous cats who are convinced the universe revolves around their needs. They are not wrong.

ChristinaPhillips.com

Have you read the first two books in the Realm of Flame and Shadow series?

Redemption

Haunted by his past, the Archangel Gabriel's a mercenary for hire and if the price is right, he'll do anything. Anything but fall in love again.

Nemesis

The Archangel Azrael and Rowan's romance

Falling for his nemesis is the most dangerous thing he's ever done...

Also available in paperback: Historical Fantasy Romances

The Highland Warrior Chronicles
Set in 9th century Pictland

Her Rebel Scot, a Prequel

Her Savage Scot

Her Vengeful Scot

Her Baseborn Scot

Her Wicked Scot

Her Outcast Scot

The Druid Chronicles: Fantasy Historical Romance

Set in 1st century Britain

Forbidden

Captive

Enslaved

Tainted

Standalone:

Bloodlust Denied A Gothic Regency Vampire Romance

A vampire duke. An immortal slayer. A dangerous obsession that could destroy them both...